BAKED WITH LOVE

A LONG VALLEY WESTERN ROMANCE NOVEL – BOOK 9

❦

ERIN WRIGHT

WRIGHT'S ROMANCE READS

Copyright © 2019 by Erin Wright

ISBN: 978-1-950570-12-6

This book is a work of fiction. The names, characters, places and incidents are products of the writer's imagination or have been used fictitiously and are not to be constructed as real. Any resemblance to persons, living or dead, actual events, locales or organizations is entirely coincidental.

All rights reserved. No part of this book may be reproduced, scanned, or distributed in any manner whatsoever without written permission from the author except in the case of brief quotation embodied in critical articles and reviews.

For Heidi, who's as strong as Cady. Keep fighting.

For Logan, who's showing us all what it means to be true to yourself. So proud of you.

And for Aunt April – I'm so very glad we're making up for lost time, and that at least one person in the family appreciates the "good parts"

CHAPTER 1

CADY

JANUARY, 2019

Cady Walcott squinted into the bright sunshine bouncing off the thigh-deep sparkling white snow, stretching out as far as she could see, broken only by the greens and browns of the pine trees and boulders of the Goldfork Mountains. It was a gorgeous winter day – one of those brilliant days that just didn't happen often enough during the normally dreary Idaho winter.

Or maybe they happen all the time and you just don't know it because you're too busy hiding away from the world to notice.

She ignored the Negative Nelly thought. Today was the start of the new year, and she wasn't about to lose sight of that.

Well, fine, *technically* it was January 3rd, not January 1st, but she'd always been a little slow, so maybe today could just be considered the start to the New Cady Walcott Year instead.

Either way, she was officially done. Done hiding in her bed. Done trying to sleep until her life faded away into nothingness. She'd taken the bold step of coming up to Long Valley – forcing herself out of the comforting embrace of her flannel sheets instead of lazing the day away – and now, she was going to enjoy the world she found herself in, dammit.

She scrambled up a giant boulder, the tip of it sticking out above the snow, warmed by the sun and blessedly clear of ice or moisture of any form. She could warm herself in the sun while taking a bit of a breather – the air up here was thin and sharp and cold, forcing her to take it slow.

She instinctively patted the emerald green pendant hanging around her neck, making sure, as always, that it was there and then pulled her cell phone out of her back pocket to look at the calendar app. Huh. Apparently, today was a Thursday – who knew? – so it was possible Hannah Lambert, her old college roommate, was at the elementary school teaching her 5th grade class.

On the other hand…Cady wasn't an expert on the scheduling practices of elementary schools, but it seemed a bit early for the school district to be back in session. Surely they'd wait until next Monday before forcing all of the students to go back to school, right?

Which meant that Hannah probably had the day off.

Which meant that Cady should probably call Hannah and tell her that she was in the area so they could meet up for coffee or something.

She stared sightlessly down at her calendar app, the *should* taunting her. That morning, Cady had managed the miracle of making herself drive up to Long Valley and her old favorite hiking trails, but she hadn't *quite* managed to make herself also call Hannah.

That just seemed so…sociable.

So…outgoing.

So…*normal*.

Am I ever going to be normal again?

Probably not.

The very idea seemed exhausting, quite honestly.

She shoved her cell phone into her back pocket. New rule: One major step forward per day. The next time she came up to Long Valley, she'd call Hannah. Today wasn't that day.

After a few pulls on the water hose snaking out of her pack, Cady pushed herself off the rock and began walking again. Despite the bright sunshine, it was still too cold to sit still for very long, no matter how lovely it was to just sit and take in the vitamin D. Carefully, she wound her way through the forest, sticking to the parts of the trail where the weak winter rays had melted the snow down to a more manageable depth. Cady breathed in deep, almost enjoying the painful crispness of the air, the icy oxygen burning its way into her lungs. It was winter's way of reminding her that she was still alive.

Whether or not she wanted to be.

You want to be. Look around, Cady. Look at all that you'd be missing if you'd given up.

Apparently, her Negative Nelly and Cheerful Cady personalities were at war with each other this morning, both of them insistent upon her seeing the world through their viewpoint.

Well, both could stick a sock in it. She just wanted to *be*.

She paused on the nonexistent trail and sucked greedily on her water hose again. Even at the shallower depths, it was still a good workout to slog through the snow. Instead of feeling worn out by the exercise, though, she felt invigorated. Alive. Her heartbeat was in high gear, her lungs had that pleasant burn feeling from breathing in the icy air, and she felt *good*.

But, she realized after sucking down more water, her legs were shaky as hell and she was running out of energy a whole lot faster than she used to.

This is what happens when you lie around for months on end. Your body atrophies. You know that.

Yeah, she did know that. After years of working in sports medicine and rehab, she hadn't exactly missed that fundamental point.

"I wish I had a dog to talk to," she told a chattering squirrel, watching as it bounced from pine tree to pine tree, dumping snow off the branches in a shower of white with each jump. "I wouldn't seem so much like a crackpot if I had a dog on a leash that I talked to as I walked."

The squirrel bounded off into the pines, snow swirling to the ground in its wake.

"Thanks for listening!" she called out after the squirrel.

No response.

Squirrels aren't great listeners. Who's surprised?

With a sigh, she turned and headed back down the trail towards the trailhead. She should get going back to Boise. Darkness came early in the mountains, the tall, icy peaks blocking out the winter sun and forcing the valley below into hours of prolonged twilight. Up here, it wasn't unusual for it to start getting dark at four in the afternoon during the deepest winter months.

It really is too damn bad that all of this gorgeous scenery and snow comes part and parcel with limited daylight hours.

After a hard slog through the snow and a careful winding of her way down the Goldfork Mountains in her Jeep 4x4, Cady took a left and headed towards Sawyer. A blink of the eye and she'd be through the tiny town and back on her way to Boise. Once she made it home, she could...

Well, she'd have to start making decisions. Decisions she'd been avoiding for the past six months. Because this was the start to the New Cady Walcott Year, and that included doing things like acting like an adult, not a neurotic, scared child hiding from the world.

And anyway, she wasn't neurotic. She just had quirks. Lots and lots of quirks. Which, by definition, made her quirky.

A *totally* different thing.

She was squinting into the bright sunshine that was reflecting off every car and window, practically blinding her as she drove through the quaint town, when she noticed a charming storefront. *The Muffin Man*, the sign proudly proclaimed, and beneath it, the large plate-glass windows were decorated with gingerbread men, snowflakes, and cups of coffee with steam swirling out of them. It was *adorable*, and absolutely fit the vibe of the tiny mountain hamlet.

Impulsively, she flipped on her blinker and pulled into a parking spot out front. She could grab a to-go cup of joe to drink on the way home – it'd warm her up *and* keep her awake for the 90-minute drive at the same time.

A win-win.

She took a few steps towards the front door, the sugar and yeast and coffee aromas floating on the air and tempting her before she could even get inside, when a forlorn For Sale sign in the window of the business next door caught her eye. Hesitating, she paused for just a moment, and then shrugged, changing directions and heading to the connected storefront to the right of the Muffin Man. She wasn't sure why she was even looking – it wasn't exactly like she needed a store. They weren't an item that a person collected, like adding to a scarf or handbag collection, but there was something a little sad, a little pathetic about the place, that begged for her attention.

Like it needed some love, and wanted her in particular to give it.

Great, now storefronts are talking to you.

She ignored that bit of input from Ms. Negative Nelly and instead scrubbed at the dirty window pane, pressing her face against it, trying to peer into the darkened, abandoned building. Squinting as hard as she could, she worked to make out the details. The flooring was composed of large white-and-black tiles in a checkerboard pattern, set on edge to create rows of black and white diamonds that marched off into the darkened rear of the store. About a third of the way in were…

"Are those hand-carved wooden countertops?" she asked herself under her breath, scrubbing at the window pane again and pressing her face to the freezing glass. Everything about the shop screamed quaint and adorable and lots of character and charm…

Huh. Except for the left-hand wall, that was. The wall of the shop that it shared with the Muffin Man next door was a dark charcoal gray with what appeared to be smoke damage.

Shit. Fire damage…that could be trouble.

She squinted hard, peering around at the shop

through her limited peephole, but couldn't spot any other signs of fire or smoke damage. Had an electrical outlet gotten hot, but was quickly put out before it could set the whole place on fire?

She took a few steps back from the window and looked at the storefront as a whole. It actually looked a lot like the Muffin Man next door…minus any care or attention for the last 25 years, that was. All of the huge glass-paned windows facing Main Street were in one piece, which she considered to be a big plus, but the awning over the front door hung at a steep, awkward angle, obviously broken after a large snowstorm had piled up too much snow, testing – and breaking – its structural integrity. The brickwork also wasn't in great shape – the red bricks were worn and pitted, with a couple missing to the right of the front door, below one of the large windows.

Then there was the fact that everything was *beyond* grimy. It would take countless hours of scrubbing just to make the place inhabitable.

A store? Cady, you can only barely handle getting out of bed on a regular basis, and you think you want to buy a store*?!*

But despite Negative Nelly's best efforts, she still couldn't quite stomp the excitement into oblivion that was bubbling up in her. She'd come up to Long Valley several times when she'd been roommates with Hannah, and she'd always loved the area. There was a reason that when she was trying to make herself move and *do* something today, she'd come to this magical valley.

A store would require something to sell, though, and she didn't make things by hand. She wasn't crafty. She didn't paint, or sew, or quilt, or carve, or scrapbook, or cook—

Hold on. There's *an idea.*

She wasn't a cook – at least, not much of one, although she'd managed to survive 33 years without starving to death – but she was good at smoothies. When she'd worked at the smoothie shop and health food store in Boise last year, those five months had been the happiest of her adult life. She'd been making a difference – serving up *good* food to people, not junk food full of additives and sugar. There was a satisfaction there, and even better, a barrier between her and the public.

A shocking fact for anyone who knew her: She was good with people...*if* there was something between her and said people. The counter at Give It A Whirl had separated her from the strangers off the street, and that had meant that she could relax while working. Working in a clothing store or restaurant where she'd be forced to mingle in amongst everyone simply wasn't an option, but Give It A Whirl had been ideal.

She pressed her face against the window again. *Hmmm*...She could work behind that beautiful countertop, creating smoothies, and then in the front third of the store, she could have some tables for people to sit at on one side, and shelves with health food on the other. As long as she made sure to not create any dead ends where someone could trap her in, she should be able to handle the occasional venturing out from behind the counter. Especially if the shelves were low enough that people could see over them, even her.

Pulling back from the grimy window, she turned in a wide circle, taking in Main Street as a whole. There was a fountain in the middle with the water turned off – she guessed it only ran during the summer – and a big planter area filled to the brim with bright snow. If memory served her, someone took the time to fill it with flowers during the summer.

Across from her was the pharmacy and gift shop, and up the street was the hardware store. If she squinted, she could see Betty's Diner further down the street with its iconic giant waving woman statue out front, and some businesses beyond there, although she couldn't tell from this spot what they were.

Overall, it was a cute area, if a little rundown. The benches along the sidewalks had seen better days, and some of the stores were edging past quaint and straight into rundown territory, but…

She turned and looked back at the storefront for sale. There were possibilities here.

She looked up at the brilliant blue sky arching above Sawyer, no chemtrails in sight. The whole day up in the mountains and now here on Main Street in Sawyer, and not a single airplane had flown overhead at any point.

Yeah, she could make this work – she really could.

She, Cady Walcott, could actually *do* something with her life that didn't include her bed and/or her flannel sheets.

The bubble of hope rising up inside of her felt... weird, honestly. She headed next door to the Muffin Man, the doorbell tinkling as she stepped inside, her mind running a million miles an hour. Considering the state of the building next door, she could probably get a good deal on it, which meant her nest egg would last longer. She stared sightlessly at the bakery display in front of her, her mind on everything back in Boise that would need to be dealt with before she could move forward.

Move forward...there was a phrase she hadn't used in relation to her own life in a very long—

"My personal favorite are the cream puffs," a deep, male voice said in her ear. "If you're—"

But she was screaming and jumping and turning in a half circle all in one terrified movement, her hand over her racing heart, backing instinctively away from the man who'd spoken. He jerked his head back and his friendly smile slowly faded away. "Sorry," he said, not looking very sorry. He looked more... surprised and annoyed by her response than sorry. "I didn't mean to scare you."

The haze of panic was settling over her, though, thick and blinding, as she stared at his biceps. They were bulging, holding a heavily laden tray of brownies that he'd apparently brought out to put into the display case. But they were huge – *he* was huge – and all she could think was that he could hold her down so easily, like a giant holding a baby in place. She could fight with all her might and not move him an inch.

She shook her head, backing towards the door, looking around wildly for someone else, *anyone* else, to step into view. Someone else being there would be her protection against this man. He would never attack her with a witness present. But the bakery was empty, just him and her, and she didn't know him at all, and—

He slid the tray onto the countertop and then held up his hands. "I'm sorry," he said again, but this time, his tone all but screamed, *You're taking this way out of context.* "Are you looking for something in particular?"

She stopped her retreat to the front door, her gaze swinging wildly between the display case and the massive employee who worked there. She was almost to the front door. She was almost free. If she went on the offensive, then maybe he wouldn't look at her as easy prey and she could make her escape.

"You know," she said bitingly, "you shouldn't serve up such large quantities of sugar. They've done a lot of studies on it. It's terrible for the human body. It's places like this that have caused the obesity epidemic in our nation."

His smile completely disappeared then, replaced by an increasingly pissed-off glare. "Hey, *I* didn't force you to come in here," he practically growled. "If you don't like it, you can leave."

"Well, maybe I will!" she shot back as she swung

around, the bell ringing wildly above her head as she pulled the door open and ran blindly down the street, panic and anger nipping at her heels. *Get away, get away! Escape!*

Finally, she forced herself to stop, slumping up against an icy brick storefront and gasping for air.

She was fine. Everything was fine. She had taken control of the situation and had escaped.

She sucked in a lungful of air, trying to slow her breathing down.

She was fine. Everything was fine. She'd escaped. She was fine.

She forced herself upright and looked up and down the street, hunting for her Jeep, finally spotting it several blocks up. *Whoops.* She'd apparently run right past it in her pell-mell escape from the bakery and the wall of muscle who snuck up on people for fun and scared them half to death.

Man, what a jackass.

With any luck at all, that guy's boss would've overheard that little exchange, and he'd be gone by the time she actually moved up here. The sweet, elderly lady who surely owned the Muffin Man would be unhappy to have such a muscular man practically attacking defenseless women in her bakery.

With that pleasant thought, she began marching back up the street to her Jeep. She was going to head back to Boise, make some decisions that she'd been putting off for a very long time, get her life in order, and be back in just a couple of months. By that point,

Muscle-Bound Man would be gone, off to go terrorize some other store, and she could settle into a quiet existence in her smoothie and health shop.

She slid into the driver's seat and turned the heat on full blast as she headed back home. Finally, she was getting her life back into order. She wasn't about to allow anything – or anyone – to get in her way.

CHAPTER 2

GAGE

April, 2019

*I*t was the banging that got to him.

It'd been a pretty quiet morning – not bad for a Monday, anyway, with the regulars stopping by for a cup of coffee to get their day going, and a donut if they thought they could get away with it, or a muffin if they didn't. Gage'd been able to keep up with the flow of traffic without falling too far behind, although it was damn useful that a few of the regulars had simply helped themselves to the coffee when a line had started to form.

Sugar'd had her baby three weeks ago – a tiny bundle of human being hardly bigger than a mite, but she sure could make herself known if she thought her momma had waited too long between breast-feedings. It was a damn lot of fun to see Sugar, Jaxson, Rose, and the two boys when they stopped by the bakery once a week, but a small part of him was dearly missing his only full-time employee and the one person who'd been there for him through thick and thin. Sugar's hard work and loyalty to the bakery was what had allowed him to build it up to what it was today, and her remaining three weeks of maternity leave stretched out in front of him, desolate and exhausting.

He wasn't entirely sure if he could make it another three weeks without her help, honestly. He'd thought about pressing some of the regulars into service – asking them to walk around with a carafe and refill mugs at regular intervals – but then had thought better of it. Mr. Maddow, the most dedicated of his regulars, also had shit for eyesight and it'd be just Gage's luck that Maddow would pour coffee all over someone's expensive iPhone instead of into a coffee cup, and Gage'd end up on the hook to replace it.

Bam, bam, bam.

"What the shitting hell *is* that?!" Gage yelled at no one in particular as he glared at the offending wall. On the other side of that wall was an abandoned storefront – a piece of real estate that as long as Gage could remember, no one had occupied. Hell, the For Sale sign was so old, it probably needed to register to vote.

Over the past four years since he took over the bakery from his grandparents, he'd toyed with the idea of buying the storefront and expanding next door, but he wasn't real sure what he would sell over there, plus it'd be twice the space to heat and cool and staff, not to mention all of the renovation work that needed to be done to the storefront, and he had his hands full just trying to keep the Muffin Man above water—

Bam, bam, bam.

"That's it!" he announced to the world, or at least the few patrons of the bakery. "I'm going next door. I'll be back."

Mr. Maddow raised his coffee cup in salute. "Go get 'em!" he said with a cackle. "Tell me what's going on when you come back." Mr. Behrend, sitting across from him, raised his cup in a matching salute.

But Gage was already out the door and heading down the sidewalk to the vacant storefront attached to his. The weak warmth of April in the mountains felt good – a nice change after months of nothing but snow and cold and ice – but Gage wasn't about to be mollified by the blooming schedule of the flowers in town square, dammit. He'd lived through months of construction after the bakery fire last April, and had only *just* kept a hold of his sanity by his fingernails through it all. Construction noise had never been something he would consider to be soothing and beautiful, but after months of listening to it up close and personal, he'd downgraded construction noise to *just* above hell on earth.

He yanked at the handle of the door for the abandoned storefront, but it didn't budge. He pressed his face against the dirty glass, cupping his hands around his face to block out the light. If he could just spot whoever was making the noise and gesture at them to stop—

"Shit!" he hollered, yanking his head back in shock when a face appeared on the other side of the glass, just inches away from his.

It took him a moment to place the jaw-droppingly gorgeous female face.

"*Double* shit," he muttered to himself.

It was Skittish Girl from three months back.

He saw a lot of people come through his bakery and after a while, they tended to blur together, but this one…he'd *never* forget her. The whole thing had just been too bizarre. He'd recommended the cream puffs to her, and she reacted like he'd just suggested that he should rape her for kicks and giggles. He'd never seen someone go from normal looking to completely freaked out in under two seconds like that.

And then the way she'd talked about the sugar content of his goodies, like he was lacing his food with crack cocaine or something…

The whole thing had stuck in his craw, to say the least, and now she was banging up a storm in the abandoned store next door.

She was still just standing there, though, not moving an inch towards letting him in to talk to her, so he simply crossed his arms and glared at her through the dirty glass, *clearly* conveying that he wasn't going to leave until she opened the damned door and gave him some answers. After endless moments where he could practically see the gears turning in her head as she scrambled to find a reason not to let him in, she reluctantly flipped the lock on the door and then stepped back, not even pulling the door open for him to welcome him inside.

"What are you doing here?" she demanded before he even got through the door.

"What…" he stuttered, staring at her in disbelief. "What am *I* doing here?" he finally got out. "What are *you* doing here?"

"I asked you first," she volleyed back, glaring up at him, arms crossed protectively across herself. She was just a tiny thing – about Sugar's size and build, actually, with the same dark brown hair but this lady's hair was wildly curly, strands and curls going every which way in a cloud around her head. She looked like an angel – a very pissed-off angel, that was, with a very bad attitude.

Honestly, that was the hardest part for him to understand. Gage wasn't arrogant; he didn't think of himself as God's gift to women. But he was aware that women found him attractive, and when he put his mind to it, he could charm any woman from age 2 to 102.

Which just made this woman's reaction to him, as if she knew some deep dark secret about him that no one else knew and despised him accordingly…it just didn't make sense.

"I'm here because I own the bakery next door," he

finally answered, "and your banging was causing a racket and disturbing my customers." Technically, that was true – she'd been so noisy, even mostly deaf Mr. Krein who'd stopped in earlier had heard her – so he didn't feel too bad blaming this encounter on someone else. "So! What are *you* doing here?"

"*You* own the bakery?" she whispered under her breath, staring up at him with horror in her light golden eyes, the exact color of crème brûlée. "Oh no. Oh *nooo*. The Muffin *Man*. Of *course* it'd be a guy who owns it."

Gage just cocked an eyebrow at her, waiting for her to invite him back into the conversation. As it was, she seemed to be conducting this one all by herself.

She drew herself back up to her full height, which had to be a whole five-foot-nothin', and announced, "I bought this store. It's mine now. So I was just working on some…repairs."

Gage wasn't a male chauvinistic pig – he believed that women could do anything they set their minds to, and if that included carpentry and repairs, then by God, they could do carpentry and repairs. But there wasn't a damn thing about this petite woman in front of him that led him to believe that she actually knew which end of the hammer to swing. She was so damn tiny, anything but a kid-sized hammer would probably be too heavy for her anyway.

Maybe, if he just pointed out the flaws in her plan, she'd pack up her bags and go back to wherever the hell she came from.

One could always hope, right?

"If you actually paid money for this building, you got ripped off," he said bluntly. "Hell, they probably should've paid you just for being willing to take this piece of shit off their hands. There's a reason why it's been vacant for so long. It's got a list of problems longer than my arm, and how on God's green earth did it pass an inspection from any bank with two pennies to rub together? I can't *believe* you got a loan on this place."

"For your information," she said icily, her curls of mahogany flying around her face with every word, "I paid cash. Which I *really* don't see is any business of yours. Now, if you will kindly leave, I've got work to do."

Cash? She had enough money to just buy a building, even a rundown, piece-of-shit building, with *cash*?

She was obviously playing in a different league than he was financially, and was also just as obviously willing to waste said money for the fun of it.

"It's your money to set on fire," he tossed out as he headed for the front door. "Be it far from me to tell you what to do."

"I'm glad you understand," she tossed back and then just stood there, arms crossed, waiting for him to get out of her store.

Her store. He shook his head at the shock of it.

Well, he decided as he stomped back to his bakery, there was no way she would last long. Once she found the leak in the roof, the asbestos in the tiles, and the smoke damage from the bakery fire – if she'd somehow missed the fact that one of her walls was a deep, dark gray – she'd be out of his hair, tail tucked between her legs.

And, in his not-so-humble opinion, it couldn't happen a moment too soon.

CHAPTER 3

CADY

*W*HAT. *An. Asshole.*

How *dare* he come in here, telling her what to do and how to do it, like he'd been put in charge of her life and finances when she wasn't looking. It wasn't any of his damn business how she got the money to buy the building; it wasn't any of his damn business that she'd bought the building. This was America, and she could buy and sell buildings all day long if she wanted to.

She picked up her hammer and began banging again, right about where she thought his kitchen for the bakery would be. Not that the man had exactly given her a tour of the joint, but it made sense it'd be right – *bam!* – about – *bam!* – here – *bam!*

She sat back on her heels and stared at the wall in satisfaction, the rotting 2x4 she'd been whacking at finally detached and out of the way. It was in slivers, beat to smithereens, but she'd won, and that was what mattered. It was all going in the trash anyway, so it wasn't like it had to look good while being pitched into the dumpster.

A part of her really wanted to continue banging as loudly as she could, but she didn't actually have another rotten 2x4 to remove, plus there was the pathetic fact that her arm was getting sore from lifting the heavy hammer.

She shouldn't have sold the carpentry set that she'd been using most of her life – unlike what she'd bought from the hardware store just down the street, her own tools had fit her hand just right, and hadn't worn her out just from lifting the damn things in order to pound on something. But her set had been given to her by her dad and every time she looked at it, the memories of him showing her how to hold a hammer and how to measure a piece of wood accurately had…

Well, they were overwhelming. Wonderfully touching memories that she wanted to treasure but they mostly made her just crawl into bed and inspect the backsides of her eyelids for days at a time, and if she were stronger, she wouldn't have had to rid herself of everything but she wasn't strong – that much was perfectly clear to everyone, even herself – and so it had been sold to a little girl, blonde hair in pigtails. The kid had fallen in love with the purple and pink case that Cady's dad had made for the tools, and had begged her dad to buy the set for her.

"Your dad might be dead tomorrow. Don't waste

your time with him. Treasure every moment," Cady had wanted to tell the little girl, but who told a little girl a thing like that? And so she'd simply sold the set to the kid and then closed her garage door and crawled into bed and stayed there for another three days.

And now Cady had to make do with the carpentry supplies she'd bought from Long Valley Hardware. She'd picked up screwdrivers, screws, nails, a measuring tape – all of the essentials – but when she'd come to the hammer display, she'd balked. She'd asked the crotchety old man behind the counter if he sold smaller hammers than the ones on display (which all looked more like sledgehammers to her than regular hammers) and he'd simply looked at her like she was nuts and then ignored the question.

Great customer service 'round here. First, muscle-bound men practically attack women and then grumpy old men ignore women. Great start to this plan, Cady. Why did you think this was a good idea again?

With a groan, she pushed herself to her feet and headed for the sink, cleaning up before starting in on Phase Two of her plan – scrubbing everything to within an inch of its life. The place could only look better after some elbow grease was applied to it. There was charm here, sure, but it was well-hidden under a layer of grime an inch thick.

She'd die before she admitted it to the jackass next door, but she'd already been unpleasantly surprised by a few problems that she hadn't noticed during her hurried inspection of the business before she'd bought it.

For starters, she'd found some *really* old wiring that appeared to have been installed at the turn of the last century, and after a quick Google search on her phone, she'd confirmed it – she had something called knob-and-tube wiring in a couple of different spots in the store. Not all of it – some of the wiring looked like it'd at least been installed since her birth – but according to her Google search, knob-and-tube wiring was nothing short of a death trap.

Just then, Skittles nudged her leg, begging for some lovings, and Cady picked her up, snuggling the calico against her chest. "I bought this place for a good price so I'd have enough money left over to do extensive remodeling, right?" she told her purring cat. Skittles began kneading her shoulder with her claws, clearly delighted at having been picked up. Cady tried to ignore the fact that she'd just turned into a human pincushion and continued on. "Between the life insurance, the settlement, and the sale of Mom and Dad's home and both of their cars, I have a nice financial cushion. I *refuse* to let myself become intimidated now. *Ouch!*"

She yanked Skittles away from her shoulder, forcing her to extract her claws from her skin.

"I happen to like my skin," she told her seriously. She meowed, unhappy at being dangled up in the air instead of snuggled against her. "Well, I'm unhappy, too. I already smashed my thumb using that damn oversized hammer; I don't need your help in beating me up." She meowed again, piteously, and with a sigh, she snuggled her back up against her abused shoulder. "I don't quite know why I like you," she said, even as she scratched her under the chin, right where she loved it best. Her purrs of pleasure vibrated their way through her chest.

She turned in a circle, looking at the storefront she'd bought. There was a part of her that questioned this particular life choice – okay, a very large part of her – but she also knew that if she didn't make a radical change, an over-the-top, can't-come-back-from-it change, that she'd slide right back into her bout of depression. She had the money; she probably could've hidden away in her childhood home for the rest of her life.

But what kind of life would that be?

It was better that she pushed herself out of the nest, even if the fall to the ground was scary as hell.

CHAPTER 4

GAGE

*W*ITH A SATISFIED SIGH, Gage closed the door to the oven, two angel food cakes tucked safely inside. He'd gotten so far behind with Sugar being on maternity leave and all, he'd been out of angel food cake for a whole week, and a couple of the regulars didn't hesitate in telling him that he was falling down on the job. His regulars weren't exactly wilting wallflowers, and tended to tell him whenever they thought he was screwing something up.

As Gage had told the new fire chief when the guy had moved up to Sawyer a year ago, Sawyerites weren't ones to bite their tongues. If they liked you, you knew it. If they thought you were a worthless son-of-a-bitch, well, you knew that, too.

According to his regulars, his inability to supply them with an endless quantity of angel food cake over the past week had put him squarely on the worthless son-of-a-bitch list, but now that the angel food cake supply was replenished, he could—

The bakery went black.

Gage froze for a moment, so disoriented that he couldn't quite figure out what was going on. As his mind ticked through the situation, though, he realized something much worse than a lack of light was happening: His gas ovens had shut off. Although they ran off gas, the blower and pilot light were all electric, which meant that his long-awaited angel food cakes were in the process of deflating and self-destructing at that very moment.

Double shit dammit all to—

He let out a string of curse words that would singe the eyebrows off any poor soul who was listening, and pulled his cell phone out of his back pocket. Flicking the flashlight app on, he made his way out of the kitchen – which was completely devoid of any windows – and up to the front of the bakery.

Mrs. Gehring, who'd been working her way through her maple donut and coffee, looked up at him with a worried look on her face. "What happened, do you know?" she asked. There was still plenty of light up in the dining area, all of it streaming through the large plate-glass windows, but it wouldn't take a sleuth to notice that every piece of electrical equipment in the building had gone silent.

"The lights went out in the pharmacy," Mr. Maddow chimed in, jerking his head towards the building across the street. Gage looked through the front window and saw that sure enough, the pharmacy was pitch dark. They didn't have nearly as many windows there as he did in his building, so probably more than a few of their customers were busy walking right into shelves—

Which was when he spotted it – *Watson's Electrical Service*. The bright yellow service truck was parked a block up the street. A flash of cold sweat flushed through him from head to toe at the sight. That damn yellow service truck was a harbinger of doom, and it was surely no coincidence that the electricity went out just as Watson's had shown up.

Stomping over to the front window, he let out a string of swear words that easily put his last string of swear words to shame, and Mrs. Gehring gasped audibly.

"Gage Dyer!" she snapped, her cloud of gray hair bobbing around her face as she scolded him. "Your mother would be very disappointed in you if she heard you talking like that."

"Watson's Electrical Service is here," Gage said simply, pointing down the street at the bright yellow truck. He said it as if that explained everything, because honestly, it did.

"Ooohhhhh…" the bakery patrons all said in unison, as if they'd been practicing the line together for years.

"Well, shit," Mr. Maddow finally said, a deep scowl on his lined face, working his way over to stand next to Gage. "We'll be lucky if we have electricity again this year."

"I thought they took his license away," Mrs. Gehring said, clearly forgiving Gage for his swearing and moving onto the more important topic at hand. "Didn't they take his license away?"

"Last I heard, they were still investigating," Gage murmured, his mind going a million miles an hour as he stared out onto Main Street. No one in Sawyer was stupid enough to hire Watson's Electrical Service, which meant that…

Sure enough, he saw the balding man in question crossing the street towards his truck, his trajectory exactly what it would've been if he'd just exited the shop next door.

Dammit all.

Of *course* she had – who else would Skittish Girl hire, other than the most incompetent electrician to ever string two wires together? It was just the kind of stupid-ass stunt she'd pull. Gage ground his back teeth together as he imagined wrapping his hands around her neck and squeezing. Tight. The last two times that man had actually snagged a job, his clients had ended up homeless, after Watson had done such a shitastic job of "repairing" their wiring, their homes had burned to the ground before they could even be inspected by the city inspector.

And now the man had darkened at least part of Sawyer, if not all of it.

What did I do in a past life to deserve this woman as my neighbor?

"I'm going next door," he announced to the bakery. "Considering Watson had a hand in this, it's gonna be a while before everything's back online. When you're done with your food, I'd appreciate it if you headed on out. I'll be shutting down for the day, after I've had a little *chat*," he sneered the word, "with our new business owner next door."

There were a few murmurs of discontent among the ranks, but Gage ignored them, rage boiling inside of him. He was gonna give Skittish Girl hell. Enough of this playing nice bullshit. She'd ruined two cakes, a morning of baking, *and* cost him his sales for the rest of the day.

No, he wasn't about to pull any punches. Girl or not, tiny or not, curly hair or not, it didn't matter. She deserved everything he was about to dish out to her, and more.

This time when he yanked on the door handle, it opened up easily. She'd apparently been leaving it open for Watson to come in and out.

Why in the hell does she trust Watson of all people to come and go freely, but not me?

His eyes searched for the tiny slip of a woman in the semi-darkness of the building, every swear word he'd ever heard and some he'd just invented for the occasion on the tip of his tongue, ready for delivery, when he heard it.

Crying. Someone was crying.

They were quiet about it, but there was no mistaking that sound. Gage had a younger sister – he knew *all* about crying females.

Gage ground his back teeth together, sure his teeth were going to dissolve into powder by the end of the month if this kept up. Dammit all, he didn't want a crying woman on his hands. He wanted an angry woman so he could yell at her like she deserved.

Yelling at a crying woman...that was akin to kicking a puppy.

Speaking of things his momma wouldn't allow, that would definitely top the list.

He finally saw Cady's huddled form in the deep shadows at the back of the store, and he made his way towards her, cursing his luck under his breath. First Watson had to up and destroy the electrical grid of Sawyer, and now Gage couldn't even vent his anger about it.

Seriously – what did I do to deserve this? It had to have been something bad.

He must've stepped on something or his shoes squeaked because her head snapped up and a dark form streaked off her lap and into a side door. A cat? It had moved like it, but Gage couldn't tell for sure in the poor lighting.

Skittish Girl scrambled to her feet. "I...I didn't tell you that you could come in here!" she announced, turning to the side and quickly wiping tears away with the backs of her hands, trying to pretend as if she hadn't been crying.

Good. Gage much preferred anger over tears. He was loaded for bear and ready to let it all loose. "That's because I didn't ask," he retorted. "What in the *hell* were you thinking, hiring Watson's Electrical Services of all places?"

"I...I found him on Craigslist," she stammered, clearly taken aback by the question. "He was available and he was cheap. What in the *hell*," she was mimicking his question, "does it matter to you?"

She had the balls to mimic him when he was so angry, he wasn't seeing straight? Didn't her momma teach her not to poke and taunt a pissed-off man?

"Because he just shut down the electricity to the whole block," he snapped. "Maybe the whole town, I don't know."

"He...he *what*?!" she stuttered, pushing past him and heading up to the front plate glass windows to peer out into the street. "Oh, *shit*," she murmured under her breath, staring out the window at the darkened businesses, her shoulders slumping in defeat. "When we lost electricity in here," she said so quietly, he wasn't sure if she was talking to him or to herself, "he said he had to go get some parts and he'd be right back. He didn't mention anything about it affecting anyone else."

"*Shit*," Gage growled as he came up behind her, not in a particularly forgiving sort of mood, "is right—"

And then instinctively, he was ducking because a fist was coming straight at him and he was doing his best to avoid her wild punch while not also reflexively punching her in return like his gut was demanding that he do. "What the hell?!" he yelled, stunned, forcing his balled-up fist to his side before it connected to her face. "What was *that* for?"

"Would you *stop* sneaking up on me?" she demanded, breathing heavily, eyes wild with panic.

He stared at her.

She stared back.

"I am just standing here," he pointed out, as quietly and logically as he could. He'd always been a live-and-let-live sort of guy, but he was beginning to think that the City of Sawyer should start conducting sanity tests before allowing people to buy businesses within city limits. This lady was *clearly* missing more than a few screws. "What is wrong with me just standing here?"

"Because you're in my personal space! It's a thing, you know, even if *you've* never heard of it."

"Maybe you need to eat more sugar," he snapped back. "It could sweeten you up, and then you'd be less likely to think every person on the planet is about to attack you from behind."

Yeah, fine, her sugar comment from all those months ago still stung, he'd admit it. He'd just never had anyone look at the baked goods that he'd worked so hard to make like they were laced with poison.

Who didn't like donuts, for God's sake? Was that even legal?

"I do not think everyone is attacking me." She

folded her arms across her chest defensively and stared past him, into the dark interior of the business.

"So, it's just me that you treat like a potential rapist?" he asked sarcastically. "Any particular reason that you'd like to share with the class?"

Dead silence.

If he hadn't been watching so closely, he would've missed the slight tightening of her mouth at his question. She was otherwise a statue, devoid of anger or happiness or any other human emotion.

"Rule number one when hiring electricians," he said heavily, deciding to drop the rapist discussion. Whatever her major malfunction was, he wasn't gonna get the answer out of her. Not today, anyway. "Never choose someone who advertises themselves as available and cheap. Any electrician worth a bucket of warm spit will have high prices *and* a schedule packed to the brim. Based on your license plates on your Jeep out back, you're from Boise. Is that right?"

One jerk of her head that could *almost* be termed a nod was all he got.

"So I get," he continued, as if it were perfectly normal to have a one-sided conversation, "that you don't know the local workforce, but why in the hell didn't you ask around? Anyone from Sawyer – hell, anyone from the whole of Long Valley – could've warned you away from him."

"I didn't know to ask around!" she protested. "He's a certified electrician. I looked at the certificate myself before hiring him. Doesn't that mean something?"

"Usually," Gage said sarcastically, fighting back the urge to shake some sense into her. "But last I heard, they're in the middle of trying to decide whether or not to pull that certificate. His last two clients are now homeless because after his handyman work, their homes are now smoldering piles of lumber."

"Wha..." Her gaze, which had been firmly planted somewhere behind him, finally shot up to his face. "Are you being serious?" she breathed. For the first time since he met her, she didn't look combative or pissed off. She looked genuinely worried.

Good. Finally, he was getting through to her.

"Yes. Unfortunately. Since you're from Boise, he probably thought he could actually get a job working for you. No one around here will hire him anymore. Honestly, I was hoping he'd moved on and was terrorizing someone else's town. I can't say I'm thrilled to see him back here."

"What...what do I do?" Her voice was small, as small as her, and Gage felt a little of his anger seep away in the face of her bewilderment. "He said he'd be right back after he got some parts from Franklin. He told me what was wrong, but it didn't mean much to me – it just sounded like a bunch of gibberish, honestly. I don't know much about wiring and electricity..."

She trailed off.

It probably was *gibberish*, but Gage managed to keep that uncharitable thought to himself, if only barely. There was no doubt about it: Watson had seen this lady coming from a mile away. He'd probably told her that the warp core was out of alignment, knowing that she'd just nod and agree that this was a terrible problem to have.

Shit, shit, shit.

She'd shrunk in the last three minutes, her outsized personality deflating right before his eyes and finally matching her tiny body. He didn't want to see that. He wanted to be pissed at her. He wanted to shake her by the shoulders and demand to know where her common sense ran off to. He wanted to demand to know if she was going to reimburse him for missed sales and the two ruined cakes in his oven.

And yet…

"C'mon," he sighed, pulling the front door open. "We need to call Idaho Power and tell them what's going on so they can send a truck up here and get the electricity back on. You need to lock this door and refuse to let Watson back in. When he comes back, tell him he's fired. Better yet, let me tell him. If he doesn't understand the concept, I'll explain it using my fists." The idea held more than a little appeal to him, honestly. Watson was a guy who Gage would gladly chew up and spit out just for fun. "In the meanwhile, I have two ruined cakes in my oven that I need to throw away."

Skittish Girl stopped rummaging through her

purse for a moment and looked up at him apologetically. "That's my fault, isn't it?" she asked in a small voice.

Gage from twenty minutes ago warred with Now Gage, demanding that he say, "Yes, yes it is!" She'd mucked things up and he should make her pay for it, and…

"Don't worry about it," he finally said. "They had a lot of sugar in them anyway."

The corners of her mouth quirked up just a bit at that, and he grinned to himself. So, she had a sense of humor after all. Good to know.

Finally, she produced her keys and locked the front door behind them, and then followed him back to the bakery. He noticed that she was careful to walk behind him, not in front of him like women usually did – women first, and all that – and he wondered for the millionth time exactly what her story was.

But if there was one thing he was sure of, it was that she wasn't about to tell him. He was fairly sure she'd rather eat a bucket of rusty nails than open up to a stranger.

He pulled the bakery door open to the sounds of chaos.

"There you are!" Mr. Burbank from the hardware store snapped. "What is going on? The power's been out for a half hour now and Mr. Maddow here says that the girl next door hired Watson's Electric–you!" He cut himself off, rounding on Skittish Girl as she followed Gage into the bakery. "Did you hire Watson?"

The bakery was quiet as a church as every eye swiveled to her, waiting for her answer. Gage was close enough to see her swallow hard, her hands trembling, and then she hid them behind her back and said, "I did. I didn't know—"

"And you didn't ask!" Mr. Burbank interrupted. "If you'd spent more time researching electricians and less time trying to find tiny hammers, you would've known that Watson is nothing but a worthless pile of sh—"

"She's not going to have him come back," Gage said, interrupting the tirade he could tell wasn't going to end on its own any time soon. He shouldn't, of course – he should let Mr. Burbank give it to her with both barrels. Ignorance didn't make his cakes any less ruined. But he'd been raised to pick on people his own size, and in this moment, this woman wasn't anywhere close to Mr. Burbank's size. "She's going to call Idaho Power to explain the situation; they'll get us up and going. In the meanwhile, everyone in here needs to clear out. Take your donuts and coffee and go home. I'll see you all tomorrow, I'm sure."

Mr. Burbank glared at the woman as he stormed out, muttering not so quietly under his breath about "big city girls too stupid to live" as he went. Mr. Maddow and Mr. Behrend threw back the last of their coffee and also left, avoiding the gaze of both Gage and the woman as they exited. Mrs. Gehring patted the woman on the shoulder as she passed, her cane firmly gripped in her other hand.

"Everyone does dumb things, dear," she said. "Just do try not to shut down the whole town next time, eh?"

And then she too was outside, leaving just Gage alone with his neighbor, who looked distinctly miserable.

"What's your name?" he asked bluntly. Although appropriate, Skittish Girl wasn't going to work if he was going to be stuck with her as a neighbor.

"Cady with a C," she said, and he could tell she'd said that a thousand times. "Walcott – one L, two T's." That, too, was well rehearsed.

"Well Cady with a C, I'm Gage Dyer." He stuck out his hand and they shook, before she pulled her hand away and hid it behind her back again. "This was my grandparents' bakery, and until I took it over from them four years ago, it was named the Dyer Bakery."

"Die-her?" Cady's horrified gaze met his. "Like, the bakery that *kills*?"

"Now you know why I renamed it," he said with a small laugh. "I don't think they'd thought much about their last name before they went with it."

"I guess not," Cady said, still in awe of the horrific name. And, he noted, a little less cowed and angry. He felt a flush of pride at that.

"You can get away with that kind of thing in a small town," Gage said with a shrug, pulling his cell phone out and flipping on the flashlight app as he went on the hunt to find the phone book. "The hospital in town used to be Harm's Hospital, named after Dr. Harm."

"Now you're pulling my leg," Cady said in disbelief. He noticed she stayed up in the front, where the bakery was lit by the light coming through the window, instead of following him around the bakery on his Easter egg hunt. She still didn't trust him one little bit.

"Wouldn't dream of it," he tossed over his shoulder. "He was the only town's doctor for years. They thought it was a good way to memorialize everything he'd done for the community. It wasn't until about ten years ago that they renamed the hospital to Long Valley County Hospital." He dug underneath the cash register through the pile of shit that seemed to accumulate all by itself, courtesy of the Random Shit Fairy, until he finally found the phone book. "There you are, you little bugger," he said, pulling the thin volume out of the pile. "Ready to talk to the power gods?"

CHAPTER 5

CADY

*C*ADY'S THUMB HOVERED over Hannah's name on the screen of her iPhone.

I can call her, I can call her, she's nice, I like her, she'll want to hear from me—

She tapped her thumb on Hannah's name before she could talk herself out of it. It was Saturday, which meant that Hannah wouldn't be working at the school – probably – and might actually have time to go hang out and do something fun.

I can do fun things. I'm a totally fun person. Why, just a couple of weeks ago, I went for a walk around the greenbelt in Boise, and visited the library! Totally living the crazy life—

"Hello?" Hannah sounded confused and hesitant.

Cady shoved down her knee-jerk reaction to hang up and simply pretend that the technology wires of the world had gotten crossed and certainly no, she hadn't called anyone at all—

"Hi Hannah, it's Cady, your long lost roommate!"

she blurted out, trying to act natural and cheerful, as if she called Hannah every weekend just to chat, even as her heart hovered right next to her vocal chords, cutting off her air supply, which totally explained why the world was going a little dark around the edges.

It's fine, everything is fine. You like Hannah. She's nice.

"Cady! Oh my goodness, it's so wonderful to hear from you! When your number popped up on my screen, I thought for sure that I must've entered it wrong into my phone and it was actually a telemarketer calling me. I can't believe you called! How *are* you?"

"Good, good," Cady said automatically. What else could she say? *I know you probably thought I was quirky when I was your roommate; you should see me in action now! Hahahaha! Isn't life grand?!*

She swallowed those all-too-telling words down. "I have a confession to make, actually," she rushed on, before she could change her mind or hang up the phone or swallow her own tongue. "I've moved to Long Valley. Sawyer, to be exact."

There was dead silence on the phone for three very long heartbeats, and Cady wondered if Hannah hadn't hung up instead.

"Wha…what…are you freakin' *kidding* me?! That is the best news ever! When? Why? What are you doing for a job? Cady, I can't believe you moved here! Hold on, just a sec," and then there was the muffled sound of Hannah talking to someone with a suspiciously deep voice, a feminine giggle – Hannah did *not* giggle – and then...

Was that kissing? Hannah was *kissing* someone?!

Cady pulled her phone away from her ear and stared at her screen. Surely she'd dialed the wrong number. It had *sounded* like Hannah before, but... Hannah did not date. That's what had made them such perfect roommates – they'd spent their Friday nights going down to the local coffee shop and reading books while completely ignoring each other and the world around them. They had laughingly called it their socializing time, and Cady had loved every minute of it.

No dates, no boys, no pressure...it had been heaven on earth.

"Sorry about that!" Hannah chirped, her voice barely audible because Cady was still holding the phone away from her cheek and staring at it like it was actually an alien form in disguise.

She quickly shoved the phone back between her ear and shoulder. "No problem," Cady said airily, as if her entire world hadn't just been turned upside down. "Was that...did I just hear you talking to a *guy*?"

"Oh, I forgot you haven't met him yet! Elijah Morland – he's my boyfriend, although no one in town knows it, or at least no one at the school does. I'll tell you all about it in a minute, I promise. But you were telling me how you moved to Long Valley. Spill!"

Hannah sounded giggly and excited and...was

that an edge of *authority* in her voice? It took every ounce of willpower in Cady not to pull her phone away from her ear to check it again. It was Hannah's voice, sure, but absolutely nothing else was right.

I really, really need to meet this Elijah dude. Like, yesterday.

"Oh. Well…ummm…you know about my parents, of course." It was a statement, not a question. Hannah had come to the funeral last summer, an event that Cady vaguely remembered, like the wisp of a dream that hovered on the edges of her mind, not fully formed, always on the verge of slipping away. She'd been in shock that day, and the crushing sense of non-reality had made it hard for her to function. She'd been so sure that at any moment, her mother was going to sweep in and say, "Now why is everyone so sad? Darrell and I are just fine! Look! Do I look dead to you?"

Except she hadn't. She'd stayed dead, laid out in her coffin, her face that terrible ashen gray of the dead, and Dad did too, and…

Cady gulped in some air. She couldn't pass out. She wouldn't.

"Of course," Hannah murmured, suddenly quiet and respectful, the way people always were when the dead and funerals were mentioned.

"I'm…well, I'm afraid I didn't deal with it very well." *Understatement of the century.* "Actually, to be completely honest with you," and she didn't know *why* she was being completely honest with Hannah but the words were spilling out before she could stop them and it felt *good* to talk to someone who cared, dammit, "I spent six months hiding in their house, not going out, not working...Mom had always said that because I was an only child, she wanted to make sure that I would be well taken care of if they died, so their life insurance policy was...large, shall we say." *Stupidly, horrendously large.* "Between that and the settlement with the chartering company...I guess there was a part of me that figured I had enough money to hide from the world for the rest of my life, so I was going to, you know?"

She played with the emerald green pendant hanging from a silver chain around her neck, soothing herself with the edges of the gem.

"And then...well, I'm not sure. I started pushing myself to do things – just little things – and one day, I made myself come up here to Long Valley and hike around, and I'm sorry, *so, so* sorry, that I didn't reach out to you then—"

"Cady," Hannah broke in quietly, "it's okay. What you've lived through...it's more than most people could bear. Just getting out and leaving the house – that was a big step for you to take, and I'm proud of you for doing it. Calling me on top of it all? That would've been asking too much. So don't feel like you need to justify yourself, because you don't."

"Thanks," Cady said, her voice quavering and she *hated* that – *hate, hate, hate* – so she breathed in deep, forcing her pain further down, until she could talk again without the tell-tale quiver in her voice. "It was right around New Year's when I came up here, and I went hiking in the Goldfork Mountains. I loved it – so peaceful, and no planes flying overhead, and... anyway, on the way back out of town, I saw the Muffin Man and decided to get some coffee to drink on the way home, but instead, I was drawn to the storefront next door."

"There's something next door to the Muffin Man?" Hannah asked, more to herself than to Cady. "Wha...oh, right! Doesn't it have a broken awning over the front door or something? No one's had a business there for decades? *That* one?"

"I know how to pick them," Cady said with a strangled laugh.

"Don't tell me you bought that building. You *didn't* buy that building."

"I bought that building!" Cady tried to say it as if it was funny – just a wild thing she did on impulse on a Friday night – and Hannah fell for it.

"Cady Walcott bought the crummiest building in town!" She started laughing. "Oh Cady, when you do stuff, you really do stuff. Just a second!" she gasped. "That means...are *you* the one who knocked out power to the whole town?!"

"Oh God, you heard about that?" Cady wanted to bury her head underneath her couch cushions and never come back out again.

"Did I hear about that..." Hannah laughed again. "Oh, Cady. The principal talked about cancelling school, once he'd heard that someone had actually hired Watson's Electric Service to do work in town. He was sure we wouldn't have power back for a week. Idaho Power had to work overtime to get the power up by the next morning. I'd just heard it was some out-of-towner – I had no clue it was *you*." She was laughing *again*, but finally, what seemed like years later or so, she sobered up. "Seriously, though, ummmm….don't share that tidbit of knowledge with anyone if you don't have to. It…uhhh…wasn't exactly an endearing move, honestly, and people in small towns have long memories."

"Thanks," Cady said sarcastically. "I'll keep that in mind, the next time I have a chance to make an announcement in the town square."

"Sooo," Hannah said, clearly struggling *again* with containing her laughter, and if Cady didn't love Hannah and consider her to be her only friend on earth, she might've hung up just then on her giggly ass, "you bought an abandoned storefront and then proceeded to take out the power to the whole town by hiring the worst electrician this side of the Mississippi. What are you going to sell there, once it's fixed up?"

"Smoothies, combined with a health food store," Cady said, choosing to ignore the phrasing of the question. "Natural food, wheatgrass, no sugar or preservatives…things that are *good* for you." She couldn't help the excitement in her voice – here was something she actually knew something about, and up to this very moment, she'd had no one to tell her big plans to. Trying to start this business had made her miss her mom more than ever, because her mom would've cheered her on, and listened to every moan and groan, and would've driven up to Sawyer to help her clean, and would've...well, just *been* there.

Having someone to talk to who wasn't a guy, and didn't think she was nothing but a giant screw-up... she'd missed this most of all.

She pushed herself up off the couch and began pacing around her small living room, gesturing around the featureless, mostly empty room as she went. "So, I'm sure you've noticed that Franklin is only growing as a tourist town, and Sawyer is on its way there, too. If you're coming from Boise and going up to Franklin to go water skiing during the summer or snow skiing on the mountain in the winter, you're *forced* to go through Sawyer. You can't get to Franklin any other way, period. I think more businesses need to take advantage of that fact. I bet that a lot of the people coming through to play up in these mountains are fitness buffs, and they're gonna want energy drinks to refuel and refresh after a long day of exercise."

"A health food store in little ol' Sawyer, eh?" Hannah said thoughtfully. "I wouldn't have thought to try that, not in such a small farming community, but you're right – all of the hordes of tourists on their way to Franklin *do* drive through Sawyer. I wonder if tourists stop at the Muffin Man. Have you gone next door and introduced yourself to Gage yet, and asked him?"

"Uhhh...we've met," Cady stuttered, her enthusiasm suddenly gone. She dropped back down onto the couch – the only piece of furniture in the room – and pulled a throw blanket around her shoulders. The world was so much nicer when she was under the protection of the crocheted blanket her mother had made for her 10th birthday. "He helped me when Watson shut down the power. I... uhhh...haven't talked to him about tourism traffic, though."

"I'm not surprised to hear that he helped you with the power problem. Gage is a genuinely nice guy – really, one of the good ones out there."

Right. Except when he's busy sneaking around and scaring people half to death.

Cady just made a non-committal noise, hoping Hannah wouldn't pry any further into *exactly* what it was that Cady and Gage had talked about thus far.

"Darn it, I hate to do this," Hannah said regretfully, "but Elijah and his daughter Brooklyn are waiting for me – we were just about to head out the door when you called. Can I call you back later, when I don't have two pairs of sad eyes staring at me pathetically, waiting not-so-patiently for me to finish up?"

"Sure, sure!" Cady said, a part of her relieved that the phone call was over so quickly. *See? You lived. This wasn't so painful.* "Tell Elijah and Brooklyn hello from me, and tell them that I appreciate their patience in letting me borrow you for a bit."

"I can't wait for you to meet them! You'll absolutely love them."

It was on the tip of Cady's tongue to point out that Elijah was a male and thus Cady really, really doubted it, but she just said goodbye to her former college roommate instead and hung up.

"That," she said to her empty living room, "was weird."

Skittles, asleep in the deep basement windowsill and enjoying the spring sunshine, lifted her calico head to stare at Cady quizzically. Deciding that she wasn't offering anything of interest, like fish or tummy rubs, the cat promptly went back to sleep.

"You're a great listener, you know that?" she asked her sarcastically.

This time, she didn't even twitch an ear.

With a sigh, she dropped the fluorescent-pink-and-purple blanket off her shoulders and pushed herself up off the brown-and-gold lumpy couch. The decades-old couch wasn't any more attractive than her well-worn throw blanket was and the two items together were *especially* hideous, but bonus points – the couch came with the furnished basement apartment that she was renting, and that made it perfect. She'd left most everything behind in Boise when she'd moved up to Sawyer. New start and all that. It made for a rather…*white* existence – white walls, white doors, white ceiling – but there were also no memories here to haunt her.

She headed to her bedroom to change. Part of her

wanted to crawl back into bed and laze the day away, but she fought the urge to give into her depression again. It was a sunshiny day – cold but not bitterly so, and in the patches of sunlight between the pines, the snow had completely disappeared, leaving behind tiny tufts of brilliant green as the world struggled to come back to life again.

In other words, it was a great day to go back up into the Goldfork Mountains again and go for another hike. See how different the world looked now that spring was making an appearance.

She scratched Skittles behind the ears as she bade her goodbye. "If I had a dog, he'd be a much better listener than you are," she told the cat as she ratcheted up the purring volume, clearly thrilled with Cady's choice to pet her while talking to her. "It'd serve you right if I came home with a dog in tow." She wondered for a moment how Rochelle, her landlord, would take to the idea of her having a dog, too. She'd convinced her landlord that Skittles was well-behaved and wouldn't cause any problems, an argument that was "helped" along by a healthy pet deposit, but a dog…she'd probably have to double her pet deposit, or more.

But a dog would go out hiking with me, something I'm never going to convince Skittles to do.

Choices, choices…

She grabbed her water pack, filled to the brim with snacks, water, and a windbreaker in case the wind was stronger up in the mountains, and headed out into the brilliant spring sunshine, squinting at the brightness of it all. Going for a hike was an excellent idea. If she kept this up, she just might get back into shape again.

And wouldn't that just be something.

A hike and a phone call, all in one day.

She had to admit, she was pretty damn proud of herself.

CHAPTER 6

GAGE

*G*AGE TUCKED HIS CELL PHONE between his cheek and his shoulder, typing the column of numbers into the adding machine as he suffered through his younger sister's masterful guilt trip. "C'mon, Gage, you gotta come home," Emma said in her best wheedling voice. "The party is about to start. Well, it will as soon as you let Sugar leave and come over here. It's bad enough that you're going to be late for the party – you better not hold the other half of the party hostage, too."

"Sugar's just cleaning a few things up," Gage said distractedly as he compared the two tapes against each other. He was off somewhere and he was damned if he could figure out where. "She'll be over at the house for the dual birthday party soon, I promise."

"I drove all the way from Denver for this," Emma

reminded him, as if he was in danger of forgetting where his only sister lived.

"And I'm excited for it. I'll see you soon."

"But—" And then her voice was gone as he tapped the red phone icon.

It never ceased to amaze him how people's minds worked. They wanted him to do well as a business owner, sure. They supported him wholeheartedly. Cheered him on when he posted a profit or was able to hire another part-time employee.

But if that work ever interfered with him spending time with them, or taking a vacation, or just hanging out for an evening…well now, he needed to sort out his priorities. He should stop being such a workaholic. Didn't he know how important family and friends were?

It didn't seem to *really* matter to anyone, when it came right down to it, that him working hard was how his grandparents enjoyed their retirement. He had to make his payment to them every month without fail – they depended on him. If he got behind financially, he couldn't just declare bankruptcy. It'd ruin his grandparents. He had to make this work, and that took time—

"Hey Gage, I'm heading out," Sugar said, looking tired but pinning a valiant smile on her face as she went.

"Thanks for coming in today, and letting me get caught up on paperwork," he said, for probably the millionth time. "I know you weren't due back until next week and I promise not to keep asking you to come in—"

"It's okay, really. Jaxson was happy to hang out with Rose and the boys were at school for most of the day, so it worked out just fine. Any excuse that he has to play with his daughter, Jaxson is all over. Other than the dirty diapers," she wrinkled her nose a little at that one, "he's a terrific dad. No surprise there."

"No, no surprise," Gage agreed. He hadn't been too sure about the new fire chief when he'd moved into town – actually, Gage had been sure he wouldn't last a week, so it really didn't matter what he thought about the guy. But the day of the bakery fire…Jaxson had saved both of their lives, and that wasn't something Gage would ever forget. "I'll see you over at the house soon. Tell my sister if she'd stop calling me every ten minutes, I'd get more work done."

"I'll make sure to mention that to her," Sugar said dryly, "but I presume you've met your sister once or twice, so I'm fairly sure you know how well that line of reasoning will work."

"Tell her I know how to block phone numbers, and she's treading close to the line – how about that?"

Sugar threw her head back and laughed. "I'll pass the message along. See you soon."

She slipped out the back door and into the parking lot behind the bakery, there only for employees, closing the door quietly behind her.

Gage turned back to the pile of paperwork on his desk with a groan. Despite his brave words to Sugar, he knew what Emma was like, and knew that if he was too late to Emma and Sugar's dual birthday party, she'd still be flipping him shit about it when he was 90. Best friends from the moment they met, Emma and Sugar had been even more delighted when they'd compared calendars and had realized that they were only born four days apart from each other. It'd been years now of celebrating their birthdays on the same day in the same huge party, and it had turned into a bit of a community event, honestly.

One year, Emma's boss had brazenly informed her that she couldn't take the weekend off to go back to Sawyer because they had a big project on the line. She'd told him in no uncertain terms where he could stuff that big project and that she'd see him on Monday, either to pick up her last paycheck or come back to work, and then had walked out. She'd still had a job when she went back, of course – she was too damn good for them to give up, even if she was mightily un-flexible about taking the third weekend in April off every year.

If Gage could just reconcile these two inventory sheets, he might call it good for the night, and head out. Maybe if he brought a tray of lemon poppyseed muffins with him, he could buy Emma's forgiveness. It couldn't hurt, anywa—

"Hey, quick question."

The feminine voice came out of nowhere, and Gage jumped, shoving his chair backwards as he shot to his feet, automatically dropping into a fighting stance as he peered through the poor evening lighting, his desk lamp casting a concentrated pool of light onto his desk but leaving the rest of the kitchen in semi-darkness.

"Oh," he gasped, slowly straightening up, trying to get his heart rate to slow down when he spotted Cady's slight form just inside the doorway that led out to the main dining area. "It's you. I think you just took ten years off my life." The thundering in his ears made it hard for him to hear or think or breathe properly. As his heart began to slow down, though, he could finally ask the obvious question. "Hold on a sec, how did you get in here?"

Even in the dark, he could tell that Cady's eyes were wide – probably with panic, knowing her – and he cursed his instinctual aggressiveness. He'd just been so sure that he was completely alone, so to suddenly hear someone, even a female voice, coming out of the darkness…

"It's okay," she said, backing slowly towards the swinging doors that led out into the main dining room area. "I didn't mean to bother you. I'll just go—"

"No, really, it's fine." He was tempted to put his hand out and stop her, but he somehow knew that it'd just scare her even more. "But really, how *did* you get in here?"

"The front door was open…?" Cady said slowly, as if that should've been obvious. "The bell over the door jingled and everything."

"Dammit," he cursed under his breath. "Sugar's been gone for a while on maternity leave," he explained to Cady, even as he was wondering *why* he was telling her, "and I think she got out of the rhythm of our shutdown procedures, forgetting a couple of important steps like actually locking the front door. Well, whatever." He waved his hand in the air to brush all of that away, and then flipped on the overhead fluorescent lights, bathing the kitchen in brilliant stark white light. He didn't like to have them on in the evenings – it was too sterile and made him feel like he was working in a hospital or morgue or something – but somehow, he figured Cady would feel better if she could see clearly. Sure enough, as soon as the lights flipped on, she stopped doing her backwards shuffle towards the swinging doors, and stood up a little straighter.

"So, are you going to tell me what you needed?" he asked, casually leaning against the cinder block wall of his kitchen, trying to convey a sense of openness and calm.

Red climbed up in her cheeks and she looked positively miserable. "I hate to…I just couldn't…"

She was stuttering, and he wondered for a moment if she was going to finish her thought or if they were just going to have a staring contest all evening. He didn't say anything, though, and didn't move a muscle. It was like trying to interact with a wild animal that might bolt at any moment.

What in the hell happened to this lady? There is nothing about this that's normal or healthy.

"I looked it up on my phone," she finally blurted out, "and I can't find any restaurants in town that are open past two – in fact, I only found one restaurant in town according to Google – Betty's Diner, and I haven't eaten there yet but they have good reviews but they're a breakfast diner and it's a little late for breakfast of course but I am *starving* and I don't really want to drive to Franklin so I thought I'd come over here and ask if you knew of another restaurant that was open that just wasn't showing up on Google. I tried calling my friend Hannah but she didn't answer, and you were the only other person I could think of."

The torrent of words finally dried up, and Gage just stared at Cady for a moment, trying to think through everything that had just spilled out of her, because there was a hell of a lot to unpack there.

"You know someone in town named Hannah?" he asked, knowing that wasn't the point but still, too surprised to let it go. He'd somehow thought that Cady didn't know a soul up in Long Valley – at least, he'd never seen anyone come into her business to help her out with the cleaning and remodeling.

"Hannah Lambert – she's a fifth grade teacher over at the elementary school. We were roommates at BSU."

"Oh, I know Hannah," he said with a bright smile. She was a regular at the bakery, along with Carla from the flower shop and Michelle from the city pound. The three of them had been meeting up at the bakery as long as Gage had owned it. "A *real* nice lady. Well, that aside, Google was right. The only restaurant in town is Betty's, and they're only open until two. Their food *is* good, but you're not going to have much luck there right now."

"Dammit." Cady looked completely deflated by this information. "I thought for sure that Google was just missing something. How does Sawyer only have one restaurant?!"

Gage shrugged. He hadn't thought about it much – it was just the way it was. "Well, one and a half if you count this bakery," he pointed out, his pride a little bruised at her complete dismissal of his business. At her skeptical look, he was of course obligated to push back. "Not *everything* I sell is laced with sugar. My muffins are pretty healthy, and I do have whole wheat bread for sale."

"Well, I better get going," she said, pointedly choosing to sidestep any discussion on the healthiness of his wares. He narrowed his eyes at her, but she seemed completely oblivious to how her dismissal of his business might be a blow to his pride. "Franklin is, what, 30 minutes away?" She was already turning to go when he reached out and stopped her, his hand on her shoulder. She flinched and he hastily dropped his hand down to his side.

"I just thought I'd offer," he said before he could think better of it, "my sister and her best friend's birthdays are only four days apart, and so during

Birthday Time, Emma comes back from Denver and they throw this *huge* party at my parents' house. Half the town shows up. You could come over with me. It's a potluck so every kind of food you can imagine will be out for you to choose from, and because it'll be so crowded, no one will think twice about me showing up with you. It won't be like I'm bringing you home to meet my parents as my date or something."

He laughed at the sheer ridiculousness of the idea, but her eyes went wide as dinner plates at the thought. She *clearly* hadn't considered that possibility as she'd listened to the invitation, and now that it'd been introduced to her, she was well on her way to freaking out about it.

He mentally kicked himself for even bringing it up. "But like I said," he hurried on, "that's not going to be what anyone thinks, because most of the town will be there, and everyone just hangs out with everyone else. You should meet someone else here other than Mr. Burbank, and the world's worst electrician, and Hannah. It wouldn't hurt to get to know other Sawyerites if you're going to open up a business here, right?"

She nodded slowly as she thought through that. "Yeah, you're right. So, we're just going as friends?"

"Just friends," he repeated, and held out his hand to her to shake. It was a weirdly formal thing to do, but then again, that was a phrase that summed up Cady perfectly: Weirdly formal. And skittish. And prickly.

And downright gorgeous the few times he'd actually managed to make her smile.

Not a full-blown smile, of course – he was charming, not a miracle worker – but even the small quirk of her lips had made all the difference in the world.

She put out her hand and they shook quickly, her grip surprisingly forceful, and then she pulled away, clasping her hands behind her back. "I'll go get my purse and stuff and meet you in the parking lot in the back and follow you over, okay?"

"Perfect. But—" He touched her lightly on the shoulder before she could turn away completely, and then pulled back when he saw her flinch again. "I just wanted to make something clear…my sister, Emma, is a matchmaker of extreme proportions. She had Sugar, her best friend and my only full-time employee, convinced that I was desperately in love with her, and it caused problems for a while between us. So, I wanted to say upfront that no matter what insanity my sister spouts, *please* don't believe her. She's sure that without her help, I will die an old and single man, never having tasted true love."

He laughed because obviously, you can't get any crazier than that, but Cady just arched an eyebrow at him.

"I'll do my best to remember you're not madly in love with me," she said sarcastically. "See you out back," and then she was walking quickly through the front dining room area and out the front door, leaving him standing and watching her go.

"Sometimes, you're a real idiot," he said aloud to the empty bakery. "Inviting Cady to this party just tops the list. You might as well have invited the offspring of a porcupine and a rattlesnake mating." He rubbed at his forehead wearily, and then grabbed a to-go box and began filling it with lemon poppyseed muffins, Emma's favorite. Something made him think that a little bribery could go a long ways with his sister tonight.

CHAPTER 7

CADY

She followed Gage's tail lights in the darkness, winding their way to a part of town she hadn't been to yet. With the setting of the sun, all of the warmth of the day had disappeared, and Cady found herself shivering violently as she drove.

Was it the cold, though, causing the shivers? Or was it panic?

I am not panicked. This is a fun event; an easy and low-stress way of getting to know my neighbors. I am going to have fun and hang out and I shall not throw up or pass out. Not even once. Not even a little bit.

She could tell which house was the Dyer's house from a block away – there were cars and trucks parked up and down the street, people walking every which way, laughter and music ringing out…

It appeared that Gage was not exaggerating when he said that half the town would be here tonight.

I am not going to panic – it's good *that so many people are here. Makes it easier to hide in the crowds. No one will notice me.*

She clung to that thought, hanging onto it for all she was worth. She wondered what Emma and Sugar were like. She'd never met either one of them, and with the size of the party that was in full swing, she doubted that'd change tonight. No doubt there'd be crowds of people around the two of them.

They slowly drove past the Dyer house, finally finding a place to park big enough for two vehicles a block down. Cady sat in the darkness of her car, gripping the steering wheel and chanting to herself.

"I'm fine. Everything is fine. This is going to be fun. I'm going to enjoy myself. Everything is fi—"

Knock-knock.

"Are you coming?" Gage asked, his breath in clouds around his head in the freezing mountain air as he stared through her driver's side window.

She swallowed the yelp of pure terror that was strangling the breath right out of her, and instead slowly peeled her fingers off the steering wheel, one finger at a time. She really, really, *really* wished he'd quit doing that. Was it too much to ask that he stop jumping out of the shadows and scaring her every time she turned around?

On wobbly legs, she got out of her Jeep and followed him back towards the brightly lit house, balloons and twinkle lights strung across every available surface, twangy music thumping out into the night. Cady concentrated on the lyrics of the song rather than on the rippling muscles of Gage's arms as he carried the overloaded tray of baked goods, and realized to her horror that the country singer was singing about a red solo cup.

I have officially moved to Hickville. No wonder I'm not fitting in around here. I don't own a single pair of cowboy boots, and I'm in full possession of all of my teeth.

She wanted to turn around and go back to her Jeep and drive away, but the smells were too enticing and her stomach was rumbling too loudly. She followed him up the front steps and into the brightly lit house instead, the warmth and cheerfulness immediately enveloping her. It gave her the strangest sense of déjà vu, and it took her a moment to figure out why.

The bakery. Other than the moments when Gage is freaking me out completely by sneaking up on me, the bakery has always felt warm and welcoming. His parents – he must've gotten this talent from his parents.

As strange as it was, the sheer number of people there made her feel more relaxed. In a crowd this size, no one was going to jump her or attack her – they wouldn't dare. She was safe here.

She felt the knot in the pit of her stomach unwind just a little, and her breath came a little easier.

"There you are!" She heard a woman's voice ring out above the general roar of the party and then a female was launching herself at Gage, hugging him and practically knocking the tray of goodies to the ground in her enthusiasm. Cady watched with detached interest, wondering if this was Gage's girlfriend, when the girl slung her arm through Gage's and then turned towards Cady, her bright smile growing even brighter. The woman's eyes skittered up and down Cady, clearly checking her out, and Cady gulped. Dammit. Was she going to get pissy because Cady'd arrived with her boyfriend?

She opened up her mouth to proclaim defensively, "We're just friends!" when the woman turned back to Gage and punched him on the shoulder. "She's even prettier than you said!"

Cady's mouth snapped back shut as she took in two things:

1) This most definitely couldn't be Gage's girlfriend, if he'd been telling her that he thought someone else was pretty; and

2) He'd told this woman that he thought Cady was pretty.

Eyes wide, she turned to Gage, waiting for an explanation that made sense.

Clearly unhappy, Gage muttered, "Cady, this is my loud-mouthed sister who is turning 27 years old. Emma, this is Cady, my new next-door neighbor at the bakery. I am going to go deliver this tray over to the dessert table and see what else there is to eat." He turned and marched away, back ramrod straight, his muscles rippling with every step.

"Ignore him," Emma said freely, slipping her arm through Cady's. "He's just a sourpuss because I spent the last hour hounding him to actually leave the bakery behind and spend time doing something other than adding up numbers or baking up cookies. The man has no concept of how to have fun. Over here," and she began dragging Cady towards the overloaded buffet tables, apparently not needing a word in response, "is all of the food for the party. Pick out what you like, and then meet me through those doors," she pointed at the sliding glass doors at the back of the house, "and you can sit with Sugar and me while we discuss Gage's many failings together. He is my favorite older brother, but that doesn't mean that he's perfect." She slipped her arm out of Cady's and headed out towards the sliding glass door, skillfully winding through the crowds, glad-handing and chatting as she went.

Cady watched the woman in awe for a moment – she deserved to be in the halls of Congress with that kind of personality – but finally turned back to the overloaded tables with a quiet murmur of appreciation. Food, after all, was why she was in this mess to begin with, and as hungry as she felt in that moment, she was more than a little tempted to just pick up a casserole dish and tip the whole thing towards her mouth, skipping the niceties of plating the food beforehand.

She was a big city girl – maybe she could convince everyone that this was how it was done in Boise nowadays. The latest trend or some such bullshit.

Reluctantly, she gave up the dream and instead

picked up a sturdy paper plate – no flimsy, cheap plate here; the Dyers obviously knew what kinds of food quantities to expect – and began working her way down the buffet tables, spooning out tiny portions of every delicious dish and still running out of room all-too-quickly on her plate.

As she went, she sensed...something and looked up to see Gage standing next to an older woman – his grandmother, perhaps? – an unhappy look on his face as they talked, pushing his glasses up the bridge of his nose absentmindedly. The older woman, her steel-gray hair pulled up in a severe bun, noticed that Cady was looking at them and instead of smiling at her in greeting, the woman turned her back on Cady in a clear sign of disapproval.

Is she mad about the power thing? Did I ruin her cakes like I ruined Gage's? Or is it something else...?

Clutching her paper plate carefully, she wound towards the glass sliding doors, trying to pretend as if she hadn't noticed the woman's clear-as-a-bell unhappiness at her presence.

I'll go outside and hide from her. Maybe she'll forget all about me.

It seemed like just as good of a plan as any; Cady wasn't about to give up her plate of food and drive to Franklin at this point based on a crotchety old woman. Not when she had sustenance right there, ready to be eaten, the smell drifting up to her nose in tantalizing waves.

The Dyers, having spent years holding an outdoor

party every April when the weather could be warm, cold, or Antarctic-frozen, had apparently gotten smart and invested in heat lamps that they'd placed throughout the backyard, providing light and much more importantly, heat to the groups of people huddled around them. Cady scanned the crowds, worried that she'd taken too long to get out there – Emma would probably have a hundred friends hanging around her, all wanting to talk to her by now – but finally she found Emma and another girl huddled towards the back of the yard, chatting and laughing freely as they practically hugged the heat lamp they were standing next to.

With a grateful sigh, Cady made her way over to them, thrilled that she recognized at least one person in the huge group. She hadn't spotted Hannah, so she was guessing her friend either wasn't close to the Dyers, or had schoolwork to grade, or maybe Elijah didn't like parties much more than Cady did.

I really need to get around to meeting this guy. Hannah, dating someone…will miracles never cease.

"Hi," she said shyly as she came walking up to the pair of best friends. There was an energy – a level of comfort between them that spoke of their familiarity with each other – and they turned as one to Cady.

"Cady!" Emma exclaimed excitedly, greeting her as if she hadn't just chatted with her five minutes earlier. "I was just telling Sugar here that you were going to come out back and join us. Sugar, this is Cady, Gage's new next door neighbor at the bakery.

Cady, this is Sugar, my best friend and Gage's only full-time employee."

Carefully, Cady balanced her loaded paper plate in one hand so she could shake Sugar's hand with the other. Looking the woman over, she could see why Emma had thought her brother should date her. She was petite, despite having just given birth recently, with generously sized breasts for someone that small, and straight brown hair in a braid over her shoulder.

"So good to finally put a face to the name," Sugar said with a warm smile. "I've been gone on maternity leave for the past five weeks, so I haven't been at the bakery a whole lot, but starting on the 26th, I'll be back to work full-time. I heard you've been having some…problems getting the store next door up and going."

"Oh?" Emma said, looking at Cady quizzically. "Spill. With me being all the way over in Denver, I'm the last to hear any of the local gossip."

With Hannah's warning blaring in her mind, Cady did her best to downplay her disastrous first couple of weeks. "I apparently have terrible taste in electricians," she said around a mouthful of potato salad, too starved to wait one more moment to start shoving food into her mouth. "I didn't know that, of course, so…things got a little interesting." She shoveled a bite of fruit salad in, hoping to stave off more questions by clearly being too busy chewing to talk, not realizing that Sugar would ever-so-helpfully take up the story instead.

"She hired Watson's Electric," Sugar told Emma, as if that one statement should explain everything. Emma turned back to Cady, her eyes wide.

"Oh dear God, tell me you didn't."

Cady shrugged her shoulders and sent her a grimacing smile as she began working on a juicy slice of ham.

Food. Give me food.

"Knocked out power to the whole town," Sugar continued, when Cady didn't. "They almost cancelled school over it because the principal didn't think they'd get the power back online within the week, once he'd heard who the electrician was."

"You're lucky you didn't get hauled out into town square and drawn and quartered for that one," Emma said, starting to laugh at the idea of someone intentionally hiring Watson's Electric, and then abruptly stopped. "Hold on," she said seriously, every trace of laughter gone, "you're not telling a lot of people about this, right?"

"I've managed to keep myself from making an announcement in town square," Cady said around a delightfully moist and soft roll. "I've been informed that wouldn't be in my best interest."

"Definitely something to keep under wraps," Emma agreed dryly. "Hey, I don't know if you know this, but I'm actually an architect over in Denver and although the firm I work for specializes in new build projects, I could probably also help with a remodel. I could stop by this weekend before I head back to work and look over your building – tell you what I think you should spend money on, and a rough idea of how much each project should cost."

This, finally, was enough to get Cady to stop shoving food in her mouth.

"Wow," she said softly. "I...that would be great." She wanted to hug Emma, but she kept her hands occupied by the plate of food instead. Having someone on her side, giving her guidance, not just shaming her for stupid mistakes she'd already made... there was no more perfect present than that.

Emma shrugged nonchalantly. "I like challenges, and helping you put together an action plan for a remodel of that piece-of-shit building would totally be a challenge." Cady couldn't help her shout of laughter at that. She wasn't about to admit it to the other Dyer sibling, but the more she worked on the building, the more she realized that it really was a piece of shit.

At this point, she was sticking to it out of sheer pride and nothing more, something she wouldn't admit to if her life depended upon it.

"I thought you said you were on maternity leave?" Cady asked Sugar hesitantly. "Where's your baby at?"

"Jaxson, my husband, has her. It's too cold to keep her outside, even next to the heat lamps, and at parties like this, I wouldn't be holding her anyway. If you ever want free babysitters, just show up in a crowd of Idaho women with an adorable newborn in your arms. You won't see your baby again until she either needs fed or her diaper changed. From age 10 to 100, Idaho women have this instinctive maternal love for every bundle of drool within ten miles. It's a thing you have to see to believe."

Cady nodded as if she totally understood but honestly, she didn't. Unlike Hannah, her gift had never really been with the tiny human population; she preferred her humans to be able to pee in a toilet without help, and once they got over the age of 15, she also preferred them not to be in the possession of a penis *or* too many muscles.

Really, though, she was easy to please. People who had a high tolerance level for quirkiness were also a huge plus, along with the ability to appreciate a good book…or a guilty pleasure book.

As long as it was a female, someone who could pee and poop without Cady's help, read novels like they were going out of style, and put up with things like Cady not wanting to be around other men, why then, they were destined to become best friends.

Easy to please, honestly.

Before Cady could figure out a socially acceptable response to Sugar's statement – never her strong suit to begin with – a commotion broke out up on the deck of the house, leading from the house into the backyard. Cady squinted, the bright flames of light from the heat lamps making it more difficult to see in the darkness, when a drunken voice drifted towards them. "It was shupposed to be *my* baby." It was a very male and very angry voice, and Cady felt panic shooting through her just from hearing him speak.

Bad guy, bad guy, very bad guy, run away—

"Shit!" Sugar and Emma exclaimed in unison and they took off running towards the back porch.

Cady hesitated for a moment – honestly, running *towards* the pissed-off male struck her as a Very, Very Bad Idea – but they were also the only two people at the party that Cady knew other than Gage and she didn't know where he was at, and so despite her very large misgivings, she wasn't about to let them out of her sight. She dogged their steps, and drew to a stop when they did.

"I knew it!" Emma groaned under her breath. "Hey, Dick," she called out, "no one invited you here, so why don't you just leave, and we'll pretend this never happened?"

A man turned towards them, a hand gun glinting in the porch light, and everyone in the crowd took a step back while inhaling simultaneously...everyone, that was, except for Sugar.

"C'mon now, Richard," she said softly, placatingly, moving slowly towards the swaying man, his breath coming out in puffs around his head, ringing his head like some sort of dragon breathing fire. "You know this won't help bring our baby back."

Why is she moving towards this man? Sugar, you need to run away. Run away! Didn't you see the gun? Run!

"Sugar and Richard had a baby together?" someone whispered, right behind Cady.

"She fell down the stairs to their basement and lost it before she was very far along," someone else whispered back. "I'm guessing that he's taking it personally that she actually had Jaxson's baby."

Cady looked at the clearly drunk Richard, waving a gun around in one hand and a beer around in the other, and at Sugar who was only a few steps away from him, doing her best to soothe him. Sugar had seemed so nice, so friendly, so…so *normal* when they'd stood in the backyard talking. How was it that she'd lived through something so horrendous and had come out the other side still sane?

Because she's stronger than you are.

"Where is it? Where's the baby?" Richard demanded, his words slurring together, and then he began stumbling towards Sugar, trying to attack her, his muscles rippling in the porch light, and this time, Cady felt the panic completely overwhelm her, paralyzing her. She couldn't breathe or think or scream and she wanted to run and hide or kick him in the nuts or *something* but instead she was just watching as this man attacked a defenseless woman right in front of her—

CHAPTER 8

GAGE

With a grumpy sigh, Gage rearranged the decimated platter of goodies that he'd brought, absentmindedly staging them for maximum appeal just as he did daily at the bakery.

Not that the guests really needed any encouragement to inhale his baked goods; he probably should've brought another tray, actually. Last year, the miniature cinnamon rolls had been a crowd favorite but this year, the cream puffs with chocolate inside were pulling ahead.

With another disgruntled sigh, Gage looked around the crowded living / dining room of his parents' house, hoping to spot the Birthday Girls, but he couldn't catch sight of either one. He hadn't seen hide nor tail of Cady, either, since she'd made a beeline for the buffet table. He'd been caught when he first got there by his grandmother, who'd been supremely unhappy to see him showing up with someone of the female persuasion, and by the time he'd finally convinced her that he and Cady were simply friends, Cady had pulled a disappearing act.

It wasn't any of his business, of course – this had been a good idea to invite her here so she could get to know other people in the community. She was clearly busy doing that, so he should be happy. And he was. He just…

Restless, he headed for the sliding back door that led out into the backyard. Maybe she was back here, hanging out with Emma and Sugar. That was probably it. Emma could make friends with a taciturn hermit who hadn't stepped foot outside of the Amazon for the last twenty years. She could surely make friends with Cady, who at least had flashes of friendliness…whenever she was brave enough to let her guard down.

He was stepping through the sliding glass door when movement to the right caught his attention, *right* before a heart-stopping scream grabbed his attention by the balls.

"Let me *go!*" Sugar yelled, her arms flailing as her ex-husband pulled her backwards across the porch, holding her in a chokehold as he went, and was that…? Dear God, the man had a gun shoved underneath her chin.

Gage didn't pause or think or breathe but only launched himself at the man who dared to hurt Sugar. For just one moment, he was back in high school again, going for the tackle to bring down the other team but this time, so much more than *just* a championship was on the line.

Dick's eyes, bleary and unfocused from the massive amounts of alcohol he'd consumed before crashing the birthday party, swung towards Gage, realizing a bit too late that he was going to go down. Instinctively, he threw Sugar off to the side, probably realizing that even as tiny as she was, she could still slow him down just by fighting him tooth and nail, and turned to make a run for it.

Which was when Gage hit him with an oh-so-satisfying crunch of bone and muscle beneath him. They skidded across the deck with Dick on bottom, thank God, no doubt depositing slivers where the sun didn't shine as they went, until they came to a stop next to the railing.

"Stop! Help! He's attacking me!" Dick yelled like the little girl he was, throwing his hands up in front of his face to protect it.

"It doesn't feel so good to be on the receiving end, does it?" Gage asked, rolling to his feet so he could get some good leverage behind his punches. He'd hate to land only light taps on the worthless son-of-a-bitch. He was just debating whether he should do an uppercut to the jaw or a fist straight into Dick's stomach when he heard Abby Miller's voice behind him.

"I've got it from here, Gage," she said calmly, stepping up beside him. A Long Valley County cop, she was apparently on duty tonight, decked out as she was in her police uniform.

"Oh hey," Gage greeted her, cool as a cucumber, even as he drew back his booted foot and kicked Dickwad in the side as hard as he could. "I didn't know you were here," he said calmly over the screams from the worthless conglomeration of cells writhing on the deck.

"Just stopped by while on my rounds to wish the Birthday Girls a happy birthday," Abby replied easily, not batting an eyelash at the kick Gage had delivered, but when he drew his foot back for round two, she put her hand on his arm. "We don't want to give this man any reason to be able to talk his way out of jail, right? Because we all know what happened the last time someone tried to teach this guy a lesson."

With a regretful sigh, Gage stepped back to give Abby the space she needed to work. She was right, of course – a beat-down on Richard Schmidt was how Abby fell in love with her prisoner and future husband, Wyatt Miller. Because the damage to Dick's face wrought by Wyatt's fists had been so extreme – requiring facial reconstruction surgery to get him back to semi-normal looking – his lawyer had been able to successfully argue that he'd paid for his mistake of driving while fall-down drunk, and Dickwad had walked away without having to serve even a day behind bars.

It didn't hurt that Richard Schmidt's father was

the judge in town. In small counties like theirs, it never did.

Gage straightened his glasses on his face – they'd been knocked askew during the fight – and then looked around to try to figure out where Jaxson was, and if Sugar was okay, and where were Emma and Cady? He found that Jaxson was holding Sugar who was holding their one-month-old, Rose, and even as the beautiful baby slept peacefully in her momma's arms, Sugar kept cooing to her, "It's okay, baby girl. No one's gonna hurt you. You're all right. Uncle Gage saved us."

Uncle Gage...It was an honorary title Sugar had granted him the day of her wedding to Jaxson, and it'd touched Gage every time he heard it but tonight, it meant so much more.

But what if he hadn't been there? What if Dickwad's finger convulsed out of panic or fear, and Sugar had died? Terror spiked through him at the thought and he caught the gaze of Jaxson, whose arms were protectively wrapped around his wife. Jaxson mouthed, "Thank you."

Gage nodded once in acknowledgment, and he felt his panic over Sugar's well-being subsiding just a smidge. Jaxson would take care of her. He would make sure she was okay, but who would look after Emma and Cady? He'd come out partway through the confrontation – it was possible that Dickwad had put his hands on them also. He pushed his way through the crowd, nodding as people clapped him on the back and congratulated him on being the "hero of the night," until he finally found Emma and Cady together, clinging to each other, a terrorized look on their faces.

"There you are," he said, surprised at the strength of the relief that washed over him. "Are you guys okay?"

Emma straightened up first. "That son of a bitch!" she spat out. "He didn't love Sugar while he was married to her; I don't know why he thinks he deserves anything more from her. Did you *smell* the alcohol coming off him? I swear to God, I was getting drunk just breathing in the fumes!"

Satisfied that Emma was indeed just fine, Gage turned to Cady. "How are you doing?" he asked quietly, not making a move towards her, waiting for her to think through the answer before giving it.

She looked up at him, her golden brown eyes huge with sheer panic and terror. *Shit.* She was spiraling and Gage knew that if he didn't break through to her and pull her back from the abyss, she'd go tumbling over. What she'd just seen was traumatic, sure, but somehow, Gage knew it had been a thousand times worse for Cady than anyone else in the crowd. He didn't know how he knew that – he just did.

Cady continued to stand there, blinking, not saying a word, and the longer she said nothing, the more worried Gage got. This wasn't good. She wasn't going to be fine. She wasn't going to snap out of it and come out fighting on the other side, like Emma had.

And then without a sound, she turned and sprinted around the side of the house, through the gate that led into the front yard, disappearing into the shadows as if she'd never existed. Emma turned to Gage, her eyes wide with surprise. "Is there something wrong with Cady?" she asked quietly.

"I think so, but...well, she hasn't exactly been confiding in me. I'll be back," he promised his sister, and then took off in a jog towards the front of the house. She probably didn't want to hear from him or see him, but since he was the only one there who even had a chance of getting through to her, he had to try. There was a primal terror in her eyes that called out to his protective nature – he wanted to care for her; to help her realize that she was going to be okay. There was a small part of him – okay, a very large part of him – that doubted that he'd succeed, but still, he had to try.

She'd made it to her Jeep by the time he finally caught up to her, but she was just sitting in the darkness, not moving, not turning the key, just staring blankly ahead of her, a frozen statue of a person.

He hesitated for a moment, and then pulled on the door handle to the passenger door, sending up a silent thank-you when it swung open for him. He'd been a little worried that she'd locked herself in, and he was a thousand percent sure there was no way he'd be able to talk that statue in the driver's seat into letting him in.

"Cady," he said, his voice just above a whisper, as he struggled to get comfortable in the cramped quarters of her Jeep. Her back seat was filled to the brim with junk, and she obviously hadn't had someone in the passenger seat who was over 4'10" in a very long time. Finally, he managed to get his legs in just the right spot and he turned towards the statue sitting in the driver's seat, still not moving, not blinking, not…breathing?

"Cady, you gotta breathe."

Nothing.

He reached over and patted her roughly on the shoulder, much like he'd burp a baby, hoping to force some air into her lungs.

He'd known to expect an explosion from her – she didn't appreciate being touched, no matter the circumstances – but still, the ferocity of her attack was shocking. She went from perfectly still to launching herself across the console between them and straight at his eyes, howling as she tried to blind him with her fingernails. He found himself wrestling with her, pulling her arms down by her sides, pinning them there, doing his best not to hurt her even as he kept her from hurting herself.

"Cady, it's me. It's Gage. You're okay. You're safe here. You're fine. Just breathe." He kept his voice low and smooth, not even winded by Cady's struggles in his arms. She was such a tiny thing, the only way she'd manage to hurt him was if she got access to delicate parts of him, like his eyes or his nuts.

Yeah, even a tiny slip of a human could do real damage there.

Finally, she wore herself out and collapsed against him, her breathing harsh and ragged in the darkness. "You're okay, you're all right," he kept murmuring, finally moving his hands to her cloud of wildly curly hair and stroking it out of her face. "You're gonna be fine."

Eventually, she made a move to clamber out of his arms and back into the driver's seat, but Gage ignored that, instead settling her more comfortably on his lap, where he held her loosely. *Please, dear God, let my dick stay down. Even with her sliding her very curvy, very delicious ass across me, this is* not *the time to sport a boner.*

"You wanna tell me what's going on?" he asked in the darkness – a statement, not a question.

CHAPTER 9

CADY

"You wanna tell me what's going on?" Gage asked her quietly, his breath hot on her neck as he held her captive. He was trying to nestle and hold her in a reassuring way – the rational part of her could tell that was true – but as far as she was concerned, trapped was trapped, and whether the trapping was done with ropes of silk or metal chains, she was still stuck exactly where she didn't want to be – on a guy's lap.

And not just any guy. Oh no, of course not. This was a huge, muscle-bound, could-squash-her-flat-if-he-wanted-to guy.

She wanted to struggle again but she was tired from the first bout and then there was the awful fact that he sounded so reasonable. So calm and friendly and caring, as if spilling her guts to him should be an easy thing to do.

"No."

She sounded truculent even to her own ears, probably because she *was* being truculent, but despite her best truculescent (*was that a word? It should definitely be a word*) efforts to drive him away, he seemed completely unmovable. A human version of the granite cliffs that made the Goldfork Mountains so beautiful.

But this…this wasn't beauty. This was him being a jackass. She *wanted* him to pull away, to wash his hands of her and leave. Why did this bastard insist on *being* there? Couldn't he just walk away? Couldn't he just abandon her like everyone else had and get it over with already?

Waiting for the other shoe to drop was exhausting.

Terrifying, honestly.

But he didn't leave and his muscular arms were still there, encircling her, holding her loosely. She'd already figured out that that was a trick, though. Like those Chinese finger traps she used to play with as a kid, the harder she struggled, the more trapped she was. She'd already tried every self-defense trick in the book on him and it hadn't made a damn bit of difference.

Self-defense…She'd studied up on that particular topic like her life'd depended on it – because it did – and it was from that in-depth study that she'd learned that a woman of her stature had to go for the more delicate parts of the male body: The eyeballs or the groin.

No matter how Goliath a guy was, *nobody* could handle being hit there.

But as hard as she'd fought, Gage had deftly protected those delicate parts of his body, all while simultaneously keeping her from wiggling free of his grasp. If she didn't know any better, she would've sworn he had ten hands.

"Wanna tell me what's going on?" he repeated in the darkness, just as quietly, just as…as caring as before, and somehow, this broke her. Broke through her defenses. Or maybe it was because she had no choice. Or maybe it was because he was so quiet, so calm, no matter what she threw at him.

Whatever the reason was, she found herself talking, almost without meaning to, but before she could stop herself or reconsider, it was all just spilling out, an avalanche of pain tearing through her.

"I was an assistant physical therapist," she said in a monotone voice. "Went to school at Boise State and got my degree in sports medicine. Afterwards, I started working for a physical therapist's office in Boise that specialized in working with the student athletes who were attending BSU. It was…fine. I'm actually not much into sports – like, at *all* – and had stupidly thought when I got my degree that I'd be working with people who hurt themselves doing yoga or something. Which, in retrospect, was a really idiotic thing to think." She laughed bitterly at her ignorance. She sure had been dumb. "Of *course* I'd be working with football players who got hit wrong at practice. Why I ever thought otherwise…" She sighed.

He was rubbing her back in small, slow circles, and it was soothing, and for a moment, she wondered if this was how a baby felt – wrapped up in someone's arms who was bigger and stronger than them, being soothed by hands that seemed to be large enough to take on the world.

She wasn't sure what that meant, comparing herself to a baby. Nothing that she really wanted to think too hard about, that was for damn sure.

"There was a football player from BSU who came in – took a fall wrong during a game and did a real number on his knee. We worked together three times a week on it, and he was starting to make great strides. The entire time that we worked on his knee, he would brag to me about some amazing pass he'd intercepted or caught or thrown…I don't even know. I'd just nod and say 'Uh-huh' occasionally, and that satisfied him that I was listening. He acted like he was God's gift to the earth because he had 'mad handling skills.' I didn't think much about it, or about him – if nothing would've happened, a year later, I wouldn't have even been able to tell you his name or what he looked like. He was just one more dumb-as-a-box-of-rocks jock who had three brain cells to rub together, and two were preoccupied with his dick at all times."

She stopped then, waiting for him to jump to the guy's defense. She'd seen the way that Gage had tackled Richard just minutes before. He looked like he'd done it hundreds of times. Cady was willing to bet next year's salary that Gage had played football at least in high school, if not in college.

So Gage would pipe up here and say that playing football was difficult and required lots of brainpower and then she could argue back that the mere ability to catch or throw a piece of pig skin around did not make you special, and then they could get off on that topic and never, ever come back to this one and…

Nothing.

He didn't rise to the bait. He refused to get sidetracked away from this godawful story and onto a topic that was impersonal and not in the least bit painful.

She really, *really* hated him now.

Finally, the infernal silence got under her skin, and with an irritated huff, she continued on. "It was our last appointment together. I was just checking him over – doing some range of motion tests – and then turned to get his paper file from off the counter when he…"

Except now that she'd gotten to it – the bad part, the part she relived again and again in her dreams – her throat was tightening and the panic that was beating through her made it hard to think – *run away, run away* – and she wanted to throw up on his shoes – it'd serve him right for pushing her to talk like this – and her breaths were coming in short bursts and the world was turning dark around the edges and she was struggling to get free because she wanted to be anywhere, anywhere at all but there.

Please just let me go…

"Oof!" A puff of air blew out past her cheek and she realized that Gage was gasping for air and somewhere in the dim recesses of her mind she realized that she'd elbowed him in the stomach in her panic but *still*, he wasn't letting her go.

"Then what happened, Cady?" he asked quietly, but there was an edge of pain in his voice that wasn't there before.

She was torn between feeling guilty for hurting him, and feeling triumphant for hurting him.

"He grabbed me," she whispered, trying to push back the darkness crowding in around the edges of her vision. *Breathe, Cady. Breathe.* "I hadn't been expecting it, and was just reaching for that damn folder – I was just about there – and then his arms were around me. Pinning me down. Hand over my mouth. Told me to shut up. That I wanted this. That I'd been teasing him and taunting him for months now, and it was time that I got what I'd been begging for." The words were acrid on her tongue and the bile was rising higher, the acid burning her throat, and she was quite sure then that she'd throw up all over Gage and a small part of her mind wanted to, in retribution for forcing her to go through this pain.

Bastard, bastard, bastard – why are you making me tell this story?

"Then what happened, Cady?" he whispered in the darkness.

She swallowed hard, forcing the bile down enough to let words out. Just a little bit longer, and it'd be over.

Just breathe, Cady, breathe.

"I bit down on his hand as hard as I could," she admitted. "I heard later that he had to get stitches."

She chuckled a little at the thought, a dry, humorless laugh. Oh, the number of times she'd dreamt about him being stupid enough to stick his dick in her mouth. She would've *really* extracted some revenge then.

Except then she would have the memory of the feel and taste of his dick in her mouth and…

She pushed that horrific thought aside.

"He yanked his hand back," she continued on, monotone, "but I still wasn't free because he was stuffing his shirt into my mouth instead, and my arms were pinned by my side, and I couldn't get any leverage to kick him in the balls. I don't know…this next part…"

She drew in a deep breath. *Almost there, almost there, almost there.*

"I've tried to remember what happened next – even went under hypnosis one time to see if they could help me remember – but it's just this blur and in the end, all I know is that my clothing was either torn to shreds or gone completely, and that I finally got my foot free enough to kick as hard as I could against the examining table. It was steel and the heel of my knee-high boot against it caused quite the racket. A nurse walking by popped her head in to see what was going on and found us rolling around on the floor…"

Gage was smoothing his hand down over her hair, again and again, saying nothing, just listening.

"The police came, my boss was in there, and I couldn't stop shaking…I was mostly naked other than my boots and finally, one of the nurses found some blankets and wrapped me up in them. The police took the guy away as soon as they got there so I didn't have to look at him, but I'll *never* forget what he looks like."

She cuddled against Gage's broad chest – his frighteningly huge, muscular chest – and sighed. She'd only gotten through the story in its entirety from start to finish one other time – when she'd told her parents what had happened – and she felt boneless now, as if every bit of what made her *her* had been sucked out and wrung out and hung out to dry.

"What was the guy's excuse?" Gage asked, and she swore she could feel the question as much as she could hear it. The rumble against her cheek…she nestled down further. It was warm here in his arms, even with the cold nighttime temperature outside trying to seep in through the doors and windows, and if she could just melt into his body heat, she'd be happy then – happy for the rest of her life.

Never move again.

It sounded lovely.

"Excuse?" she finally mumbled.

"Yeah. He would never admit that he'd actually tried to rape you. So what piss-poor excuse did he try to give?"

Cady could've kissed him then.

Could have, but didn't, of course.

He believes me.

No questions.

No, "Are you sure you didn't lead him on?" No, "Are you sure it wasn't just some sort of crude come-on move?" No, "What did you wear to work to make him think he could do this to you?" No assumptions at all that she was at fault when you got right down to the heart of the matter.

She wasn't sure how she felt about that. A little too stunned to take it in properly, honestly.

"He said..." She drew in a deep breath. "He said that it was all a big misunderstanding." She snorted a little at that. It really was the most ridiculous defense on the planet. "That I had started to fall over and that he'd tried to catch me, and that this had made me think that I was being attacked so I'd fought him and he'd just tried to protect himself from me...it was total bullshit. Everyone knew it. The story had more holes in it than a block of Swiss cheese."

"What happened to him?" Quiet. Steady. Unwavering.

"The usual," she said sarcastically. This part – this was almost more painful than the attempted rape had been. The aftermath. She'd been so scarred by it all, and he went right back to his life as if nothing had happened.

Because to him, it *had* been nothing.

"He was forced to write me a letter of apology for the 'misunderstanding,' the university paid out a large settlement to keep me quiet, and he was back on the field the next season. He's playing in the NFL now. I hate it, you know – part of the agreement is I can't ever speak publicly about this. I can't even tell you his name. Last year, a small story showed up about a domestic violence charge being brought against him by his girlfriend but she dropped it soon after and it didn't make big waves. I only know because I have a Google Alert set up for the bastard. I want to know every time he twitches his nose. He's playing for a team on the East Coast, far, far away from here, so at least *that's* a consolation."

It was quiet then between them as Gage thought through what she'd just said.

"Why aren't you still working as a physical therapist?" he asked, still just as quiet and steady as ever.

What would it be like to be this steady and calm?

She had been once. If she strained hard enough, she could remember back to a time when she'd been friendly and outgoing and cheerful and steady as a rock.

That was Innocent Cady, though, and that version of her was long gone.

"I tried," she admitted. Failure. She was nothing

but one big ball of failure. "I went back to work the next week. Walked into an examination room – not the same one; they weren't stupid enough to give me the same room again – and the panic just closed in on me from all sides and I threw up in the trash can. Told them I had the flu and went home. Tried one other time, and...couldn't. Suddenly, every athlete was just way too big and strong for me and every one of them freaked me the hell out just by walking into the room. I know you probably haven't noticed," she said wryly, "but I tend towards the smaller side, and pound-for-pound, I was outmatched. Even the long-distance runners on the BSU track team had a weight and height advantage on me. Women get hurt too, but not nearly as often or as badly as guys do, and anyway, the little appeal that physical therapy had held for me had disappeared completely by that point."

Another long silence and then, "Is this why you hate it when I walk up behind you?"

She flinched. She wanted to lash out at him. What made him think he had the right to ask all of these questions? What business was it of his anyway?

But then a small voice peeped up, quiet and niggling and oh-so-terribly correct, that the *real* reason she hated the question was because he was right.

Why did he have to be right? Why did he have to keep pushing and prodding at every single sore spot on her soul?

"Probably," she equivocated, and then paused.

And groaned.

"Yes," she finally admitted. "I know it's hard to believe, but I didn't used to jump at every little sound and noise and movement. That's definitely a new development. And someone coming up from behind? That's the *worst*."

She felt his chin rub up against the top of her head as he nodded, and then, just as she thought they were done excavating her soul and they could go on to do something fun for a change, like shoving wooden toothpicks under her fingernails or something else equally as delightful, he went a step too far.

"Have you talked to someone about this? A therapist or something?"

And with that, the loose-boned feeling disappeared – gone in the blink of an eye. She bolted straight up and folded her arms over her chest protectively.

Dammit all, he'd really gone and stepped in it this time. It was bad enough that he thought he could force her into talking about the worst day of her life – he didn't need to imply she was insane at the same time.

"I don't need a psychiatrist!" she snapped. "I'm not crazy. I just went through something hard, is all. People go through hard things all the time, and aren't crazy afterwards."

"Whoa, whoa," he said, holding up his hands. "No one said you're crazy—"

She shifted on his lap so she could really glare at

him – she could get a good glare going when she had a mind to – when they both felt it.

Directly underneath her ass was the start of a hard-on. Her eyes got wide, his eyes got wide, and they just stared at each other, dead silence between them for a moment.

"It's just a biological reaction," he blurted out. "I'm sorry. You're a cute girl, wiggling your ass across my lap…I can't control…"

But that didn't make her feel any better. A guy who's not able to control his lust?

No, no, no, that did not make her feel better, not one little bit.

The panic was welling up again and instinctively, she fumbled for the door handle and this time, he didn't try to stop her. She spilled out onto the cold ground and then scrambled to her feet, brushing off her knees even as she demanded, "Go! Go away. Get out of my car. I'm going to go home now."

He looked around the interior of her vehicle as if surprised to see that he was, in fact, in her Jeep, and then pushed himself out of it, palms out. "It's fine. I'm not going to attack you," he said slowly. "I'm just gonna walk back up to the party. You could come back with me. Are you sure you want to leave?"

That was such a ridiculous question, she didn't even bother answering it. Did he honestly think she'd stay now? After what just happened?

They sure did grow them big and beautiful and stupid up in the mountains of Idaho.

She was shaking – shaking *so* hard – and a part of her realized that she was right back where she'd started. Except now, Gage knew everything there was to know about her. All of the bad stuff was laid out in the open, and she *still* didn't feel any better.

She marched on wobbly legs to the driver's side and slid in, slamming the door closed behind her and breathing in deep. *Calm down. It's going to be fine.*

Except the faint smell of sugar and yeast and flour was left behind, a smell she was beginning to associate with Gage. It was drifting through the car, taunting her. Even a simple birthday party ended in disaster when she was involved.

Her Jeep roared to life and, slamming her foot to the floor, she tore backwards out of the parking space and into the street. She realized with an inward grimace as she threw her Jeep into drive that she'd forgotten to check her mirrors before roaring out into the street. It'd been nothing but sheer luck that she hadn't run straight into someone.

Well, at least she'd had one tiny piece of luck today.

God only knew that in every other aspect of her life, she hadn't had even that.

CHAPTER 10

GAGE

Slowly, Gage made his way around to the back of his parents' house, working his way through everything that he'd just heard as he walked. He'd known it was bad. Every warning sign that'd blared off Cady like a nuclear reactor about to explode had said that whatever had happened to her in the past hadn't been pretty.

But still…somehow, the truth had been even worse than Gage had imagined. This nameless football player – he'd noticed how careful she'd been not even to mention which position he played – was now in the NFL, eh?

Sure did make it hard to believe in karma.

The partygoers were a blurry group around him and a part of him knew he was being rude by not talking to anyone, but it was hard to focus. Everything he'd just heard…

Well, it definitely made a certain Cady Walcott a lot more understandable.

More than anything else – and he was dead sure she'd hate this analogy, even though (maybe especially because) it was totally accurate – she reminded him of a feral baby kitten who'd been hurt. Tiny, defenseless, completely untrusting of any human, hissing and swatting and doing its best to fight against the mean world it'd found itself in.

Underneath all of that hissing and tiny claws, though, was the heart and soul of someone who *wanted* to be loved.

But how to make the little hissing kitten trust me? I can't just slide tuna cans under Cady's front door, although I'm gonna guess Skittles would appreciate that…

Emma hurried up beside him, worry stamped across her face, jerking him out of his thoughts. "Is she all right?" she asked. "Where is she?"

"She…uhhh…she went home." He paused then, trying to decide what else he could safely tell his sister without breaking Cady's confidence, and then realized the answer to that was: Nothing at all. "I can't really say more than that. So, what happened to Dickwad?" he asked, before she could brazenly ignore that statement and press him for more anyway.

"Abby carted his ass off to jail. We'll see if the county prosecutor has the guts to go after him, though." She screwed up her mouth in disgust, *clearly* doubting the chances of that happening, and Gage couldn't blame her. No county prosecutor would want to piss off the only judge in town, and to boot, their current prosecutor wasn't exactly known for his backbone and high sense of morals.

But *still*. Waving a gun around at a party? Trying to kidnap Sugar? Surely Dickwad's father couldn't fast-talk his son out of *that* one, right?

He's in the NFL now.

Cady's simple statement of fact about her attacker reverberated in his head, and Gage winced. If karma wasn't at play with the nameless football player, why would it be at play with Dickwad?

"Is Sugar okay?" he asked, needing to hear something reassuring.

"Yeah. Jaxson took her home, and then went to go pick up the boys from the babysitter."

"Oh, shit," Gage said, surprised. "I didn't even notice it, but you're right – Aiden and Frankie weren't here." Damn. Sherlock Holmes he was not, at least not tonight. He decided then and there to blame it on Cady being at the party. It seemed only fair. He found it damn hard to think with her around, for reasons he didn't really want to think about too hard.

"Rose is too little to be left with a babysitter, of course, but Sugar wanted to have fun and not worry about corralling two little boys the whole night, so they dropped them off at the babysitter's before coming over. And then…" She shrugged morosely. "So much for having fun."

Gage leaned over and gave his only sister a quick squeeze. "I'm sorry Dickwad ruined your birthday party," he said quietly into Emma's hair before letting her go.

Emma shrugged again, not making eye contact, clearly trying to act as if it wasn't a big deal when it really, really was. Emma was a social butterfly, and her combined birthday party with Sugar was a Very Big Deal in her life. Having Dickwad ruin it for her made Gage want to hunt him down and get in that uppercut to the jaw after all. He was beginning to regret listening to Abby on that topic. Surely one punch wouldn't change anything, except to make him feel a hell of a lot better.

"I saw you chatting with Grandma after you and Cady showed up," Emma said quietly. "She didn't seem happy. Does she not like Cady?"

Gage chuckled a little at that. "That'd require Grandma to know Cady," he pointed out dryly. "No, she's just…you know how she is about me dating."

"Creepily protective?" Emma offered up. He narrowed his eyes at her. She shrugged unrepentantly. "You asked for my thoughts," she pointed out.

Gage decided to ignore that. Just because his sister was right didn't mean he had to acknowledge that fact out loud.

"You know why Grandma is the way she is," he said heavily. "Her only child, leaving town after his high school graduation and joining the Marine Corps? She pretty much didn't get to see her son or any of us grandkids for twenty years, and whether or not she should, she places the blame for that squarely on Mom's shoulders. It would only make sense that she'd be a little more protective of me."

Yeah, his grandmother was a little more protective of him than most grandparents would probably be, but Gage tried to see it from her point of view, even if that viewpoint was a bit smothering at times.

Emma *clearly* had more she wanted to say on the topic, but in a rare showing of self-control, she just nodded noncommittally and gestured towards the only remaining item on the dessert table – a huge birthday cake. "Since Sugar isn't here to blow out the candles with me, wanna help?"

"You don't want to ask Chris to help you?" Gage asked with a teasing laugh. It'd always been Gage and Emma together, with Chris as the annoying younger brother who got away with murder just because he was the baby of the family. And baby was what he damn well acted like, too. "Where *is* our erstwhile younger brother, anyway?"

"Erstwhile…nice one," Emma said approvingly. "And, I have no idea. Probably hiding down in the basement and playing video games."

"Shocking," Gage said dryly. "A teenage boy, hiding out and playing video games? I never would've seen that one coming. All right, old woman," and he slung his arm around Emma's shoulders, "just because you asked, I'll help you blow out your candles."

"You know you're older than me, right?" Emma asked sarcastically, slinging an elbow into his stomach for good measure as they walked towards the dessert table.

"Older *and* wiser," he said with an air of self-importance, and it was an indication of just how upset Emma was over Dickwad's appearance that she didn't have anything better to dish back at him than a dignified sniff.

CHAPTER 11

CADY

*C*ADY SQUINTED in the quickly enveloping darkness. Dammit all, another day gone and she still hadn't gotten half of the things done that she'd wanted to. It would help if she could work past sunset, but even though Idaho Power had been kind enough to get the rest of the town connected back up to power, their help (understandably) only extended to the front doorstep.

Unfortunately for her, since Watson's Electric had managed to blow her main breaker box *inside* of the building past the point of no return, she was now waiting for the only reputable electricians in town, Goldfork Mountains Electrical Service, to make it over. Just like Gage had warned her, they were good, they were expensive, and they were booked. It was going to be at least another week before they could get her up and running again.

She'd tried buying battery-powered lanterns so

she could have light in the evenings, but they'd ended up casting just as many shadows as they did light, and the other night, after fifteen minutes of scrubbing at a particularly stubborn spot, she'd realized that it was just a shadow she'd been trying to scrub off the floor.

Whoops.

She'd given up on working past dark after that.

With a groan, she pushed herself to her feet and headed to the sink in the back to wash up. It'd only been three days since the disastrous birthday party, and she'd been quite happy to spend all day Saturday and Sunday hiding in bed, telling herself that this was her rest time. Her therapy time. She'd be back at it on Monday. She wasn't slipping into a depression again; she was just taking it easy for the weekend.

There was *totally* a difference.

She didn't much like to think about how hard it'd been to force herself to actually get back to work that morning. Every bone in her body had begged to sleep one more day. She could tackle the store on Tuesday. People took long weekends all the time. She was entitled after everything she'd been through on Friday night, right?

In the end, it was Skittle meowing piteously to be fed wet cat food that'd forced her out of bed, and once she was standing up, she'd had to go pee, and once she'd made it into the bathroom and used the toilet and washed her face and brushed her teeth… well, she'd ended up feeling a whole lot better. Going into the storefront and cleaning some more hadn't ended up being such an overwhelming idea after all.

"You may be an atrocious listener and a complete asshole when I try to put a leash on you," she'd told Skittles after she'd finished her wet cat food and had begun her daily routine of napping for hours in the sun, "but you're at least good for getting me out of bed."

One ear had twitched.

She'd taken that as her hearty congratulations on a job well done for not slipping back down that bottomless pit, just as she'd intended it, Cady was sure.

Now that she'd gotten at least a few things done, and all of her light was quickly disappearing for the night, it was time to head home. *Ugh.* With a mental sigh, she reviewed what was in her fridge, but from what she could remember, it wasn't much. Her two-day bender of not getting out of bed except to go pee and stumble to the kitchen to eat some breakfast cereal, hadn't also miraculously included a trip to the grocery store.

It was definitely one of the major downsides to living out in the middle of Nowhere, Idaho – unlike Boise where she could order her groceries online and they would be delivered automagically to her doorstep, that just wasn't an option here.

Why did you want to live in Sawyer, Idaho again?

Dammit, she really wasn't in the mood to cook, but going out to eat by herself was always awkward as hell. Everyone else in a restaurant had someone to talk to; someone to laugh and chat with. It seemed like the waitresses always had a slightly pitying look in their eyes when they served her just by herself. Maybe it was all in her head – God knew so much else was – but still, it took all of the fun out of eating out. Last Friday – when she'd been downright *desperate* not to cook – that'd been the exception, not the rule. Usually, she hated going out to eat more than she hated cooking, and the lesser of two evils tended to win out in her world.

She was digging her purse out from underneath the back counter so she could find her keys and lock up for the night, when she heard someone loudly open up the front door. "Hi, Cady!" she heard Gage call out, and the panic that'd begun to bubble up inside of her instantly dissipated. It wasn't lost on her that he was making a big production out of coming in to keep from scaring her in the process. It was damn thoughtful, and honestly more appreciated than any gift he could ever give her.

She swung her purse over her shoulder and headed through the swinging door up to the front. "Hey, Gage," she said, flashing him a quick smile, fiddling with the strap on her purse, not *quite* able to meet his eye. She'd spent the weekend in bed, sure, but she'd also spent it thinking over Friday night, so she'd consoled herself with the idea that it hadn't been a *complete* waste of time.

And after two days of thinking about almost

nothing else, she'd came to the conclusion that as tough as it'd been to talk to Gage, she'd also realized that having him simply listen and not judge her had been a Damn Big Deal in her world.

She wasn't blind, or ignorant, or stupid. She'd seen all of the online comments on news articles whenever a woman came forward with accusations of rape. She'd heard the unspoken questions in the commentator's voices when discussing it during the evening news. Had it *really* happened? Or was the woman just overreacting? And even if it had happened, had the woman somehow brought it on herself through her own actions?

But none of that had been there with Gage. It'd taken her the whole weekend to process that, and to truly realize how much that meant to her.

That hard-on thing, though? It still made her as nervous as a long-tailed cat in a room full of rocking chairs, and she was pretty damn sure that wasn't gonna change anytime soon. Lust and her just didn't mix.

"I wanted to stop by and see how you were doing today," he said by way of greeting, pushing a hand wearily through his thick dark blond hair. "I kept meaning to come over earlier, but it was nuts at the bakery. Every person in town wanted to come over and congratulate me on taking Dickwad down," he sent her a laughing grin at his proud usage of such a terrible nickname, "*and* to tell me that his dad got him out of jail already." At that, his smile had disappeared and he looked downright pissed. "He's out on bail, but everyone thinks the prosecutor is just going to drop the charges."

"Shit, *honestly*?!" Cady just stared at him, open-mouthed. "What? Why? Who the hell is his dad? And how could the prosecutor even *think* about dropping the charges?! That man had a gun! At a *birthday* party!"

Any semblance of calm that she'd managed to gather over the weekend blew away in the wind. That man was out there still? Just roaming the streets?

What kind of small-town bullshit is this?!

"I forgot you don't know the Schmidt family," Gage said thoughtfully. He followed it up with, "His dad is the Long Valley County judge," as if that was supposed to explain everything.

She just stared at him, totally lost. "His dad is a judge?" she finally prodded him. "So what?"

"No, not *a* judge. *The* judge. He's the *only* judge in the entire county. Every single court case in the county is heard by him. Now, imagine you're the county prosecutor, and you've pissed off that judge by throwing the book at his only son. His darling, can't-do-anything-wrong son."

"Oooohhhhhh..." It was like the air slowly escaping a balloon, her breath just hissing out of her as she stared at Gage wide-eyed.

"Sometimes, small towns suck," Gage said succinctly, and then chuckled. "Don't get me wrong –

I love it here. But I'm not oblivious to what can happen in a small town. It's not all Mayberry."

She nodded slowly, trying – and failing – to push down the seemingly ever-present panic that had begun to well up inside of her. Again. Dammit all, she'd wanted to move to Sawyer because it *had* looked like Mayberry to her. So quaint and cute and safe.

But this was proof that the safety she was seeking was just an illusion.

Run away, run away, go somewhere safe. You can't stay here. He could attack you. He's evil. Out of jail. No one's going to stand up to him. He's going to come back. Run! Run! Run!

The world was going black around the edges and she slid down the interior brick wall into a heap on the floor, the world disappearing in a haze around her. She was coming apart – flying into pieces and shards and she couldn't stop it. She couldn't be saved.

Someone was talking, but they were far away. She shook her head, pushing the sound away.

Run, run, run, run—

She forced herself to pull in a deep breath, hold it for five seconds, and then slowly exhale it.

Run, run, run, run—

She pulled in another deep breath, held it for five seconds, counting as slowly as she could manage, and then exhaled, letting the self-imposed calm ever-so-slowly creep back in.

After her first panic attack, just a week after the attempted rape, she'd done research online of what to do while in the midst of them. It wasn't easy – there was a loud and rather opinionated part of her brain that was still chanting *run away, run away, he's evil, get away* – so concentrating and making herself focus on calming down was akin to trying to solve a calculus problem while juggling chainsaws, but she forced herself to continue the slow-and-steady breathing technique anyway.

Finally, she was able to force her eyes open…and saw Gage's face just inches away from hers. She let out a little yelp and he jerked back.

"Sorry, I didn't mean to scare you! I was just worried. Can you hear me now?"

She nodded numbly.

"Thank God," he said with a heartfelt sigh of relief. "I was really worried there for a minute."

"Panic attacks," she said through dry lips. "They're…not pretty." She dug around in her purse and pulled out her mostly empty bottle of water, swigging the rest back, wishing she'd thought to bring a second bottle to work that morning.

Gage stroked her hair out of her face. "I'm just glad you're back," he said softly. He eased his huge body down onto the floor across from her, sitting cross-legged on the cold tile as if it was the most normal position in the world.

No judgment at all.

What was it like in his world, all calm and sane and rational and shit? She'd never know again, that was for damn sure. She'd known once but that was so long ago, it might as well have been someone el—

"I know you won't believe me," he continued on easily, "but I actually came over to invite you to dinner."

"Dinner?" she squeaked. *Dammit.* And her heart rate had *just* started to come back down into normal range. Her hands flew instinctively to the necklace around her neck, playing with the gem, her protection against the men of the world. "I can't—"

He held up a hand. "Not a date. Just the two of us eating at a restaurant as friends. Nothing more. I realized that inviting you over to my parents' house for the big birthday party doesn't help you the next night when you still don't want to cook, and don't know where to go out to eat. You can't just keep showing back up at my parents' house, especially since Emma went back to Denver. My favorite place is…I don't know."

She cocked an eyebrow at him. "Well, if you don't know, *I* certainly don't know," she felt obliged to point out. "I really don't know Franklin all that well."

"C'mon," he said, ignoring that and extending his hand out to her. After a moment's hesitation, she clasped her hand in his and they pulled each other up into a standing position. He dropped his hand next to his side, and she found herself missing it, just for a moment. "You can even follow me over in your own car. That way, no one will get the wrong idea. Dates don't arrive in separate cars, right?"

She let out a little whoosh of relief at that – if she was in her own vehicle and things went sideways on her, she could just drive back home. She had an out. It made her feel a little more secure. A little more willing to say yes.

"Sounds good." She couldn't believe her own ears. She sounded so…so *normal* in that moment. "I'm parked out back – do you need to go lock up?"

"Nope. I already did that before coming over. This way, I could walk with you to the parking lot out back."

There was a part of her that wanted to inform him she wasn't some maiden in the Dark Ages, needing an escort everywhere she went, but then she remembered that Dickwad was out on bail and decided she could whip out her women's lib card some other time.

For now, having an escort felt…nice.

Gage waited quietly as she locked up behind them, and then walked her over to her Jeep, even though the parking lot was small and it was obvious no one else was around. She almost teased him about it, but then decided not to. After all, what if that caused him to stop?

She wasn't about to say this out loud, but no matter how huge his muscles were and no matter how much the beginnings of that hard-on had scared her, she was also beginning to believe Hannah's assessment of him.

He's one of the good guys.

It didn't make her less jumpy around him, but it

did mean she was able to relax faster *after* jumping, and that was some sort of an improvement, right?

After she'd unlocked her Jeep and had gotten inside without a problem, Gage hurried to his truck and they caravanned out of the parking lot, her once again following his tail lights.

An uneventful thirty minutes later, and they were pulling into the parking lot of a diner. *I Don't Know* was flashing in a brilliant neon above the front door. She was laughing as she got out of her Jeep. "Really? The name of this place is *I Don't Know?*" she called out to Gage as he swung down from his truck.

He flashed her a wide grin as he walked over. "I asked the owners – they said that everyone seems to say 'I don't know' when asked where they want to eat for dinner. So, they figured they'd *be* I Don't Know, and get all of that business."

"Makes sense to me," Cady said admiringly. She followed him up to the front door, which he held open for her. *A gentleman, through and through.* "I've been toying around with names for my business, and I haven't found quite the right one yet."

Just then, the waitress hurried over to seat them, and they fell silent as she escorted them to a booth. After promising to return with their drinks, she disappeared as Gage and Cady perused their menu. From what she could tell, the diner specialized in burgers and had combos on the menu that she never would've dreamed to put together. Who thought that peanut butter was a good idea on a *burger?*

But some of the more normal options looked appealing, and she finally forced herself to make a choice.

"So, what names have you come up with so far?" Gage asked after the waitress took their order and disappeared into the back again.

"What? Oh, right. Ummm..." She began ticking them off on her fingers in no particular order. "The Banana Blender, Smoothie Time!, The Juice Box, The Smoothie Stop...I'm sure there's more but I left my list at home." Alphabetized, of course, with stars next to her favorites. She'd almost rewritten the list in order from shortest to longest – a name that was *too* long would be a pain to fit onto a logo or a sign, after all – but at the last moment, she'd managed to stop herself.

He nodded thoughtfully as he pondered her list. "As I already told you, I renamed the Muffin Man after I bought it from my grandparents. It took me forever to find just the right name but I'd known for years that I was going to take it over, so I had a lot of time to make my choice. Hey," he said, brightening, "you could be the Smoothie Queen!"

She laughed, and, clearly emboldened, he added, "Or the Hippie Chick Smoothies...Hmmm...I'm not sure how much you want to emphasize being a hippie in Sawyer, though."

"Smoothie Queen," she murmured to herself, testing out the name, ignoring his second suggestion, a clearly horrendous one. She already knew that she was pushing it by putting a smoothie and health food store in Sawyer. She didn't need to make things worse by choosing a name with 'Hippie Chick' in it. "A play on Dairy Queen. Huh. I actually like it."

He beamed at her and she blinked. Twice. Having the full strength of Gage's smile turned on her was...

Wow.

A *clearly* inappropriate reaction. They were just friends, only friends, and never to be anything but friends. No matter how much wattage his smile put out.

The waitress showed up just then with their food, saving Cady from having to come up with something intelligent to say. After laying out enough food to feed at least three or four people, the waitress headed off to go help another table, leaving Cady behind, staring at the massive amounts of food with an open mouth.

"Have I mentioned that they dish up generous servings here?" Gage asked, laughing at her expression. "Just one of the many reasons to love this place."

As they dug in, they began chatting, first about small town life and then about Gage's family and then they drifted to Hannah...the conversation just seemed to flow between them, something Cady tried very hard not to think about too much, and thus ruin it all by freezing up. Gage was a naturally outgoing person, and when they weren't discussing the worst day of Cady's life, she found his questions easy to answer. Thankfully, he seemed to have decided that that was a verboten topic, and also steered clear of any mention of football or BSU.

Finally, they both sat back with a happy sigh, and Cady eyed the remains dubiously. Somehow, Gage had managed to eat a double-patty burger with cheese and bacon, a serving of french fries, jalapeño poppers, *and* onion rings, and she honestly thought he'd be up for more if the opportunity presented itself.

How is this man not 400 pounds of flabby fat?

It really wasn't fair.

"Ice cream time!" he announced, and waved the waitress over.

"Ice cream?" Cady wasn't sure if she should laugh or cry. "Where on God's green earth am I supposed to fit ice cream?" She may not have eaten quite as much as Gage, but she'd certainly eaten more than she normally did, and felt stuffed to the gills.

"There's always room for ice cream," Gage said seriously, and then turned to the waiting waitress, flashing one of his charming grins at her. She patted her hair and smiled flirtatiously in return, clearly in possession of eyeballs and thus could see how handsome Gage was.

Cady did her best to tamp down her glare. She had no claim on Gage, of course, but still. It wasn't professional to flirt with the customers. Everyone knew that.

Or, at least, *should* know that.

"What kind of ice cream are you wantin', darlin'?" the waitress asked, addressing the question only to Gage, not even seeming to remember that Cady was sitting right there.

Cady fought back the urge to "accidentally" kick the woman in the shins, but only barely.

"A scoop of mint chocolate and another of pralines and cream," he told her. "Waffle cone. What about you, Cady?"

The waitress reluctantly turned towards Cady, clearly remembering only then that someone else was at the table besides Gage.

Cady worked really, *really* hard to tamp down her irritation. "I don't need any, honestly," she said tightly. "I'm full to the brim."

"Just some for me then," Gage said, and the waitress scurried off to dish it up for him, ignoring the next table over that was trying to catch her attention to get refills on their drinks.

Cady just shook her head. "Do all women respond to you like that?" she asked. She felt embarrassed for her female comrades of the world. They ought to be ashamed of themselves.

"Uh…" He was clearly caught off guard by the question, and not sure how to answer it. Finally, "Most women seem to like me." He shrugged, one massive, muscle-bound shoulder moving under his thin t-shirt.

Shockingly enough – at least in her opinion – she was able to quell her panic at the sight instead of letting it overtake her and smother her alive. Yeah, Gage had way more muscles than she really cared for, but the more time she spent around him, the more she was beginning to realize that he was just a gentle giant.

At least so far.

"I'm a people person," he said, when she didn't say anything else. "I like being around people, and figuring out what makes them tick."

She tilted her head to the side at that, staring at him, trying to decide how to take that statement. "It sounds like you study the rest of us under a microscope," she said slowly, not liking that idea. She wasn't some strange specimen to be dissected, even if it was just figuratively.

He laughed. "Wow, then that came out wrong," he said dryly. "It's not that, promise. Humanity is just interesting to me. Everyone has their own motivations for why they do things and how they perceive the world around them. I find that fascinating. Two people can see the same exact situation and interpret it in completely different ways. The power of perception…" He shrugged again, those damn muscles rippling again, but before he could say anything else, the waitress showed up with his ice cream cone and the check.

Cady pulled her wallet out of her purse to pay her half but Gage waved her away. "This is my welcome-to-Sawyer gift to you," he said. "You can catch dinner some other time." She wanted to argue but even as she opened her mouth to do so, she let out a sigh of resignation instead. She somehow knew it would be a futile move. Signing the credit card receipt with one hand while licking at the cone in the other, he pushed to his feet. "Ready?"

She nodded, but instead of heading back to their vehicles like she'd expected, Gage led her around the side of the parking lot, through a patch of pine trees with the only spotty lighting filtering through from the street lamps and the half moon, until they came out on the other side and onto the shoreline of a lake.

"Wolf Bends Lake," Gage said, between long licks of his cone. He held the cone out to her and she shook her head. With a shrug, he continued. She tried not to stare. He seemed awfully…dexterous with his tongue.

She absolutely, positively was *not* going to imagine what else he could do with it.

"When fall hits," he continued, oblivious to her wandering thoughts, "I Don't Know serves up hot cocoa or coffee in to-go cups, and then people walk along this beach, drinking it to keep warm while listening to the waves, until the lake freezes over, of course. Then people walk along this beach and laugh at the people trying to ice skate but who spend more time on their ass than on their feet."

Cady laughed at that, imagining the scene. "I've never been ice skating," she said after a moment's reflection. Gage looked at her, surprised, and she just shrugged. "I love watching the ice skating in the Winter Olympics – it's by far my favorite sport. It never occurred to me to try doing it myself, though."

"We'll have to go this winter," Gage said. "As just friends, of course," he added quickly. "But there's an ice skating rink over on that side of town," he pointed away from the lake, "that some regional skating stars like to practice on. I like to skate – there's something about gliding over the ice that is just soothing, I suppose – and I've had a couple of women ask me to be their skating partner because I could lift them up in the air without a problem. But I have the bakery to run, so…no time. It's a nice way to pass a free day, though."

She looked furtively at his bulging shoulders, so wide they looked like they could take on the world, and didn't doubt his story for a second. A guy who looked like *that* who could also stay upright with a pair of ice skates on? He probably had women lined up down the block to skate with someone like him.

She moved her eyes up past his shoulders and up to his brilliant blue eyes – or at least eyes that she knew were a brilliant blue, but in the late spring evening with very little light, she couldn't see much past the glinting off his glasses.

"Why do you wear glasses?" she asked suddenly. At his puzzled look, she added, "Most people wear contacts nowadays. It isn't that you don't look good in glasses, because…" She stumbled to a verbal stop, wishing for the sands of the lake shore to open up and swallow her whole, but Gage took pity on her and answered her question, sidestepping her almost-a-compliment comment.

"I used to wear contacts," he said, "but after the fire, my eyes were really irritated from all of the smoke and dust, and then reconstruction started on the bakery which caused even more dust, and…well, I got into the habit of wearing glasses and after a while, I just forgot to go back to contacts. It's nice not to be trying to wake up at four in the morning by stabbing myself in the eyeball with my finger. I don't miss contacts, honestly."

Cady almost got sidetracked by the "four in the morning" comment – who woke up at four in the morning voluntarily?! – but managed by sheer dint of will to focus on an even more shocking statement: This fire he mentioned so casually.

"What fire?" she asked.

"What?" he murmured, distracted by a trail of melting ice cream down the side of the waffle cone and managing to catch it with his tongue before it dropped to the sand beneath their feet.

*You have a very nice tongue…*is what she *almost* said, but she managed to stop herself at the last moment. She really would have to be swallowed up whole by the sand beneath her feet if she made a ridiculous statement like that.

"You mentioned a fire. What fire?"

"Oh! Right. Shit, I keep forgetting that you haven't been living here for forever. Last April – the 10th, to be exact – the chimney in my bakery caught fire. I stayed too long trying to put the fire out, and tripped over something in all of the smoke. Hit my head on the way down, and completely knocked me out. We have an excellent fire crew here, though, and Jaxson, Sugar's husband, found me and got me out. Saved my life, and Sugar's too. Didn't you wonder where all of that black smoke on the wall of your store came from?"

He drew to a stop, looking out over the gently lapping lake, eating the last bites of his cone, offering her the last crunchy bite of the base of the cone but she shook her head. She'd managed to say no this long; she could continue holding out. He popped the rest into his mouth with a shrug.

"Huh," she said thoughtfully, turning to also look out over the lake. It was a safer view. "I saw that, of course, but thought that there'd been some sort of electrical fire from an outlet or something that had caused it. It was that and the knob-and-tube wiring that caused me to call Watson's."

Gage shook his head ruefully. "Let's just all be glad that he *only* knocked out the power to the whole town," he said with a dry chuckle. "He could've actually tried to wire something up for you, and then you really would've had an electrical fire. No, all of that smoke damage was actually from the fire in the bakery. The previous owner of your building had had that damn place for sale for what seemed like years but no one was interested. Too many problems and the price was too high. After the fire, he came over to the bakery to complain about the smoke damage. I told him to file a complaint with my insurance company, and gave him the info. He never did. I think he just liked to hear the sound of his own voice, preferably complaining."

They grew silent then, looking out over the moonlit lake. The ripples meant that the half-moon's reflection was distorted and ever moving, and Cady stared at that, feeling like it had more significance than most would ever realize.

Distorted, moving and restless, but still pretty in its own way.

Yeah, that could definitely be an analogy for her life.

"You ready to head back?" Gage asked quietly, breaking into her thoughts.

She nodded, not meaning it but knowing that she should. If Gage was getting up at four in the morning, she'd already kept him up past his bedtime, and as his friend, she should be focused on his well-being.

Friend.

When was the last time she'd had a male friend?

Dad. She had been closest to her mom, but her dad was a damn close second. He'd cared about her.

When they'd died…

She tried to push down the pain of that memory, and instead think back to the last male friend she'd had who wasn't related to her. Elementary school, probably. Back before boys got cooties. Back before boys became monsters without provocation.

"You okay?" Gage asked, breaking into her thoughts. She realized with a start that they were standing next to her Jeep. He must've decided to walk her to it, but instead of climbing inside when they got there, she'd gotten lost in her painful history.

"Oh yeah, I'm good. See you tomorrow?" she asked rhetorically, and her voice was too loud and forcefully happy and she knew it wasn't believable but she ignored that and climbed into her Jeep, starting it and letting the quiet rumble of the engine soothe her as she tried to breathe again.

Despite her mental meanderings, she reflected as she drove home (this time Gage following her, waiting in her landlord's driveway until she'd made it safely inside of her basement apartment and he could drive away) tonight had been fun. More fun than she'd had in a long time. Maybe years, even.

Maybe, just maybe, Gage was the perfect friend – attentive, thoughtful, protective without being overbearing, and really, what guy would dare even think about touching her with him hulking just behind her? He was like a human-sized bottle of mace, at the ready at a moment's notice to take down any asshole who dared to step inside her personal space.

Yeah, she could get used to this. As long as his dick stayed zipped up and out of sight, this could work just fine.

CHAPTER 12

GAGE

May, 2019

It, he decided as he stepped through the door of the Smoothie Queen, clomping loudly on the checkerboard floor and calling out Cady's name to keep from surprising her, was quite an unusual way to spend a day off.

After a lecture from Emma, Mom, Dad, Grandma, and Grandpa (both separately and together) – oh, and Chris just because he knew he could get away with it and he thought it was *hilarious* to get away with scolding his older brother about anything at all – Gage finally decided that he'd have set days off each week. Two whole days, back to back, every single week where he wasn't expected to show up at the bakery and count inventory or fulfill an order or bake a single thing.

Thank God Sugar was back from maternity leave – this unheard of laziness on his behalf simply wouldn't be possible without her there to take over the reins those two days. At least that part was taken care of. But as for two days off, in a row, *every single week...* Well, he wouldn't lie, not even to himself.

It was...nice.

Unfortunately, all of this free time was also becoming boring as hell.

The first week, he'd read books. All of the books he was always going to read "someday." Unfortunately, he'd never been one to read book after book, and even the classic, *Mastering the Art of French Cooking* by Julia Child, could only hold his interest for so long.

The second week, he decided to switch it up and binge-watch TV instead, ripping through every single episode of *The Great British Bake Off* he could get his hands on. This quickly backfired on him, however, when he realized that this just made him more restless and anxious to be in the kitchen, mixing up his own concoctions, and anyway, was it really too much to ask the gods that he be born in the UK so he could've competed on the show? A few of the mistakes that the contestants had made were just so...so *amateurish*. He could beat some of the contestants with one hand tied behind his back.

He was choosing, of course, to firmly ignore the fact that it was a show where one of the requirements to participate was that you be an amateur. Just because you had to *be* one didn't mean you had to *act* like one.

It was now Week Three of this two-days-off-a-week experiment, and he was quite sure he was going to go insane. He just wasn't meant to have this much free time on his hands to do absolutely nothing at all, no matter what every person in his life seemed to think.

Everyone except Cady, that was. When he'd originally told her the plan, she'd simply raised one eyebrow and then had blandly wished him the best of luck. No vanilla glaze he'd ever whipped up had dripped as much as her sarcasm did off those words.

It really wasn't fair that a woman he just met five months ago apparently knew him better than anyone else in his life, and maybe even better than he knew himself.

But all of that was why he was there at the Smoothie Queen that Wednesday morning. Cady had asked him who she should hire to do some carpentry work for her – after her electrical debacle, she'd become almost painfully insistent upon getting recommendations before hiring someone to so much as sneeze in her shop – and instead of recommending any number of handyman companies around town who'd jump at the chance for a small project like this to fill in the gaps between the larger projects, he found himself offering his own services. What else was he going to do with his Wednesday and Thursday this week? He was down to arranging the cans in his pantry by alphabetical order – he'd already done them by height – and after a five minute debate of whether "tuna fish" belonged with the T's or the F's, he'd decided that maybe something else to occupy his time might be a good idea.

A little woodworking would do the trick.

After his purposefully noisy entrance, Cady came walking up through the swinging doors from the back, an easy sway and grace to her steps as she shot him a pleased smile. He tried to force his body to ignore the appeal of that smile. His little feral kitten, all claws and hissing and angry, had finally started relaxing around him in the hardest-won fight of his life. He wasn't about to send them hurtling back to square one by letting his errant dick lead him around. Cady had so firmly friend-zoned him, he was a little surprised she didn't make him wear t-shirts while around her that said things like, "I own beachfront property in the Friend Zone" or "King of the Friend Zone."

Actually, if she thought she could get away with it…

"Hey, Cady!" he said with a matching friendly smile of his own. "Reporting for duty as promised."

"Thank you again," she said – again – shooting him a grateful smile as she shoved her hands into the back pockets of her jeans, unintentionally thrusting her perfectly proportioned tits forward as she did so. He gulped and forced his eyes up to her face. He'd simply never look below her neck ever again.

That was a totally doable and realistic plan.

Totally.

"I know this isn't normally something that someone does on their day off," she continued, "so I really appreciate it."

He shrugged, shoving his hands into his back pockets, matching her stance in hopes of keeping his hands to himself. "No one in my family seems to understand this, but I *like* working," he said. "Not all of it – spreadsheets aren't exactly the most fun I've ever had, and I'm just lucky I can afford to have Jennifer and Bonnie help me with my bookkeeping – but the rest of it, I like. There's a reason I chose to become a bakery owner. It gives me a sense of purpose."

He stumbled to a stop then, before he continued his little spiel and said something stupidly personal. He couldn't remember who he'd last tried to talk to about this sort of thing, who'd actually seemed to understand. Maybe Cady was just good at pretending, but the look in her eye…

It made him think she *got* it.

"Let me show you what's going on," Cady said, diplomatically understanding his desire to leave that topic alone and even better, respecting that desire. "I love these countertops," she said, walking over to the line of glass-topped counters that ran the width of the store, breaking it up into *customer* and *employee* areas. "They're just gorgeous. The woodworking people used to do…No one does this anymore. Everything is just a veneer of pine over chipboard or something." She ran her hand lovingly over the carved dark wood. "But," and she walked through the low swinging door that separated the retail area from the employee section and he followed, "on this side, it looks like someone let water drip down it without cleaning it up or something…? I'm not sure, but it's in shit shape. This wasn't just a little bit of water – it was a whole lot of water for a whole long time."

He crouched down next to the warped wood and took it in. She was right – someone hadn't just spilled a water bottle here or something. For the water to seep into the lacquered wood, it had to have been something much worse than that.

On a hunch, he looked up at the ceiling tiles above them, and sure enough, he spotted the tell-tale brown stains in the otherwise white acoustic tiles. Confused, she followed his gaze.

"Oh!" she exclaimed. She walked over and stood right next to him, except he was still crouched down on the heels of his boots which meant that his face was now directly in line with her perfectly proportioned (was any part of her *not* perfectly proportioned?) ass.

Completely ignorant of what she was doing to him, she craned her neck, staring up at the ceiling and then down at the countertop. "Well, duh, Cady," she muttered to herself. She looked down at him, her mouth quirked up in a self-deprecating smile. "Some business owner I am. Looking up…a new concept."

It was, unfortunately, *not* a new concept for him, because he was quickly realizing that this vantage point meant that he was also able to admire the underside of her perfectly proportioned breasts, which were just as perfect from this vantage point as they had been when he'd been looking down on them.

With a grunt, he forced himself into a standing position. He couldn't follow his new personal rule to not look below Cady's neck if he was crouched below her and looking up at her. The laws of physics and all that.

"All right, talk to me. What kind of money are you wanting to spend on this project?" he asked, leaning against the countertop casually, trying to get his groin to unclench and act just as casual as the rest of him.

"I don't know…" she said slowly. "I hadn't thought about it. What are the different options?"

He rubbed his chin as he thought about it, scratching at the stubble growing there. It was his day off, dammit, and the way he figured it, that meant a day off from shaving, too. The stubble was a little itchy, but he was determined not to give in and shave until Friday. If he was going to be forced to take two days off every single week, then by God, he was going to enjoy those two days by not shaving.

Even if the stubble was driving him insane.

"Basically," he said after a few more moments of scratching, "it comes down to whether or not you want to match the woodwork on the other side. This side is the employee-only side, so no one but you and anyone you hire will ever see it. You might want to use the money you have to focus on something that is customer-facing and use cheap wood back here just to get the counter back into functional shape. On the other hand, if you're someone who is bothered by things not matching or if the beauty of something really matters to you, maybe even more than the function, it could bother you to have ugly-ass wood right here that you're staring at all the time. Do you care what you're looking at? Or do you care only about what the *customers* are looking at?"

"Both," she said without hesitation. "It isn't such a big deal if it's just something that I'm renting – like my basement apartment is never going to win any architectural awards, you know? I love my landlords, Rochelle and Mike, to death, but it's *just* an apartment, and I'm okay with that. But if I'm going to buy something and renovate it and make it my own, I want there to be beauty *and* function. As a business owner, I'm going to be here a lot. I want to make it into a place I want to be."

He nodded approvingly. "When I first took over the bakery, I struggled with the lighting back in the kitchen. It's fluorescent and it's ugly and there are no windows where I can bring in natural light. I told myself it wasn't such a big deal and it was better to spend the money on upgrading the mixer than it was to replace the lighting. It's been four years now, and I hate that lighting just as much as I ever did, maybe more. I keep telling myself that the next thing I'm going to do is replace it, but there's always something...And that damn fire *really* set me back. It's taken the last year just to regain the ground I'd lost after that fire. I had insurance, but it never pays for everything, plus the loss of income...Anyway." He plastered a determined smile on his face. This was about her, not him. "So don't let yourself think that aesthetics don't matter," he finished lamely.

She nodded slowly, chewing on her bottom lip as she thought, and he had to shove his hands into his back pockets again to keep from reaching out to her. If there was one thing guaranteed to drive Cady away, it would be reaching out to her, unless it was to save her from falling and breaking her neck, and even then, it was debatable.

She might as well have had a giant "Do Not Touch" sign blazing above her head at all times, visible to every guy for miles around.

"Can we match the dark cherry wood, though?" she asked. "And what about this lacquer finish? I love how gorgeous it is." She trailed her fingers over the wood. "How replicable is all of this?"

This time, they crouched down together next to the countertop as they began to go over her options. She listened intently, asked intelligent questions, and made intelligent suggestions.

In other words, she seemed to know at least something about construction and woodworking. It was on the tip of Gage's tongue to ask who she'd learned from – a city girl who knew how to run a table saw? He was flat-out shocked, not gonna lie.

But he didn't want to pry into her background. She could tell him what she felt comfortable sharing, when she wanted to share it. He'd pushed her the night of the party – pushed her *hard* – and somehow, he knew that he couldn't pull off a repeat performance. There was only so much prying into her life that Cady would tolerate.

And if he could only ask a limited number of questions, he better be damn picky when choosing. For example, she still hadn't told him how she was affording all of this, and as a guy who was *firmly* in the friend zone, he had no right to ask. That didn't keep him from being observant, however, and he hadn't missed the fact that she wasn't acting as if every penny were dear and was all that was between her and starvation, but she also didn't appear to be spending those pennies excessively.

So just how did someone her age get the money to buy a building, to renovate said building, *and* have enough money to live off while renovating said building? It wasn't like he was an old man looking down at her like she was a child – he was fairly sure they were close to the same age, although he'd never asked her – but that just made him *more* qualified, in his ever-so-humble opinion, to know how much cash someone their age could reasonably be expected to have.

And there was no doubt about it – Cady had a *lot* more than that.

Just when he thought he had at least a little bit of her figured out, another mystery popped up and proved all over again that she was nothing but one big question mark.

After some last-minute back and forths, they settled on a battle plan, but Gage realized that more than the tools he'd brought with him that morning, there was a whole list of supplies that he needed to make this project a go. "Wanna head down to the hardware store with me? I've got a list a mile long of supplies to buy, and I'm going to need your credit card to make it happen."

She bit her lip hesitantly. "The owner…he doesn't seem to like me much. Not to mention, it seems like Home Depot or Lowes would be cheaper than Long Valley Hardware prices, right? Wouldn't it be better to drive to Boise instead?" There was a hopeful lilt to her voice that his dick happily matched. The idea of spending hours in the truck driving to and from Boise and maybe grabbing a bite to eat while there…

But unless his self-control levels had magically increased in the last ten minutes, spending that much time in Cady's presence seemed like a truly bad idea, no matter what his dick was trying to tell him.

"Couple of things," he said slowly as he forced his brain to think through the situation and not just be overruled by parts considerably south of it. "Nothing will win Mr. Burbank over faster than you spending money in his store. He may not appreciate you quite literally darkening not just the doorway of his business but *all* of his business, but seeing you shop local will go a long ways in making him willing to move past that. Second, we'd need to take my truck – we can't fit some of the longer pieces of wood into your tiny Jeep – and my truck doesn't get the best gas mileage, so by the time we drive to Boise and back, the chances of us actually saving money by shopping at a big box store are pretty damn small, not to mention the time wasted just driving."

He waved his hand dismissively. He didn't want to make it sound like gas money was going to make or break him, because it wasn't. Not only that, it wasn't the true issue here.

"I'm going to level with you," he said seriously, and waited for her to nod her understanding before he continued. More than anything else, he had to make her get this. "If you're gonna make it as a business owner here in this valley, the one thing you've gotta understand is how much it means to local merchants that you shop *here* whenever possible. Need a prescription? There's a pharmacy across the street. Need flowers? There's Happy Petals just down the street. Almost anything you need, you can find right here in Sawyer or with a quick trip over to Franklin." He leaned against the counter, one leg crossed over the other as he did his best to explain to a big city girl what it was like to try to thrive in a world of Amazon and eBay and 1-800-Flowers. "The thing is, it's hard for a small-town merchant because the locals expect them to always be there *just* in case they need something right at that moment, but they are otherwise willing to wait two days for some giant internet company to send them whatever they need so they can save that fourteen cents. Then when the small-town merchant closes up shop, the locals complain about how there are no shops in town and they have to drive so far to buy anything, without realizing that *they* were part of the problem to begin with."

He knew it was a long diatribe. He knew Cady didn't deserve to get the brunt of that particular lecture, but *still*…if she was going to fit into small-town life, she had to understand this. Running to Boise for every little thing would kill off her business faster than anything else. If she didn't think her fellow Sawyerite business owners would notice…well, it was up to him to disabuse her of that notion real quick.

"Wow," she finally said. "I didn't know…" She trailed off. "Growing up in Boise, I just didn't realize," she continued after a long pregnant pause. She turned her golden brown eyes up to him. "In Boise, no business owner would notice where another business owner shopped, but I'm starting to think that here, they notice if I sneeze and don't say 'Excuse me' afterwards."

"They do," he broke in to assure her. "Everyone notices everything. There's not much else to do in a small town *but* that."

"Grand," she said sarcastically, shoving some wild curls off her forehead. There was one long strand that seemed to be stuck to the side of her face, though, and Gage's fingers itched to brush that one away too.

He clenched his hands into fists and kept them by his sides.

Nothing would drive her away faster. Nothing.

Perhaps he should look at getting that tattooed somewhere…

"Anyway, it only makes sense that Mr. Burbank would notice if I came back from Boise with my Jeep loaded to the brim with building supplies. Local, it is," she sighed, not exactly looking thrilled with the idea. He wasn't sure he could blame her. Burbank was not a fan of hers, and didn't try to hide that fact from anyone at all, let alone from her. "So, do we drive your truck down to the hardware store?"

He shook his head. "It's only a block and a half down the street. If we get anything too large or heavy, we can grab my truck and bring that back. But it's best for you to be seen walking down the street, loaded down with plastic bags marked Long Valley Hardware. Every business owner who sees it will nod approvingly."

She laughed. "I had no idea buying screws was such a public action," she said with a roll of her eyes. "I'm sure glad I have you here to help me out with this. After my Watson's Electric debacle, who knows what other mistakes I might've gotten myself into without your guidance."

Not meeting her eyes, he flashed her a grin while looking somewhere vaguely to the left of her head. "What kind of friend would I be if I didn't help?" he asked rhetorically.

He was beginning to hate the word "friend," he really, really was…

CHAPTER 13

CADY

*D*ESPITE WHAT SHE HOPED was an outwardly cavalier attitude about this little outing, inwardly, Cady was quaking in her boots. Well, tennis shoes to be exact. But no matter the footwear on her feet, the idea of walking into Long Valley Hardware again and seeing Mr. Burbank…

He hadn't exactly been friendly the first time she went over there, and that was *before* she cost him a full day of sales. Based on his anger that day, he didn't seem like the understanding *or* forgiving type, and she doubted he'd had a major personality change in the last month.

By the time they'd walked the one and a half blocks to the hardware store, Cady felt like her chest was being tightened in a vise and she couldn't seem to get a full breath into her lungs. He was probably going to yell at her – again – for being such an idiot for hiring Watson's and really, what could she say in her defense?

Dejected, she trailed Gage into the store, the stacks of items for sale piled haphazardly on every conceivable surface and some, she noted with surprise, were even hung from the ceiling. Mr. Burbank clearly took *Waste not, want not* literally. How had she missed ladders being hung by cables from the ceiling last time, let alone the inflatable kiddie pool?

She hadn't realized it then, but looking back on it, she was sure she'd still been stuck in that awful hazy world where nothing had seemed quite real. What else could explain her complete lack of observational skills? She'd thought she'd already changed and grown so much by that point – look at her, buying a business, selling her parents' house and cars and personal items, and moving into an apartment in Sawyer – but just between then and now…

She had changed. Relaxed. Opened up. Stopped being *quite* so terrified of every little thing.

"Hey, Gage!" the older man said gruffly, walking up from the back and wiping his hands on a grease rag. "What're you—"

He caught sight of Cady then, and his pleasantly gruff – gruffly pleasant? – demeanor changed at the drop of a hat. "Miss," he practically growled in what could be charitably termed a greeting…*if* one was feeling charitable.

Cady wasn't so sure she was.

She nodded in return, but didn't say a word. Did

he really have to be *quite* such an ass? It wasn't like she'd killed someone when she'd knocked out the electricity. No long-term damage had been done.

"So Cady here is wanting me to do some carpentry work on her building," Gage said smoothly, as if he was completely oblivious to the stand-off happening between her and the shop owner, "and she put together a list of items we need to make that happen. Cady, you got it?"

She nodded and dug into her back pocket. The sooner she could hand the list over to Gage and let the two of them get to work gathering it all up, the sooner she could escape from this place. Gage'd seemed to think the older man would appreciate her shopping at his store, but Cady was beginning to think he'd been a mite bit optimistic. Mr. Burbank looked like he wouldn't appreciate anything more than the two of them leaving.

Or at least her leaving.

But when she went to hand the list over to Gage, she realized he'd casually walked off and was inspecting a display of power tools. He was clearly expecting her to work together with Burbank to make this happen while he just stood around and waited.

She shot a death glare at Gage's back and then turned to the grumpy store owner with a sickly smile, holding the paper out. "Here's what we came up with."

He took the proffered list and, pulling his reading glasses down from the top of his balding head, he began scanning it. Grumbling something under his breath that she was sure she didn't want to hear, he wandered off to begin gathering items up.

Cady paused for a moment, chewing her bottom lip, torn between wanting to stand next to Gage and just wait for everything to be gathered up, and going to help gather the items. After all, Mr. Burbank wasn't her servant, here to do her bidding, but it wasn't like she knew the place and—

With an inner groan, she forced her feet towards the most promising aisle for wood glue, getting grumpier by the minute. If she was helping to look for items, shouldn't Gage be helping, too? Debating between two choices, she finally snatched a bottle off the shelf and marched it back up to the front. Sure, he was there as an unpaid volunteer to help her out, but standing up at the front and leaving her by herself to deal with a crotchety old man wasn't exactly a lot of help in her not-so-humble opinion, and—

"Got the wood glue?" Mr. Burbank asked briskly, interrupting her thoughts. She nodded, and he checkmarked it off the list. "Just one item left – I'll go grab the clamps." And the older man headed down a different aisle, leaving the two of them behind.

"What are you up to?" she whisper-demanded to Gage. "You're abandoning me all alone to deal with this guy. I thought you were supposed to be helping me." She tried to keep the accusing tone out of her voice.

Okay, fine, she didn't try very hard. She felt downright betrayed by him, to be honest.

"Burbank is headed back up here," was all Gage said. She gave him a second death glare and then turned back to the taciturn old man with a patently false smile on her face. Mr. Burbank began sorting out the pile of items to ring them up, but there was something about the set of his shoulders...

Was it possible? It almost seemed like he wasn't *quite* as pissed as he had been before.

She kept a smile pasted on her face as she quickly ran through what was happening in her mind.

Gage was trying to force the two of them to talk to each other, that much was obvious. But what was surprising was that it seemed to be working, or at least Burbank didn't seem quite as happy-happy-joy-joy about the idea of ringing her neck as he had before.

Huh.

She was used to being scared of everyone and everything – at least, everyone in possession of a penis and past the age of puberty – but as she looked at the cranky old man standing in front of her, she realized that in this case, she could be fairly confident in the fact that he wasn't going to jump the counter and try to rape her. You never knew for sure, of course, but he didn't seem like the type and anyway, she had Gage by her side. Mr. Burbank would never try something with her wall of muscles behind her.

So, she decided to try extending an olive branch. See how far that got her. The worst that could happen was he could grab the branch and whack her over the head with it.

"How long have you owned the hardware store?" she asked him as he made his way through the pile of items.

"Since 1985," he said gruffly.

Dead silence.

Cady had never considered herself to be the queen of small talk, and that had only gotten worse over the years, not better. Sometimes, she could hide this fatal flaw from others if they were super chatty – Emma Dyer being a great example of that – but Mr. Burbank...

Nope, he wasn't helping the situation, not one bit.

The only semi-intelligent comment she could think of to say was that she was born in 1985, so he'd been doing this as long as she'd been alive, but that just didn't seem like a great idea. That'd only encourage him to continue to look at her like a little kid, *not* something she needed any help with.

Before she could come up with something else to ask – anything at all – he unexpectedly added, "Always thought my boys would take it over from me but all three moved away from Sawyer, and so far, they ain't had any grandkids that've made noise 'bout taking over either, not like Gage here did with his grandparents." He jerked his head towards Gage. "So I just keep working away. I s'pose I'll just be here until I keel over one day in Aisle 2." He snorted a little at that. "Joke's on them – after I'm gone, they'll have to deal with this store after all, even if it's just to sell it all off." He chortled at the thought, and then rattled off the total.

Cady smiled and nodded, sliding her card through the machine. Good manners dictated that she respond in some way to his comments about his sons but nothing appropriate came to mind, and then the moment had passed to say anything at all. Taking the receipt, she gathered up half the bags – the lighter half; her momma didn't raise no fool – and headed for the door.

"Good luck," the crotchety old man called out after her, but in that moment, he didn't seem nearly so crotchety as he had before.

"Uh, thank you," she stuttered, pushing her way through the glass front door and holding it open with her back until Gage made it through with the rest of the bags. She looked at his straining muscles and felt a flash of guilt at the sight. She really had left some heavy bags for him.

But he didn't say a word about it and fell into step beside her as they headed back down the street.

"He doesn't expect women to know a damn thing about construction supplies, does he?" she asked once they got far enough away from the store that geriatric ears wouldn't be able to overhear her. Damn the chauvinistic pigs of the world. It wasn't like she was some sort of expert, but she did know which end of the hammer to use, despite what Burbank seemed to expect. Cady's dad had done a few projects with her over the years, teaching her the basics. She wasn't about to put herself in charge of building someone a house, but she knew the difference between wood glue and cement glue.

"Not at all," Gage said cheerfully.

"And you knew that me helping look for supplies and being the one to talk to him would impress him."

"Yup," Gage affirmed, just as cheerfully.

"You could've let me in on the plan," she complained, shifting the bags in her hands. Even as light as they were, they were starting to dig into her palms.

"Don't take this personally, Cady, but you're not a clutch player."

Finally, they were back at her store, having walked right past the Muffin Man. Her stomach rumbled at the glorious smells drifting out of the bakery, but she chose to ignore them for the moment. "'Clutch player'?" she repeated. She set the bags down for a moment – glorious relief – and dug her keys out of her pocket, unlocking the door to the Smoothie Queen to let them back in.

"You know, for working with athletes for years, you sure don't know any sports terms," Gage said dryly, following her inside.

She shrugged. "I told you, sports just aren't my thing. The last thing I should've done was go into *sports* medicine." She rolled her eyes at herself. "The advisor for the major was cute, and I thought…well, anyway. So. What is a clutch player?"

Gage was already unloading the bags on the counter, spreading out the supplies to get ready to work. "When a player can come in at the last moment and save the game. A clutch player does well under pressure, and you, Cady Walcott, just don't fit that description. You tend to freeze up. I figured that the less you knew about the plan beforehand, the less you could worry and stew about it and screw it all up. Better to surprise you with the deets and let you figure it out on the fly. Less chances of you doing or saying something you didn't mean."

She crossed her arms and gave him a death glare for the third time that day. He really was on a roll.

"Your confidence in me is overwhelming," she said sarcastically.

He had the good grace to look a little guilty at that. "You have plenty of things you're good at," he rushed to reassure her. "Most women don't know what a jigsaw is, unless you're talking about puzzle pieces, and talking through what to do here…you had a couple of good ideas that I hadn't even thought of. But dealing with people you don't know well isn't a talent that tops the list for you. There's nothing wrong with that – I have plenty of things I'm not good at."

As soon as the words left his mouth, she could tell he regretted them. Naturally, Cady decided to needle him over it, because why not?

"Plenty of things, eh?" she repeated. "Care to name any?"

"Nope!" He popped the "p" when he said it, and

then flashed her a charming grin. "I prefer to keep my secrets. Makes me more of a mystery to the ladies." He waggled his eyebrows at that and she burst out laughing.

Instead of smiling or laughing in return, though, he began pulling his shirt away from his chest and flapping it, his face a bit flushed. "Does it seem hot in here to you?" he asked, his voice a bit…croaky.

"Hot?" She looked around the storefront as if a thermometer was going to pop up out of nowhere and tell her what the temperature was in the room. "I don't think so, but I also tend to run cold. Not enough body here to retain body heat." She gestured to her small figure with a wry smile. "I'm used to adding on the layers, though. Do you want me to prop open the front door and let a cross-breeze through?"

"Sure, thanks," he said, turning away from her and pulling his flannel shirt off, leaving just his thin t-shirt behind.

After finding a loose brick to prop the front door open with, Cady headed back into the storefront. She'd ask Gage how she could best help, and—

She froze.

Gage's back was turned to her as he rifled through the items from the hardware store, looking for something, muttering under his breath, but she couldn't hear what he was saying because it turned out that she couldn't hear anything at all over the roaring in her ears.

He'd not only stripped off his flannel shirt, he'd

stripped off his t-shirt too, leaving nothing behind but acres of skin. And muscles. Muscles everywhere.

So big. He was *so. big.* He could crush her with his little pinky. He could squash her flat. He could sit on her and not even notice there was a lump under his ass. Not because he was fat – oh hell no. Not that. She could describe him using a whole lot of adjectives, but *fat* was nowhere on that list.

The oh-too-familiar waves of panic began washing over her at the sight. He was big – *way* too big – and what if he decided that he wanted to hurt her? She couldn't stop him. She could no more stop him than she could stop the waves rolling up from the ocean.

But there, just on the edges, tinging her panic was…lust?

Surely not lust.

She couldn't lust after Gage.

She couldn't lust after anyone at all, honestly, but *especially* not after Gage. He was too big. Too terrifyingly gigantic. If she ever managed to find someone to date – if that not-so-small miracle ever occurred – he would have to be skinny as a rail. Preferably short, too. Shorter than her, if she could manage to find such a minuscule being, but she'd be willing to go as tall as six inches over her five-foot-nothin' height if he was skinny enough.

But Gage was over a foot taller than her and probably a foot wider and every bit of him was muscles and valleys and lightly tanned skin…

"Did you bring in the bag with the clamps?" Gage asked, turning towards her, running his hand through his hair in exasperation.

"I'm…I'm pretty sure," she said, and this time, it was her turn to have a croaky voice.

Which, obviously, when Gage'd had a croaky voice, it wasn't the same reason why she was now having one because that'd imply that he liked her and that, more than anything else, absolutely could *not* be true.

She wouldn't let it be.

Some disasters simply couldn't be.

CHAPTER 14

GAGE

*I*T WAS DAY TWO of his days off for the week, or as he had begun to call it, Hell on Earth.

Not because he was bored. No, that definitely wasn't it. He felt many a thing yesterday, but boredom was *not* amongst them.

How was it that Gage could get (almost) any woman he wanted eating out of his hand (sometimes quite literally) without breaking into a sweat, but one tiny Cady Walcott was completely immune to his charms?

It just wasn't fair, honestly.

Maybe it was because it'd been so long since he'd tried to charm a woman. During culinary arts school, business school, and then working at the Sweet Spot bakery for two years to fulfill the requirements set out by his grandparents before he could take over their bakery, he'd been *the* guy. Every waitress (and half the waiters) flirted with him. He was well liked, and he had no end to the number of women he could convince to join him in bed when he put a mind to it.

Then he'd moved up to Long Valley and taken over the bakery and…the last four years just passed by in a blur of cooking and paying bills and dealing with high schoolers who didn't have a clue what it meant to work, and trying to dodge the latest matchmaking attempts from his meddling sister, and so maybe, somewhere in there, he'd forgotten how to be attractive to women.

He pushed his glasses up the brim of his nose absentmindedly.

Hey, maybe it was the glasses. He pulled them off and looked at them for a moment. Were they Woman Repellant?

He shoved the glasses back on with a groan. If Cady was so shallow that she wouldn't date him because of his glasses, then he didn't want her anyway.

But he knew why Cady wasn't even bothering to look his way. She'd already told him exactly why it was that she didn't trust any man over the age of 12. But he somehow naïvely believed that this would only apply if she were worried about the guy in question raping her, and surely, surely by now she'd learned to trust him.

Right?

Well, here went nothing. Another day of working beside Cady, listening to her laugh, watching her wrinkle her nose up as she thought, his palms itching with the desire to tuck the curly wisps of her hair behind her ears as they flew around her face...

And then not touching her at all.

Like he said, Hell on Earth, Day Two.

He pushed his way through the glass door of the smoothie shop, and forced out a cheerful, "Good morning!"

Which, he later reflected, it was a damn good thing he'd said good morning before he saw her, because as soon as he did...

All breathing stopped. All speaking stopped.

How was it that women thought that they were ugly when they'd just thrown their hair up into a messy bun and pulled on a pair of old, ripped jeans and a tank top? Because Gage was sure of one thing if he was sure of anything at all, and that was in that moment, Cady probably thought no guy would look at her twice, *and* that she was happy about this fact. She wanted to be guy proof.

But those tears in her jeans – not expensively destroyed jeans that cost $200 down at the Boise Mall, but rips and holes that came from doing actual, honest-to-God work in them – showed small patches of skin, covering more than they revealed but his imagination was happy to supply the missing pieces and...

Whoa, boy. Down. Cady would appreciate you touching her like she'd appreciate licking an electric fence set to high.

"Hey, Gage!" Cady called out cheerfully, turning

carefully on the ladder, a small paint can in one hand and a brush in the other. She had a careless streak of white paint across her nose and Gage's thumbs itched to rub it off.

Casually, he shoved his hands into his back pockets.

"You're already hard at work," he observed, and was thrilled to hear his voice coming out all normal and shit, like he wasn't fighting a boner of monstrous proportions in that moment.

Not bad, Gage. Not bad at all.

He'd woken up at four that morning – after years of early mornings, his body refused to get on board with the idea that sleeping in was a possibility on his days off – and had forced himself to clean out his fridge, scrub his kitchen floors, and do a load of laundry, all before coming to the Smoothie Queen. No reason to act anxious and excited to please. He could play it cool, even if it killed him.

Which it just might.

All of this meant that he was arriving at the Smoothie Queen at the insanely late hour of 8:30. He was rather proud of himself for lasting that long. There at the end, it'd either been drive to the Smoothie Queen and get to work, or start arranging his canned food alphabetically, and he still hadn't decided if tuna fish should go under T or F—

"I'm a morning person," Cady said with a shrug, jerking him back to the present. "When I get out of bed, that is," she said under her breath.

Gage's eyebrows hit his hairline at that.

When *she gets out of bed? Does she normally not get out of bed? She's been coming down here to work every day. Is that something she—*

Even as he scrambled to put the pieces together, her face turned a brilliant red and she waved her paintbrush dismissively. "I mean, of *course* I get out of bed!" she said gaily, and much too loudly. "Every day!"

Curiouser and curiouser…

But in the end, Gage decided to swallow his questions and let her think that he hadn't noticed her slip of the tongue. He'd figure out a way to casually ask her about it later.

Of course, how to casually bring up a topic like that – *Do you regularly not get out of bed? Are you depressed? Do you have suicidal thoughts?* – was a whole different ball of wax.

Well, he'd let Future Gage figure that one out.

"You're making the trim look damn good," he said, bluntly changing the subject and putting them both out of their misery. Looking relieved, she nodded enthusiastically.

"It's a shame to paint real wood," she said with a sigh, "but it's been so dinged up and beat up over the years, what with the water damage and…I don't even know. It looks like chew marks?" She laughed again. Her laugh…he could listen to it all day. "But unless mice have learned how to crawl across the ceiling, I'm pretty sure it isn't teeth marks. But whatever it is, I figured some smoothing over with wood putty and then painting would hide the sins, as my dad used to say."

Gage turned back to his workbench where he'd left his tools the day before. Not staring up the ladder at Cady's ass was probably a real good idea right about then. "You don't talk about your parents much," he said as he began to put his workbench into some semblance of order. "Do they live in Boise?"

It was quiet for a long heartbeat, and then—
"Yes."

Except her voice was flat and hard when she said it, and surprised by the sudden change in emotions, Gage's head whipped up to look at her. That "Yes" sounded like Old Cady – the one he'd first met – and he hadn't seen that version of Cady in so long, he'd almost forgotten what she sounded like.

But Cady was staring intently at the wood trim she was painting, her brush moving back and forth as she worked her way down the wall.

Still, she said nothing more, and Gage realized that he'd inadvertently stumbled into No-Go Land. She climbed carefully down the ladder, moved it over several feet, and climbed back up. Still not another word.

One thing about Cady – you always know where you stand with her. Playacting is not her strong suit.

"Wanna listen to some music?" he finally asked in the strained silence. Anything to create some noise between them.

"Oh. Sure," Cady said, but he could tell her mind wasn't on the question. "I have a radio over in the corner that you can pair with your phone if you want."

Gage put on some Blake Shelton – everything was better with Blake in the house – and got to work on recreating the beautifully carved counter so he could cut out the damaged part and slide in the new. If he did it right, no one would ever know the difference.

Making an item as beautiful and perfect as it'd been before it was broken...there was something truly satisfying about that.

If only Cady would let him help her, too.

CHAPTER 15

CADY

*I*T WAS PROBABLY the fact that she was up near the ceiling and thus breathing in all of the paint and lacquer fumes that had drifted upward, but she felt lightheaded, and...just *off*, somehow. She and Gage had been working in companionable silence for a while now, broken only by that dreadful country twang that he somehow called music, and the roar of the table saw as he ran boards through it.

It had been...nice. Other than the dreadful music, of course, but she didn't think that she could complain about her free labor's horrendous choice in music. Listening to songs about a guy's dog running away was the least she could do after all of Gage's help.

Food. I need food.

"Ready for me to pay you back for the welcome-to-Sawyer dinner?" she asked, already eagerly climbing down the ladder. Her stomach had begun its low rumble and she was afraid it'd reach cacophony levels if she held off eating for much longer. "I still haven't made it down to the diner – Betty's, right? – and I figure lunch on me is a good way to say thanks for your help today."

Gage pulled his safety glasses off and wiped at his face and hair, sending a shower of sawdust into the air. They both coughed and hacked from it, until Gage could finally get out, "Are you sure you wanna go out into public with me?"

She laughed, scrubbing at her cheek with the back of her hand. "I'm sure I look just as awful," she said dryly. "I'm getting paint into places I didn't even know I had. If you're willing to be seen in public with me, I'm willing to be seen with you. Let me go clean out my paintbrush and put a lid on the can, and I'll be ready to go."

She scrubbed up in the big utility sink in the back, listening to the water running in the bathroom as Gage did his best to clean up too. She knew, of course, that there was no mirror in the bathroom – only a giant light spot on the wall where the old one used to hang – but he'd at least be able to get most of the sawdust off in the sink. Probably.

He came out of the bathroom, his hair wet and glistening – he'd apparently chosen to dunk his head in the sink – and most of his face was clean, except…

"Hold on, you've got this big stripe right here," she said, gesturing vaguely to her cheek. He scrubbed at his cheek. "No, the other side." He switched cheeks. "Now you've got a clean spot in the middle of the dirty spot," she said, laughing. "C'mon."

She slipped past him into the bathroom and wet a paper towel as he obediently pulled his glasses off. She dabbed at his face, swiping and wiping and then throwing away the paper towel and starting over again when it got too ragged and dirty to use. His face was a warm, stubbled world under her fingertips and she felt her own face warming up as she scrubbed away.

She kept her eyes glued to his square jaw, though, using her peripheral vision to clean the rest of his face. What if she looked up and caught his gaze? She couldn't look him in the eye. She was too close to him.

Finally, everything she could spot out of the corner of her eye had been cleaned and she stepped back with a forced laugh. "There, you look better," she pronounced, her gaze hovering vaguely to the left of his head.

"Okay, but now it's my turn," he said, shoving his glasses back on and turning the tap on again, grabbing a paper towel and dipping it underneath the stream of water.

She sucked in a breath and held it, hoping that if she just didn't breathe ever again, she could keep from breathing in his smell – which somehow still reminded her of bread and yeast and sugar, even after two days of him not baking anything – and thus keep from making a fool out of herself and she absolutely, positively did *not* like him because…because…

Well, because.

He gently took her chin into his calloused, large fingers, turning her face this way and that, wiping gently with the towel, more gently than a guy of his size should be able to wield a paper towel. She waited for the ever-present panic to well up inside of her and smother her; to roll over her in dark waves and keep her from breathing or thinking but only running, except…

The panic didn't come.

Here she was with a guy – a huge, muscular guy – standing in the doorway of a tiny bathroom, blocking her in, in the back of a building that was otherwise empty, and she should be terrified but…she wasn't?

"There," he said softly, and then his fingers disappeared from her chin and she heard the wet paper towel drop into the trash. "The paint is all gone."

Seemingly of their own accord – because Cady *knew* better than to open up her eyes while standing this close to a guy – her eyes fluttered open and she realized that she was just inches away from Gage and he was looking down at her and even if there wasn't lust in her eyes and she had no idea if there was because she was all turned around inside, and up was down, and right was left—

Breathe, Cady—

But even if there wasn't lust in her eyes, there was

in his. She hadn't had much experience having a guy look at her like…like *this*, but even ignorant, naïve Cady knew what *that* look meant.

It meant trouble.

Big, fat, inescapable trouble.

"Ready to go?" Her voice hit a painfully high note with that last vowel, and then she was practically sprinting out of the store and onto the street…

Where she came to a dead stop and with a painful sigh, she turned around. Purse. She needed her purse if she was going to pay for this lunch.

Gage had stopped just inside of the door and was waiting quietly for her as she came bustling back in, acting to all the world – or at least to the Gage Dyers of the world – as if absolutely, positively not a thing was wrong.

"Purse!" she said with a forced laugh, snagging it out from underneath the counter, blowing all of the sawdust off the top, and slinging it over her shoulder.

"Ready to go?" she asked again, but this time, oh thank the heavens above, her voice didn't crack like a thirteen-year-old boy just hitting puberty.

"Sure," Gage said, but his normally easy-going personality seemed to be missing. For the first time since she'd met him, he seemed awkward around her.

It was bright outside, the mid-May sunshine bouncing off every window and car on the street.

"I'm assuming it's faster to just walk?" she asked, shielding her eyes from the sun as she peered down the street towards the waving statue.

"Absolutely, and again, you're publicly supporting a local business – walking there means that everyone can see you going there to eat. That sort of thing is insanely important around here."

"Right." They took off down the street, Cady clutching her purse as they walked. Not that she thought anyone was going to jump out and try to nab it from her – even if there was a rash of purse thievery in Sawyer, no one would be stupid enough to try it with Gage by her side – but rather because she was clutching the purse to her side, she then had something to do with her hands.

Something that didn't involve reaching over and threading her fingers through Gage's.

You are being an idiot. Like, a world-class dumbass. You know you can't date someone. You know what happens when a guy tries to kiss you.

One date. She'd gone on one date since the near-rape, and only because her mom had been moaning and groaning about how her daughter never got out anymore, and how was she going to have any grandkids to love on at this rate?

You never did get your grandkids, Mom. Just one more way that I failed you.

But that one date was enough for Cady. When Tom had leaned forward to plant what was probably a perfectly innocent, close-mouthed goodnight kiss on her lips, she'd slapped him across the face, kneed him in the balls, and then had run into the house, deadbolting the door behind her.

Needless to say, Tom hadn't called to ask for a second date.

The painfully quiet walk finally reached its conclusion when they got to the front door of Betty's, the giant statue casting a shadow over them as they walked inside.

Cady immediately felt at home. There was the same homey, warm vibe here as there was at the Muffin Man, and Cady knew that more than shopping in a public sort of way, she needed to recreate this feeling in the Smoothie Queen if she was going to make it in this town.

"Hey, Gage!" A lady with short cropped platinum blonde hair waved across the restaurant at them. "Pick a booth – I'll be right over."

Cady looked Gage straight in the face – the first time since she'd stupidly done it back in the bathroom at the store – as she grinned up at him. "Eat here much?" she asked dryly as he led the way to one of the booths lining the front of the diner.

He shrugged, unrepentant. "This is Sawyer," he reminded her. "Whether I ate here daily or only once a month, I'd still know everyone. Chloe is a transplant to the area, but she's been here long enough, most of us have forgiven her for being a big city girl."

"How long will it take for people to forget that I'm a transplant here, too?" Cady asked, gnawing on her bottom lip with worry. She hadn't thought about that nearly as much as she probably should have; an oversight she was only realizing she'd made because she was finally starting to get to know this town.

And outsiders were definitely *not* the norm.

"Fifteen years?" Gage guessed. Cady gasped in horror. "If you're lucky," he added.

She glared at him. "You're teasing me, aren't you." It was a statement, not a question, but before he could affirm or deny, the waitress came bustling over.

"Hey, Gage!" she said, pushing her hand through her short blonde hair, the shiny straight hair falling back into a perfect line to her shoulder, even after she ran her fingers through it.

Cady tried not to drool with envy. She had naturally curly hair that simply wasn't something she could run her fingers through – at least not without using a pick and a whole bottle of detangler beforehand – and so naturally, she was green with envy over every woman who had straight hair.

I bet her hair never creates a halo of frizz around her head when it rains.

She heaved a sigh.

"I haven't met you yet," Chloe said, turning to Cady with a large, friendly smile. "I'm Chloe, and you are…"

Cady held out her hand and they shook. "Cady Walcott. I bought the store next door to the Muffin Man."

"Oh!" Chloe's face lit up. "I've been watching the progress on that old place. I can't believe everything you've managed to do to it so far. Just fixing that broken awning was a huge step forward. It looks a thousand times better now that you've scrubbed the smoke damage off the walls, too."

Cady smiled, trying to hide her surprise. Was Chloe pressing her face up against the window and inspecting the interior? She knew small town residents tended to stick their noses in wherever they wanted, but surely peering inside of an unopened building was odd, right?

Before Cady could ask any questions – before she could think of any question to ask – Gage broke out with, "Now lookie here – who's an expecting mama!"

Chloe's face broke out in a huge grin. "You sure are observant," she said, turning sideways and running her hand over the small bump with pride. Cady gulped. Gage was damn brave to mention it. Sure, Chloe was fairly petite and it looked like a pregnancy bump to the untrained eye, but it could've been an eating-too-many-donuts bump too. "Dawson is over the moon. He's already counted out how many days until we can go in and find out if it's a girl or a boy. He says he'd be fine with either, but honestly, I think he wants a little girl he can spoil rotten. Of course, Tommy wants a younger brother. I've tried to tell him that we don't have a choice in the matter, but he's started adding it to his prayers every night, sure that he can talk God into giving him a brother instead of an icky sister."

Gage rumbled with laughter. "You two have your hands full with that one. Well, I don't know if you were at Jennifer and Stetson's baby reveal party, but I baked the cake for it, making the inside blue. I'd be happy to do something similar for you two. No charge. I'm just excited to see you two getting around to adding to the family."

Chloe smiled then, a contented smile filled with warmth and precious memories that made Cady feel almost like an interloper, eavesdropping on an inner conversation that only Chloe could hear. "Me, too," she murmured. "So!" She straightened up, putting her back-to-work face on. "Are you two ready to order?"

CHAPTER 16

GAGE

They headed back up Main Street, Gage gallantly carrying the to-go bag from Betty's. It was Cady's leftovers and she'd tried to argue that she should thus be responsible for carrying it, but he'd pointed out that his manly man pride had already taken a beating when he'd let her pay for lunch, so she surely couldn't expect him to have her carry a bag while he was empty-handed.

He'd cheerfully ignored her not-so-quietly muttered comments about male chauvinistic pigs. He'd come to the firm conclusion in the last few weeks that teasing Cady was one of the highlights of his life, and he wasn't about to give up that pleasure now.

"So, how long have you known Chloe and Dawson?" Cady asked as they walked.

"Only since I moved back to Sawyer myself," he said, scratching again at the stubble on his jaw. At this point, he wasn't sure if he was more excited about going back to work tomorrow so he could get back to baking, or so he could shave and not feel like he was giving in.

He hated shaving. He wasn't going to do it on his days off, dammit.

But he was quickly starting to realize that he might hate stubble even more.

"I didn't know the story for a long time," he continued, "and I probably still don't know most of it, but somehow, Chloe ended up here, pregnant with Tommy, and totally alone." They paused to look both ways, and then darted across the street back towards their stores. Gage glanced up at the Muffin Man Bakery storefront, automatically noting the smudges in the corner of the far-left window and making a mental note to tell Sugar to clean it up, and then his brain was off to the races and he was wondering how sales were going that day and if the latest teenage hire was actually going to show up or not this afternoon and…

Today is my day off, dammit. I will not worry about the bakery. Sugar has everything under control. The smudge will still be there tomorrow. I can clean it then. If there are any problems, she'll come find me.

"So anyway," he said, forcing himself to keep going, "our town vet, Adam Whitaker, helped her give birth on the side of the road in the middle of a blizzard – *that's* a story you should hear her tell sometime – and she's been here ever since. Years later,

Tommy's dad, Dawson, showed up and they patched things up. Dawson started a horse breeding ranch outside of town out at the old Miller place, and they seem plenty happy now."

Cady nodded thoughtfully as they stopped in front of the smoothie store. Just as she was digging into her purse to pull her keys out, though, she froze, one hand inside of her purse, jerking her head up to stare into the sky, a look of sheer panic on her face.

"What? What?" Gage asked, twisting to look upwards, instinctively readying himself to defend her from whatever would cause her to look like that. But all he could see was a little two-seater plane flying overhead – probably a crop duster on his way to a new field.

Totally confused, he looked back down at Cady, searching for an answer from her on what the hell was going on, but she was shaking, her purse falling off her shoulder, spilling everything out onto the ground but she didn't notice. She was drawing in on herself, wrapping her arms around herself and rocking, moaning with pain.

Shit, shit, shit.

Without a moment's hesitation, Gage scooped up the keys off the sidewalk and after only two false tries, he got the right key in the lock and shoved Cady inside. Whatever the hell was going on with her, the last thing she needed was for the whole town to witness it.

She was already the big city girl with more money

than sense, who was stupid enough to buy the most beat-up, piece-of-shit real estate in town.

She was already the big city girl who killed the electricity to the whole town by hiring the worst electrician in living memory.

She didn't also need to be the big city girl who had full-blown panic attacks over nothing at all.

He grabbed her purse, still lying on the ground, and haphazardly shoved the items back in that'd fallen out, and then slipped inside the smoothie store, shutting and flipping the deadbolt behind him before dropping the leftovers from Betty's, Cady's purse, and her keys on the floor. He could put them nicely up on the counter later. Right now, he had someone falling to pieces in front of him, and absolutely no idea why.

"Cady?" he said hesitantly. She was shaking harder than ever, her teeth chattering, and she was rubbing her arms incessantly, up and down, up and down, trying to soothe herself, backing towards the wall until her back touched it and then she began sinking, sliding down the wall.

"Hold on there," Gage said, and pulled her up again, snuggling her against his chest. He didn't want to see Cady curled up on the floor – it seemed like it was too close to her giving up on the world. He wouldn't allow her. If she had to borrow some of his strength to make it through...*whatever* this was, then he had plenty to lend to her.

He stroked his hand down her back, rubbing up and down, just like she had been doing with her own arms, but he added what he hoped were sympathetic noises in concert to his movements. For what would probably be the only time in his life, Gage silently thanked God for "blessing" him with a younger sister who gave into hysterics often as a child, and who only got worse as a teenager. Emma's tears were usually caused by someone teasing her at school; over a boy who didn't like her as much as she liked him; or getting into trouble because Chris had done something awful and mean – again – and Emma had exacted revenge – again – and only Emma had gotten in trouble for it – again.

In other words, things that in that moment felt pretty inconsequential, at least compared to whatever the hell it was that Cady was going through.

Eventually, the shaking slowed down to mere shivers and Gage could feel the change wash over Cady as soon as she realized what had happened.

"So sorry," she muttered, pulling away, wiping at her eyes with the back of her hand. "I don't know what came over me."

Gage just stood there, watching her, his hands helplessly dangling at his sides. He wanted to pull her back into his arms and soothe her again, but the time for that had passed. If he did it now, Cady would fight him tooth and nail.

"You wanna tell me what's going on?" he asked quietly.

"No." But she quirked just a bit of a smile as she said it – the tiniest lifting of the corner of her mouth

– and Gage breathed a silent sigh of relief. Whatever had just happened, she wasn't blaming him for it.

Cady looked around the torn-apart store, clearly wanting something, and then spotted her purse on the floor. Digging a small package of tissues out, she blew her nose loudly. She sounded rather like a goose honking on its way up north in that moment, and Gage couldn't help the laughing smile that crossed his face. She really was too damn adorable for words.

"My parents are in Boise," she said so quietly, he had to lean forward to hear her. "That wasn't a lie."

She stopped, and Gage just held his breath, waiting for her to continue. His mind bounced around from possibility to possibility, trying to figure out where in the hell she could be going with this, but none of his half-formed guesses turned out to be even vaguely correct.

"More specifically, their cremated ashes are in the Boise River. Their spirits are…well, wherever spirits go after death." She waved her used tissue through the air dismissively, trying to act casual, as if she was just fine.

"Oh," he breathed, saying nothing else, waiting as he watched Cady struggle to tell him the story without breaking down again.

"It was their 35th anniversary, and my parents decided to celebrate by doing something they'd always wanted to do – a big trip up to Alaska. They were supposed to spend 10 days up there – bear watching, whale watching, hiking, kayaking, and…and taking an aerial tour of the glaciers."

"Ohhhh…" he said again.

He could put it together then – he didn't need to know the gory details of how and why.

But he kept his mouth shut anyway and just listened, because he knew this was a story that Cady needed to tell and if he was the only one she could talk to, well then, by God, he'd listen.

She stared at the far wall behind him as she spoke, though, like she was reciting facts about the 19th President of the United States.

"My parents aren't – weren't – rich, so they did the same thing that I did when looking for an electrician: They searched for the cheapest charter plane available. If they didn't get a bare-bones price, they wouldn't be able to afford to go, and my mom had always wanted to see the glaciers of Alaska.

"But the company they chose was the cheapest for a reason – the FAA found in their investigation afterwards that the company had been falsifying a lot of their maintenance and training records. My parents were going up in a plane that was being held together by bubblegum and string, and being flown by a guy who shouldn't have been allowed to pilot a hang glider, let alone a charter plane.

"Weather is unpredictable in Alaska, and partway through their tour, a strong wind came up, gusts blowing them around, and the pilot freaked out – didn't know how to handle it. Investigators told me that they listened to the black box, and they heard my father trying to tell the pilot to stay calm and think through it, but...I couldn't listen to the recording myself. They asked me if I wanted to, you know. I could never listen to the last moments of my parents' lives. Never, never, never."

She drew in a ragged breath, still staring at the wall, but there was a crack in her façade now – just a tiny one, but there. This was now more than just a recitation of facts that happened to someone else. It had become a little more personal.

"They...well, they hit the side of a mountain, basically. Using GPS, the first responders were able to locate the plane, but it was several days before they could pull everyone out. They all died on impact, so at least my parents didn't lie there for days, slowly freezing to death, right?"

She drew in an unsteady breath, held it for a moment, and then blew it out. "Between the Mayday calls, the black box, the weather satellites, and falsified records, the FAA investigators were able to piece it all together. I...my parents worried about me as an only child, so they'd paid for a large insurance policy on themselves for years, just in case something happened to them. I took some of that payout and I sued the charter company into oblivion, quite literally. My parents' flight was the last one that charter company ever did. They're no longer able to save a buck here and fifty cents there, and put the lives of their pilots and customers on the line in the process. Shutting that company down is the one good thing I think I've ever done in my life."

She lifted her chin and looked Gage straight in the eye for the first time since her meltdown began outside the store. "I don't do planes," she said bluntly. "Not ever, not for any reason. Just listening to them fly overhead…well, you saw what just happened. It's ironic – my parents owned a charming, small Craftsman home in Boise – nothing that anyone would take notice of, but for me, it was *home*. It was the only home I'd ever had until I started at Boise State. I could've just stayed living with my parents while going to college – I would've been perfectly happy there – but my mom knew me better than I knew myself, and she knew I needed to be out on my own, learning how to navigate the world. I ended up with Hannah as my roommate, but my parents were only twenty minutes away, so I ended up at home quite often, especially when my laundry hamper got full."

She sent him a grimacing smile, and he smiled in return, trying to mold his features into understanding and kindness, when all he really wanted to do was punch the penny-pinching owner of the charter company into oblivion.

"But the ironic part of it all was that my parents' home is close to the Boise Airport. I grew up with planes flying overhead. When I was really young, I dreamt of being a pilot, although that dream disappeared as soon as I realized that I got major motion sickness when I was up in the air." She chuckled humorlessly. "After my parents died, all I wanted to do was sleep – well, sleep and get revenge on the chartering company. But mostly sleep. I retreated to my parents' house and I probably never would've left again – I have enough money that if I lived frugally, I never would've had to work again – except day and night, there were planes, flying overhead. It slowly drove me insane. I never knew when they were coming. I didn't know if they'd fly safely over and keep going or if they'd drop out of the sky and take out the house and me in it. It was horrible – it was my sanctuary *and* a torture chamber."

She dabbed at her eyes with her tissue and honked loudly again before continuing.

"It was about six months later that I managed to make myself start participating in life again, even if it was in just little dribs and drabs. I would go for short walks around the yard. I would actually go down to the grocery store and go shopping, rather than have the store deliver the food to me.

"And then…" She drew in a deep breath and sent Gage a forced smile. "One day, I decided to be truly brave and drive all the way up to Long Valley to go hiking in the Goldfork Mountains. I'd gone a few times with Hannah when we were at college together, and had just loved it. So on January 3rd, I hiked and then stopped in town to get a coffee at some bakery called the Muffin Man – you should check it out, it's pretty great – but found a storefront next door to buy on the way over. Who finds a store on a whim?" She chuckled humorlessly. "It wasn't part of the plan but honestly, I didn't have a plan then, unless you could call 'Putting one foot in front of another' a plan. Or 'Getting out of bed every single day before noon' a plan. Then sure, I had a plan. But this store…it's given me a reason to get out of bed every single day before eight, and I promise you, in my world, that's a big deal."

They lapsed into silence for a minute, until Gage asked quietly, "Did you sell your parents' house in Boise?"

She nodded slowly. "The house, most of the items and furniture inside, and my parents' vehicles. I have a storage unit filled to the brim with some sentimental stuff I couldn't bear to part with, but even that is in Boise. I wanted my move up here to be a clean slate. Nothing holding me back. I was going to be New Cady – better than before. It was only an hour or two after I had that thought that I met this muscular baker who scared me shitless by sneaking up behind me – a real asshole, honestly."

Gage burst out laughing, laughing louder than he normally would have under different circumstances because Cady was making a joke. Listening to her make a joke just then…it meant everything.

She was stronger than she realized.

"Now hold on a good, long minute," he protested when his chuckles finally died down. "I didn't sneak up on anyone! I clomped around noisily in my work boots just like I always do."

"I wanted you fired for that," Cady said dryly. "I was just sure that whoever owned the Muffin Man would see that interaction and fire your ass over it. I thought some old grandma owned the place."

"You thought I should've been fired because I recommended brownies to you?" he asked, horrified.

"It was cream puffs," she corrected him pertly, as if that were a very important fact indeed, "and I mostly just wanted you fired because you scared me, and in my mind at that moment…if you scared me, you were a bad guy and you deserved to be fired. And keep in mind, this was *New* Cady. Be really, *really* glad you never met Old Cady." She sent him a self-deprecating smile as she said it.

It was quiet between them again as Gage struggled to process everything Cady had just told him. Between the attempted rape by the football player and then the death of her parents – her only family…it was a wonder she managed to get out of bed at all. It would've been so easy to just hide from the world for the rest of her life, especially because of the large inheritance she'd received.

Speaking of…a part of him understood why her parents chose to keep a large insurance policy on themselves, but a part of him…a part of him did not. They had good intentions, but wasn't there that saying that the path to hell was paved with good intentions? That large chunk of change enabled their only daughter to withdraw from the world for a while and not have to deal with things like going to work and paying bills and simply being a part of society.

If their house hadn't been so close to a major airport, Cady would've wasted her life hiding in it. And what a waste that would've been.

He did it then – what he'd been telling himself he absolutely could not do.

He reached out for Cady, not to scrub dried paint off her nose or to hold her while she cried, but because he wanted to hold her…and kiss her.

Time stopped as she looked at his outstretched hand, trying to decide if she'd take it or if she'd run away, and Gage worried that he'd pushed too hard, too fast, and she'd run now and never come back but before he could drop his hand down by his side and pretend as if he'd simply been wanting to stretch out his arm for no reason at all, she reached out with trembling fingers and clasped his hand in hers. Her fingers were tiny, as was the rest of her, but Gage knew that only a fool would think that her diminutive stature also meant that she wasn't strong.

Because she was, in every way that counted.

He pulled her towards him slowly, his eyes boring into hers, asking without words, *Do you want this? Are you ready?*

Biting her bottom lip, she took the last step to close the gap between them, answering his question without words, and the heat off her body was so hot, so delicious, it was hard to contain himself. He made himself move oh-so-slowly, though. He couldn't startle her. Knowing her now like he did, he realized that she had every reason to be the way she was – to react the way she did – but that also meant that she would always be in the driver's seat. He had to let her choose to move forward every step of the way, no matter how hard it was.

He pulled her against his thighs, feeling her softness cuddle against him, her curves as perfect as a newly blossomed rose. They fit together, the two of them, despite how big he was and how small she was, or maybe it was *because* of that...

He slid his hand into the thicket of her curls at the base of her neck, moving her, pulling her up to him as his lips finally met hers. She let out the tiniest of whimpers, her fingers grasping at him, hanging onto him for dear life, and he knew then that he was a goner. He wanted her to want him with all of her soul; he wanted her to want him like she wanted to breathe; he wanted her to want him as much as he wanted her.

He scooped her up, wrapping her legs around his waist and carrying her to the counter, where he set her down on it, finally bringing them eye to eye. Things moved quickly after that, everything a blur of sensations and sounds and he found his fingers trembling as he stroked her soft skin and he didn't know if he'd be able to contain himself or if he'd unman himself in front of her—

There was something strange happening, though.

Somewhere, far away but oh so persistent, there was a sound or fear or—

Feeling drugged, he forced himself to open up his eyes and pull away from the hollow of her neck where he'd been memorizing every dip and valley, forcing himself to look Cady in the eye.

She was trembling too, but not from lust. Not like Gage was. Her eyes were wide with fear and she was pushing at him, pushing with all her might against his chest, and he realized then that this was what had been bothering him. She was so tiny compared to him, her attempts to push him away had felt like the beating of moth wings against his skin, at least through the haze of lust that had enveloped him. But now…

Now he could see the panic in her eyes.

He stepped back, holding his hands up in surrender, trying to calm his breathing, trying to will his dick back down. It was pushing against the zipper of his jeans and the exquisite pain of it was surely going to drive him insane.

"You gotta go," Cady said hoarsely, trembling, shrinking in on herself. "You got to…" Her voice broke and she was shaking so hard, he was sure she was going to fall off the counter. Instinctively, he reached out to steady her and she let out a little shriek of terror, batting at his hand, swatting him away.

Like the flick of a light switch, the desire, the lust, the need to become one with Cady disappeared, his dick deflating like a balloon the day after a kid's party.

Seeing her react like this to *him*…

Without a word, he spun on his heel and stomped out of the store and towards his truck, anger radiating off him, hotter than the surface of the sun.

He was done. He was done with Cady Walcott. He was done being dragged around by a ring through his nose. He was done having her look at him like he was just another asshole in the world. He'd given her another chance, another chance, another chance…

Never again. He wasn't going to deliver his heart to Cady on a platter again. She could take her and her bullshit ideas about men and life and go screw with someone else's mind.

He was done.

CHAPTER 17

GAGE

GAGE PEERED AT HIS IPAD, propped up against a canister of cinnamon, trying to remember if he was supposed to beat the mixture until creamy or until crumbly. It was a new recipe and thus he didn't have it memorized yet – just a test run to see if mint Oreos would work both in the crust *and* mixed throughout.

As he concentrated, adding another dab of vanilla to the mixture and flipping the beaters back on, he felt the anger that had been throbbing through him the last week begin to ebb away, leaking out of him like air out of a tiny hole in a bike tire. Here, he was in charge. Here, he could make magic with his hands by pulling ingredients together that were heaven on the tongue, even if certain women thought he was nothing but a creeper with those hands and—

He slapped at the switch, shutting the beaters back off, forcing himself to take a deep breath and then let it slowly back out, pushing the mounting anger back down again.

It was fine. Here in his kitchen, he was in charge.

Sugar was out front, taking care of the customers, and he was back here, by himself, happy and creating and letting loose in the best way possible. He had to stop letting Cady get under his skin like this. She was obviously unbalanced, and trying to make someone like that happy was impossible.

He could stop driving himself insane, and just forget the smell of her hair and the feel of her lips already.

He roughly stuffed handfuls of the mint Oreos into a gallon Ziploc bag until it looked like about the right amount, sealed it shut, and then picked up his favorite rolling pin. He should be better about measuring so he could recreate this recipe later if it ended up being a winner but he just wasn't in the mood. Right then, he just wanted to create – to be free to work and not worry about every little thing. Not worry that he was making a mistake or scaring Cady—

"Hi, Gage." Cady's voice forced its way through the haze of frustration and anger and his head snapped up, shock shooting through him. It couldn't be—

It was.

Cady was in the doorway of his kitchen, looking beautiful and delicate and—

He smashed the rolling pin down on the bag,

shooting bits of Oreos into the air through a section of the zipper that he apparently hadn't closed well enough.

"Hi, Cady," he said, trying to keep his voice even, tossing the rolling pin down with a thunk and rezipping the closure along the edge of the bag, this time making sure most of the air was out of the bag and the teeth had actually grabbed securely to each other before picking up the rolling pin again. "How are you?"

His voice was flat. Harsh. Even to his own ears, it didn't sound like him at all, but it was all he could do not to lose his temper completely. She could damn well put up with a bit of rudeness.

It was the *least* she could do, honestly.

"I'm good."

Her voice was hesitant and he could tell without looking up that she wanted him to look at her; that her eyes would be begging for it if he'd just glance at her, but he didn't. He ran the rolling pin across the bag, crunching and smashing the cookies, enjoying the destruction, waiting for Cady to say her piece and then get out of his kitchen.

"I…uhhh…I started seeing someone."

Her words hit like a bolt of lightning out of the clear blue sky. He couldn't breathe, he couldn't think. How could she? How *dare* she?

"That didn't take long," he got out, viciously pleased that he sounded sarcastic. Mean. "What's the lucky guy's name?" He didn't consider himself to be a violent man, but in that moment, he would've gladly squashed the nameless, faceless man like a bug beneath his shoe. Maybe he'd pay the jackass a visit that evening and—

"Jane Wethersmith."

Gage froze. The world stopped. He stopped. Everything, everywhere stopped and he was left grasping at straws, trying to figure out what had just happened.

"Well," he finally growled, when he could get the air back into his lungs again, "this explains *sooo* much. When were you planning on sharing the news with the rest of the class?"

He'd started rolling the pin again, crushing the Oreos into tiny crumbs, much too small for what he needed and he'd have to throw them out and start again but right then, he wanted to crush something and since homicide wasn't legal, Oreos would just have to do the trick.

"*Dr.* Jane Wethersmith. A therapist out of Franklin. She…I explained that it was an emergency and she stayed late last night to work me into her schedule. I told her everything. I'm going back again next week. She thinks I should also try some sort of medication, like Prozac or Wellbutrin or something. I've spent the whole day convincing myself that taking a little pill doesn't mean that I'm crazy. Or that talking to someone doesn't make me crazy. I'm…I'm not 100% sure I've convinced my brain that this is fine, but I'm doing it anyway. I don't like being on a rollercoaster ride all the time. I don't like not knowing if something is going to freak me out and I'm going to fall apart. I didn't used to be this way; I swear I wasn't. I used to be normal, I promise."

She laughed awkwardly but the sound quickly died away as Gage turned to look at her. He didn't have words. There was a part of his brain that was whispering urgently that he was in shock, but he didn't know how to deal with that fact. Or any facts at all.

"Therapist?" he whispered.

Cady nodded slowly, her brown curls bouncing in time. "*Super* New Cady realized that if I didn't stop jerking you around, I'd lose you forever. I like you, Gage. A lot. And for some unknown reason, you've at least put up with me thus far, and that's more than I really deserve, honestly. But I have a whole bucketload of shit to work through, and if that means getting help…it's a damn sight better than losing you."

"*Super* New Cady?" Gage repeated, moving slowly towards Cady, the palms of his hands aching to touch her skin. "What happened to New Cady?"

"She got upgraded," Cady said seriously, and then took a step towards him. He wondered if she could hear his heart thundering, if it was as loud to her as it was to him. "Turns out, New Cady was getting out of bed and going to work, but she still had some fairly large flaws, like freaking out when her boyfriend kissed her."

Gage stopped right in front of her, so close that

her chest grazed his with every breath. "Boyfriend?" he whispered. He was so close, he could see her long, thick eyelashes, tangling together, brushing against her cheeks with every blink, almost as curly as her hair. "I didn't know I'd been upgraded to boyfriend status."

"Only if you want it." But before he could open his mouth to tell her how very much he wanted it, she rushed on. "I have to take it slow. I know it isn't fair to you, but I need the room to change and grow. Will you promise not to rush me?"

He stroked his hand down the curve of her cheek, feeling like he could promise her the world in that moment, and he'd deliver. "I promise," he whispered. "You're in the driver's seat. Girlfriend." He tested the name on his tongue and discovered that he liked it very, very much.

She reached up on her tiptoes and kissed him on the cheek. "Thank you," she said quietly. And then, in a clear bid to change the topic, "Now, what were you making before I interrupted you?"

"New recipe." He grabbed her hand and tugged her over to the counter. "I'll need a taste tester, and as my girlfriend, you are, of course, to serve as my primary testing subject."

Her laughter tinkled out as he tossed the annihilated Oreos off to the side and began putting together a new bag. "I didn't realize my title came with such serious duties," she teased him, standing next to him and watching his every move.

His groin tightened with anticipation as his

imagination supplied other...*duties* that she could perform, but he stomped on that thought, sending it straight into oblivion. If she wanted slow, she'd get slow, and if they were starting out at kissing-the-cheek stage…

Well, it'd be a damn long time until his dick was happy, that was for sure.

CHAPTER 18

CADY

June, 2019

This was it – their first official date since that awkward-as-hell discussion in the bakery kitchen. She wasn't nervous at all. Other than the fact that her stomach had apparently decided that now was the time to tie itself into Gordian knots and her heart was beating so erratically that it was a damn good thing she wasn't connected to a heart monitor, she was perfectly fine. And calm.

Skittles meowed loudly in protest, and Cady looked down in surprise, finding that she'd apparently squished the calico cat so hard against her chest, she was probably having a hard time breathing. She was scrabbling for purchase, trying to free herself from her embrace, and Cady quickly placed her down on the carpet.

"I'm sorry," she told Skittles as the cat stalked a

few feet away and began giving herself a vigorous bath, apparently needing to set her fur to rights after Cady's inadvertent mauling. "I...forgot I was holding you," she said lamely. "I just...I mean...what if I screw this all up? Dr. Jane says Gage wants to date me because he likes me for me, and I just need to be myself around him, but that seems like a really, *really* bad idea. After all, 'me' means what, exactly? The 'me' that freaks out when a plane flies overhead? The 'me' that flinches every time I see a sudden movement out of the corner of my eye? I'm pretty sure no one wants to date that 'me.' Hell, I don't even like that version of me, and it *is* me."

She flopped down on the ugliest couch known to man and watched as Skittles changed legs, extending the other one up in the air like a cat version of a ballerina, washing and straightening every hair, nosing and licking them into place.

"I just wish I could figure out what in the blazin' hell Gage sees in me," she mused. "If it made sense to me, it wouldn't freak me out so much."

She looked around the apartment, seeing it for the first time through Gage's eyes. The lack of personality or color had been just what she wanted when she'd moved to Sawyer two months earlier, but now, it was feeling a little...sterile. Empty. Devoid of personality.

She had that second bedroom that held not a stick of furniture. She could move her stuff out of her storage unit in Boise and into the spare room. Save herself the monthly charge for the unit and maybe even unpack a few of the boxes. Use the knick-knacks inside to decorate and liven things up. Hang up a few pictures of her parents, even.

"It'd be nice to have some pictures of Mom and Dad back up," she told Skittles. "I think—"

There was a knock on her apartment door just then, and she shot to her feet, almost toppling over from the panicky excitement shooting through her. Skittles stopped for a fraction of a second, trying to figure out if her movement meant wet cat food or pettings and, deciding it did not, resumed her elaborate bathing. Shooting her cat a look that was a cross between a scowl and a laugh, she walked sedately over to the front door, doing her best to appear calm. It was Gage – just Gage. Nothing to get worked up about.

She opened the front door to find him in a long-sleeve button-up shirt, open at the neck, displaying a tanned triangle of skin that was begging to be kissed, with the sleeves rolled up to just below his elbows, showing off his rippling, muscular forearms.

Why oh why couldn't I find a stick to like? A very short, very skinny stick?

But despite her huge misgivings, she couldn't help the heavy thump of her heart as she stepped back, letting him in, instinctively breathing in his scent as he went by – flour and sugar and cinnamon mixed with the pine smell of aftershave.

It was a combination that absolutely shouldn't work and yet, as was true about everything Gage-related, it did. *Real* men didn't bake and work in the kitchen, but Gage did. Handsome men didn't wear glasses, but Gage did.

What would it be like to be that secure in who you are?

She used to know. She would know again.

Hopefully.

"Are you ready?" Gage asked, his deep voice rumbling as he casually scratched Skittles behind the ears in just the spot that the cat loved. The cat paused her bath, arching her back and rubbing against Gage's hand, obviously hoping to coax as many pettings and love out of this human as possible.

"I think so…?" She gestured down at her short jean skirt and sandals and said, "You told me dressy but comfortable walking shoes. Does this pass muster? Or should I change?"

She'd already spent hours putting on and taking off and putting on clothes, changing out belts and shoes and earrings, until finally settling on this outfit, mostly because she'd run out of time and had to either choose something, or go naked.

Gage's eyes raked her body and for one trembling moment, she felt like she *was* naked. Guys had thought she was cute before; she knew that. But the look in Gage's eyes…

He looked back up at her and said, "You're good. Excellent," in a hoarse voice that she almost didn't recognize.

She hid her grin behind her hand. "Uh, good," she said brightly, and turned towards her bathing cat that'd apparently decided that she wasn't going to get any more pettings out of Gage, and thus should get back to work. "Skittles, hold down the fort. Don't eat anything I wouldn't." She ignored her, cleaning between each toe thoroughly and carefully, as Gage slid his hand into the small of Cady's back and began steering her towards the front door.

"So where are we going?" Cady asked breathlessly as they mounted the stairs to head up to ground level where Gage's truck was parked. The stairs weren't that steep but still, Cady had a hard time breathing anyway. "You still haven't told me."

"That's because that'd take all of the fun out of it," Gage said seriously as he helped her up into the passenger seat of his oversized truck, and then hurried around to his side. "How am I supposed to surprise you if you know what's coming?"

She turned and cocked an eyebrow at him skeptically. "I can always be fake surprised when we get there," she offered. "I'm pretty good at that. Oh my!" she squealed in a terrible impression of a high-pitched Southern gal. "I just had *no* idea."

Gage threw back his head and laughed as he began making his way out of town – towards Franklin, not Boise, which meant that they'd get to whatever it was they were doing as their date in about 30 minutes or so. "Don't ever take up a career on Broadway," he said after his chuckles died down. "Whatever you do, don't do that."

She fake glared at him but before she could come

up with a suitably hilarious and quippy response – never her strong suit to begin with – Gage asked, "Speaking of what it is that you do, how is the Smoothie Queen coming along? What major projects do you have left to complete before you can open?"

"Well," she said, settling back against the comfortable leather seat, broken in by years of gentle wear, "I've talked Emma into coming back to Long Valley to help me figure that out – did she tell you that?"

"Did she tell me that," Gage repeated, scoffing. "I'm her favorite older brother. Of *course* she told me that."

"You're her only older brother," Cady pointed out, confused.

"Exactly! Which explains why I'm her favorite. If I had competition, I'd probably lose!" He flashed a snarky grin at her and she burst out laughing.

"You guys sure make me wish I had siblings growing up," Cady said wistfully, twirling her hair around her finger endlessly. "It would've been a lot more fun if I had siblings to play with."

"Play with?" Gage said with a belly laugh. "I think we better back up this train before you get some sort of delusional idea of what it's like to have two siblings. Basically, your childhood is one long WWE wrestling match, minus the training on how to do fancy wrestling moves without killing yourself. The good news is that I'm the oldest, of course, so all I had to do was sit on Emma or Chris when they pissed me off. Turns out, you don't need fancy moves after all!"

"But, but, but Emma acts like she likes you," Cady protested. "She's not mentioned you sitting on her on a semi-regular basis."

"That's because when we got older, we started sitting on Chris, instead. Both of us. At the same time. As much fun as it is to pick on Chris, it's even more fun to pick on him with an accomplice." He waggled his eyebrows at her conspiratorially and Cady couldn't help the pity welling up in her for this Chris kid. She hadn't actually met him yet – he didn't seem to emerge from the basement on any sort of regular schedule – but surely he didn't deserve two older siblings picking on him.

"Poor Chris," she said seriously. "You really should be nicer to your younger brother."

"Nicer? *Nicer?*! To *Chris*?! Now that's just crazy talk. He's the baby of the family and as far as I can tell, my mother would excuse him murdering someone as being 'just a mistake.' He gets away with *everything*. Second, he's a sibling. If you're nice to your siblings, they take away your humanity card."

"Wha...you...what?!" Cady sputtered.

"Yup," Gage said seriously. "The government comes along and takes your human card from you. After all, everyone knows that it isn't normal to be nice to a sibling. Ergo, you must actually be some sort of alien in disguise."

"Okay, okay!" Cady said, laughing in defeat.

"You're right – I definitely didn't want a sibling growing up. Especially not a sibling like *you*."

"Hey, both of my siblings are still alive," Gage said defensively. "I mean, there's that fourth kid that no one talks about, but…"

"Fourth?!" Cady gasped in horror and Gage let a belly laugh loose.

"You didn't have to tell me that you were an only child," Gage said dryly after he gained control of his laughter. "You're way too easy of a mark to have had siblings while growing up. Siblings toughen you up – keep you from falling for jokes so easily."

"You make siblings sound like a gentler version of war," Cady said, sniffing her disapproval. "I think I'm going to send Emma and Chris sympathy cards on your birthday."

"Oh, please do!" Gage said, clearly delighted at the idea. "They would get a kick out of it. Maybe you're not a hopeless case after all – sending sympathy cards to siblings on a guy's birthday is *just* the sort of thing that would happen in sibling warfare. Stick around me for another ten years and you'll start sending flower-and-balloon bouquets instead. I think you'll realize that a sympathy card just isn't *quite* enough."

"Somehow, I totally believe that's true," Cady muttered loudly under her breath, but she was laughing, too.

Laughing…when had she last laughed like this? It

was hard to remember, honestly. Maybe at some point when she'd been Hannah's roommate?

Perhaps?

"As I was saying," she announced primly, pushing the question of laughter out of her mind, "Emma has promised to come down her next available weekend from Denver. She's going to help me put together an action plan for the store. She was going to help me the weekend of The Great Birthday Party but then…" Cady waved her hand in the air, summarizing *that* disaster with a few flicks of her wrist. "Anyway, I feel like I'm kinda going in circles at this point. Which project should I focus on? Which project needs to be completed before I can do the other projects? I need a game plan. I feel like everything is half done…or half un-done, depending on if you're a glass-half-full or a glass-half-empty sort of person. After she comes through, then I'll have a better idea of how far away I am from opening day."

"Have you been over to the farmer's market in town yet?" Gage asked, apropos of absolutely nothing.

"Uhhhh…no?" Cady said, trying to figure out where this was going. "I saw a couple of posters around town about it but I haven't gone yet. Why do you ask?"

"Well, I was thinking you might take some smoothies down to the farmer's market and give them away as samples. Get people excited about the opening of your store."

"Ohhh…" Cady breathed. "That's a great idea. It hadn't occurred to me to do that. Thank you!"

Gage shrugged, pink creeping up around his collar. "I've been a small business owner for a while now," he said, obviously a little embarrassed. "Things like that become second nature. I've thought about hiring a teen to run a Muffin Man booth down at the farmer's market every weekend – get new customers through it who aren't coming over to the store. I just haven't had the time to do it yet. Do you know Troy Horvath?"

"Troy…" Cady repeated, thinking. "I don't think so?"

"Well, unless you've been down to the farmer's market or had your business set on fire, there isn't much of a reason that you'd know him anyway," Gage reassured her. At her raised eyebrows, he clarified. "Troy is the guy who remodeled the old mill and started the farmer's market, but he's also on the city fire department. He was part of the crew that helped save Sugar and myself from the fire last year. Real nice guy, but quiet. If you manage to get ten words out of him in a conversation, feel special. The only person I've ever seen him talk to is his girlfriend, Penny. That's how everyone in town knew it was true love – she got him to talk."

Cady laughed. "He can't be *that* bad," she said, shaking her head in disapproval at him. She was starting to realize that he liked to exaggerate for comedic effect, and she really shouldn't believe every word that came out of his mouth. Why, he probably never even sat on his sister. She was so much smaller than him, he would've squished her flat if he had.

Cady made a mental note to ask Emma the next time she came up from Denver.

"Call him up. Ask him about giving away freebies at the farmer's market. You'll see."

Cady just shook her head in bemusement. She wasn't about to fall for Gage's teasing again. She was already growing wise to his antics.

"We should probably park here and then walk," Gage said, pulling into the parking lot for the grocery store. "Parking down there will be nuts."

Cady cocked a questioning eyebrow at him but he just shook his head with a grin.

"You'll see," he promised, hurrying around to her side of the truck and helping her down. "You can wait another three minutes, right?"

"I guess," she grumbled good-naturedly. Gage's boyish teasing was kinda fun, maybe even especially so because she wasn't used to it. She'd grown up as the only child and had always been "a little adult," hanging around her parents' friends and learning quickly to control her boisterousness lest she get sent to bed early. Her parents' friends had always remarked that she was so grown-up — so mature for her age. Her parents had been loving and caring, but teasing?

Not so much.

Gage snagged her hand and began heading down

the street, Cady hurrying to keep up with his long legs. She thought about asking him to slow down, but her pride wouldn't let her. She'd always hated the fact that she was so much shorter than the rest of the world; she wasn't about to start admitting now that she needed special accommodations.

"Here we are," Gage said, thankfully slowing a bit, letting Cady's breathing slow down too. She looked around, finally able to do more than just concentrate on where her feet were stepping, and realized that they were at some sort of street fair.

"Wha…" She trailed off as she realized where they were at. "Oh, the art and wine walk!" she said excitedly, grinning up at Gage. "I've been watching the posters about this all spring but haven't come over for one yet."

"I was hoping you'd be up for it," he said with a big grin. "See? I told you surprises wouldn't kill you. Hold on—" He came to a dead stop, pulling Cady to a standstill next to him. She almost told him that maybe surprises wouldn't kill her but him jerking her arm out of her socket just might when he asked, "Do you drink wine?"

"I do," she reassured him. "As long as I'm not driving, I'm happy to drink a little."

"Oh good," he said, clearly relieved. "I'll go grab the tickets then. You can go check out that display while you wait if you want." He pointed to a weird metal art display nearby that appeared to be made out of…bent spoons?

She squeezed his hand in hers. "I'll stay with you," she said. She didn't want to leave his side. She didn't want to wander off on her own. With him there, he'd protect her from any weirdos out there – no one would dare touch her with him by her side. Not to mention that she didn't want to be by herself. She wanted to be next to him because she just plain liked him.

As a dyed-in-the-wool introvert, this was unusual, to say the least. She wasn't entirely sure what to think about it – if she was happy with this turn of events or not. Did she want to become that dependent on someone else? What if he disappeared from her life like everyone else had?

Before she could decide if this was something to completely freak out about or not, Gage was tugging her forward to the front of the line, pulling out a wad of cash to pay for the wine tickets they could use to redeem for glasses of wine throughout the evening, and then they were free to wander together.

They stopped at a wine table and each redeemed a ticket for a glass, and then started walking through the crowds, sipping and chatting and laughing together at some of the more unusual exhibits, and sighing with envy over the gorgeous paintings.

Is this what it's like to date someone? Is this what it's like to be in a big crowd and not be flinching at every movement?

It almost didn't seem legal, honestly. Could she be this at home around a man? Since when was *that* a thing?

Since now, I guess.

"Oh now, look at that," Gage said with such love and enthusiasm in his voice, it jerked Cady out of her thoughts. She followed his line of sight to…a pen full of puppies?

Tumbling and growling and yipping as they wrestled and played, the puppies had to be some of the most adorable creatures that Cady had ever seen.

"Ooohhhh…" she breathed. She felt like she was being sucked towards the pen, like a paperclip towards a magnet. They were *gorgeous*.

Cady's heart flipped with delight.

A large-boned woman stood next to the pen, chatting with another family but they already had a squirming puppy in their hands and as Gage and Cady reached the pen, the family headed off into the crowd, clutching their puppy to them.

"So, I thought this was an art festival?" Gage asked the woman, clearly confused. "Why are there dogs here?"

The woman shrugged. "I had someone drop off this load of puppies in the middle of the night and the shelter is just full to burstin' now, so I asked the head honchos of this festival if they'd let me have a booth for free since I'm not selling these pups for a profit. They said yes. I figured they were so damn cute, there was no way people could pass 'em on by. Already adopted out three of them." She turned to Cady. "My name is Michelle Winthrop, and you are?"

"Cady Walcott," Cady said, putting her hand out

for a firm handshake. She liked the handshake, and the woman. She was open and friendly and direct. Somehow, Cady knew that she would never have to wonder how Michelle Winthrop felt about her. She was the kind of woman who'd say it how it was.

She didn't know how she was so sure about the woman, considering they'd just met, but she was.

"So, Gage," Michelle said, flashing a grin at Cady's date. Cady ignored the flash of jealousy at the sight. She couldn't go around telling everyone that they didn't get to smile at her boyfriend. "I didn't know you had a girlfriend. Where've you been hiding her all this time?"

"Well, next door, it turns out. Cady here bought the storefront next to the Muffin Man and is remodeling it into the Smoothie Queen."

Cady felt her cheeks go pink. Gage seemed downright proud to claim her as his own.

"Oh, damn. You don't say – you're the one who knocked out the power to the whole town?" Michelle asked, turning back to Cady, mouth agape.

"Am I *ever* going to live that down?" Cady asked rhetorically to the world at large.

"Nope!" Michelle and Gage said in unison and then laughed.

"So, are y'all interested in a pup?" Michelle asked, steering the conversation back to what she clearly considered the important topic. "Or are you just lookie-loos?"

"I already have a cat," Cady said with sincere

regret in her voice as she watched the playful puppies roll and wrestle with each other, "and my landlords only let me have him because I paid a large pet deposit. I don't think I could convince them that a puppy wouldn't cause any damage."

"I'm a homeowner so I don't have a landlord to convince," Gage said, dropping to his knees next to the pen, muscles rippling under his shirt as he went. "I've been so busy with the bakery, I haven't let myself get a pet, but maybe…maybe it's time."

"It's *always* time to have a pet," Michelle said, pulling up her folding chair and sitting down in it while Cady and Gage crouched next to the pen. "Having a dog to greet you when you get home… there's no better feeling in the world."

Gage put his fingers through the wire mesh and immediately, a puppy came bounding over, tumbling over its overly long ears and landing on its back, revealing to the world that it was actually a she.

"What kind of a dog are these?" Cady asked, trying to puzzle it out. The ears were longer like a cocker spaniel but the fur was all wrong – straight instead of wavy – and the legs were way too short, almost like a corgi or something. She'd never seen such an adorable puppy in all her life but none in the litter bore any resemblance to any breed Cady had ever laid eyes on.

"This here is what I like to call a 'mutt,'" Michelle said, and laughed. "They're the love child of about ten different breeds, from what I can tell. The good news is, they should have excellent health. No problems with inbreeding here."

"I guess there's that," Gage said with a grin as he pulled his fingers out from the wire mesh and instead scooped the girl out over the top of the cage. "You're a friendly one," he murmured as the dog whined and licked and nuzzled his hand, clearly in the throes of ecstasy over someone actually petting her.

Apparently a little *too* excited because with a shout of surprise, Gage yanked the dog up into the air and away from the widening wet spot on his jeans. In her excitement, the pup had peed all over him.

Cady laughed so hard, she snorted. She didn't even know that was something she was capable of, but she'd never seen such a hilarious sight in all her life.

"You know, there's that rule," Michelle said dryly, clearly trying to suppress her laughter and doing a shitastic job of it. "You break it, you buy it. Except in this case, it's 'You get peed on, it's yours.' Not quite the same ring to it, but true anyway."

Gage, who was holding the squirming dog up in the air, as far away from his body as he could manage, looked up at Michelle and said, "You think I should *adopt* her?"

"Well, of course," Michelle said smoothly. "I think she was just trying to mark you as hers. Show you how much she likes you."

"You could like me a little less," Gage told the puppy seriously. "My feelings wouldn't be hurt, promise."

"Poor girl," Cady crooned. "She was just excited."

"*You* want to hold her?" Gage asked, holding the puppy towards Cady with a dare in his eye.

"Sure!" Cady said brightly, holding her hands out for the darling dog. "Hell, her bladder is empty now."

It was Michelle's turn to snort with laughter. "I like you," she told Cady. "'Bout time a girl brought this handsome bachelor to his knees."

"You think I'm handsome?" Gage asked, clearly choosing to ignore the rest of what Michelle said as he handed the dog off to Cady. "All this time and I never knew."

"Well, us girls can't go around telling you that or you'd get a big head," Michelle informed him pertly, but Cady missed his retort as she began to snuggle the soft puppy against her chest. She'd never felt something so wonderful in all her life. Skittles was soft, sure, but she was a *cat*. She was happy to spend most of her day in the high window sill of the basement apartment, taking in the sun. This puppy, on the other hand…Cady didn't know a puppy could be so sweet, so soft, so loving. Sensing that Cady wanted to just cuddle, she snuggled her tiny snout into the base of Cady's neck, snoring within seconds, her soft whistling breath like a love song only Cady could hear.

She held the puppy against her, letting the world around her just swirl out of focus as she felt the love that this dog had for her wash over her in waves. How was it that a puppy could fall in love with a human so quickly? Or a human in love with a puppy?

Finally, her eyes fluttered open and she realized that Michelle and Gage were just staring at her. "I think she's found her new owner," Michelle said seriously. "She just loves you."

"I can't…" Cady said weakly, her defenses melting in the face of the overwhelming love of the dog. "My landlord…Rochelle didn't want Skittles, and she's fully house-trained *and* fixed."

"Rochelle and Mike?" Michelle asked. Surprised, Cady nodded. How was it that Michelle knew the names of her landlords? "Small town," Michelle said dismissively, answering Cady's unspoken question. "Anyway, I'll talk to them. See if I can't get them to make an allowance, just this once. They're real nice people – they had real bad renters a couple years back who destroyed the place, and they've been skittish ever since."

"I'll double my pet deposit if it'd help," Cady said eagerly. "I don't mind." She had to stop herself from promising to walk the dog twice a day and pick up her poop after her, too. Michelle wasn't her mother. Cady was just so excited about the idea of a puppy – *this* puppy…

"Well, I promise I'll adopt her even if Mike and Rochelle don't allow it," Gage said. "Like I said, I'm a homeowner. No one can tell me no."

Michelle nodded her approval. "I'm going to put you down on the paperwork then, Gage, so y'all can take her home today. There is a $50 adoption fee, to pay for her shots and her getting spayed. You okay with that?"

"Absolutely," Gage said, reaching for his wallet over Cady's protestations. He waved her away, which was probably good anyway because Cady was struggling to figure out how to get into her purse to get her wallet without waking up the snoring puppy on her shoulder. "Hell, she might end up as mine anyway. And even if your landlords say yes, well then, it'll be my gift to you. Mark our first official date together."

Things moved quickly after that. They took the pup down to the local pet store in Franklin – a tiny, overpriced shop where the dog woke up from her nap and got into a wrestling match with a rolled-up newspaper – and then once they had all of the necessary supplies, including training pads for her to pee on while being house-trained, they headed back to Sawyer, all thoughts of the art festival left far behind.

"I can't believe we went to an art festival and brought home a dog," Gage said with a laugh as he scratched the pup behind the ears. She yipped in pleasure and began licking his hand enthusiastically. "I think I'm about to become the cleanest human being on the planet," he said dryly. "I haven't had this many baths since I was a toddler and wouldn't stay out of the mud puddle."

"What are we going to name her?" Cady asked, the thrill of that sentence running through her. *We*.

What a lovely word. Could she really be co-adopting a dog with her boyfriend of one date? This should be freaking her out hardcore, but somehow, it wasn't. "We can't keep calling her 'She.' She needs a good name."

"With her *creamy* light coloring, I would've thought it'd be obvious." Gage sent her a challenging look, as if daring her to figure out where he was going with this.

He'd emphasized the word *creamy*, as if that was the key to what he was thinking, and Cady's mind tore through their time that they'd known each other. *Creamy? Creamy. Creeeaammmyyy. Cream—*

"Oh, Cream Puffs! You want to call her Cream Puffs?!" Cady asked, laughing, retrieving the end of her braid from the dog's mouth and flipping it over her shoulder and out of reach. "What kind of name is that for a dog?"

"You have a cat named Skittles," Gage reminded her, as if she was in danger of forgetting that. "For a girl who hates sugar, you sure seem to surround yourself with sugary names."

She narrowed her eyes in mock disapproval at him. "Her name is Skittles because she's every color of the rainbow," she informed him pertly. "*And,* I haven't agreed to Cream Puffs yet."

But at the words "Cream Puffs," the pup let out a yippy yowl of happiness, her tail going a million miles an hour, and then she was tugging on Cady's necklace, trying to pull it off from around Cady's neck.

"Oh no you don't," Cady said, gently extracting the necklace out of the dog's mouth and rotating the emerald pendant to the back of her neck and out of reach. She had a feeling she'd be doing a lot of that over the coming months. "And fine. Cream Puffs it is."

With a sigh of regret, Cady let Gage drop her off at her apartment, wishing she could be there with Cream Puffs that night as she tried to settle into her new home, knowing that the puppy would be lonely and would want to snuggle with Cady.

No matter how much Rochelle and Mike wanted for a pet deposit, Cady resolved to pay it. Now that she'd had a taste of how much fun a puppy was, it was hard to let it go.

She let herself into her apartment and Skittles did a big Halloween-cat stretch and then padded over to greet her. As Skittles wound her way around her ankles, hoping for attention or at least wet cat food, Cady headed for the couch where she collapsed and let Skittles sniff and inspect every inch of her. "I know, I know, I smell like dog," she said, laughing at the disgruntled look on Skittles' face. "Just wait until I manage to bring the puppy home. You're going to love her. Actually, you're probably going to hate her guts but someday you guys will be best friends, I'm sure of it."

As she idly scratched Skittles behind the ears, she thought about the least romantic goodbye in the history of goodbyes. Gage had been trying to keep Cream Puffs from jumping out of the truck and following Cady into the house and had only barely managed to hold onto her slippery body. Cream Puffs hadn't been let in on this plan and kept wiggling and clawing her way towards Cady, yipping when Cady closed the passenger side door behind her. Cady'd been hoping that she and Gage would kiss goodbye at the end of the date, but there'd been no chance of that with Creamy there.

She let out a disgruntled sigh. She'd told Gage that she wanted to move slow, of course, but there was slow and then there was slooowwwww. What if he was waiting for Cady to make the first move?

If so, they were going to be waiting a *very* long time. It'd taken them a month to go out on their first official date, since that day she'd apologized to him and told him about going to see Dr. Jane. If it took another month for them to kiss again…

"C'mon," she said to Skittles, a little sharper than she probably should have. "Time to go to bed. You and I can snuggle together. It'll be almost exactly the same as snuggling with Gage."

Officially making that statement the biggest whopper Cady had ever said.

CHAPTER 19

GAGE

September, 2019

"Hi!" Mom said happily, kissing Gage on the cheek and pulling him into the house. "And now, this is your girlfriend, right?" she asked, turning expectantly towards Cady, already holding out her arms for a huge hug.

Cady plastered on what Gage was sure was supposed to be a cheerful grin, but instead looked more like a painful grimace as she stepped towards his mom, dutifully accepting the incoming hug. She seemed to understand that she was going to get hugged, whether or not she wanted to be. Watching the awkward-as-hell exchange, Gage was torn before laughing and worrying to death. His mother could be a little overwhelming even to the most extroverted people, and that *definitely* didn't describe Cady. But if

Cady was going to get intimidated by his mother, just wait until Grandma showed—

"There you are, Gage," Grandma said primly, stepping up behind Mom as Cady quickly pulled back from his mom and turned towards this new threat. Seeing the austere woman in front of her, she seemed to drain of all color, quickly matching the pale beige of the door jam. If she lost any more color in her cheeks, she was liable to pass out. "And this is…?"

"Mom, Grandma, this is Cady Walcott. Cady, this is my mother, Donelle Dyer, and my grandmother, Nana Dyer. My grandma and grandpa are the ones who owned the bakery before me."

Cady put her hand out to formally shake Donelle's hand but his mother pulled Cady in for a second big bear hug instead, even more enthusiastic than the first one had been. "I'm *so* glad to meet you! I'd just about given up on Gage bringing anyone home to meet the family."

"Gage has a lot of life left ahead of him," Nana said stiffly. "Plenty of time to bring girls home." She put her hand out to shake Cady's, the differences between her and her daughter-in-law stark and raw.

Scrambling for something – *anything* – to say, Gage was saved by his younger sister. "I'm so glad you came!" Emma said, crowding up behind their grandmother. "I told my big lunk of a brother that you were too good for him and that he ought to count his lucky stars that you keep saying yes to dates but still, I'm glad you continue to take pity on him, even if you're just doing it because of me."

"Are you trying to say that Cady is dating me so she can spend more time around *you*?" Gage asked incredulously.

"If the shoe fits," Emma said in an overly sweet voice. "C'mon, Sugar's in here," she told Cady as she began dragging Cady out of the overly crowded entryway. "I told her to bring Hamlet to keep Cream Puffs company."

"Hamlet?" he heard Cady ask before the door to the study closed behind them.

"Thanks for letting me drop Cream Puffs off beforehand, Mom," Gage said, turning back to his mother, avoiding the reproachful gaze of his grandmother. Creamsy had ended up settling into his house quickly and they'd decided that it would be best for all if she just stayed with Gage full-time. "Trying to juggle the puppy and Cady in my truck…I need to get a dog carrier. Somehow, we didn't think of that while we were picking up supplies in Franklin after the arts festival back in June."

"No problem, dear," Mom said. He could tell she wanted to nag him about cutting his hair – her fingers had even reached out to touch it before dropping down to her side – but in a spate of self control he didn't know she possessed, she managed to keep her thoughts about his hair to herself. After looking at her husband – Gage's dad – for twenty years in the Marine Corps, she tended to think that anything longer than a buzz cut was simply out of control. "Hey, you want to go tell Chris that it's time to eat? Dinner's on the table. I think he's down in the basement."

Of *course* he was down in the basement, and probably playing video games to boot. Despite having graduated from high school back in May, he was still doing almost nothing of value with his life.

Hell, at Chris' age, Gage had been in charge of dinner three times a week, helping out as his mother worked late night shifts down at Kmart to make ends meet on military pay – not always an easy thing – and taking care of his younger siblings to boot.

He doubted if Chris even knew how to make a grilled cheese sandwich.

Biting back his thoughts on his parents' parenting choices when it came to the baby of the family, Gage moved past his mother and grandmother and thundered down the stairs to find Chris lazing on the couch, controller in hand, blazing his way through Call of Duty. "Ah, shit," Gage said, feigning worry. "You're about to have your ass kicked when you go around this corner."

"What do you mean?" Chris mumbled, not even looking up from the TV to greet his older brother. "There's no one around this corner—"

Gage pushed the power button on the game console, plunging the giant TV into blackness.

"Yup, dead," Gage said in a very cheerful voice, over the curses his brother was hurling at his head.

"Oh, dinner's ready, by the way. And my girlfriend, Cady, is here. Try not to be a troll."

"You shithead!" Chris was yelling. "I can't believe—"

"Better hurry up," Gage said mildly, talking over his teenage brother without a smidgen of guilt. "Everyone's waiting." He took the stairs two at a time, listening to the insults grow quieter as he left his brother behind. He used to be like a second dad to Chris – with a 12-year gap between them, he'd helped bottle feed and change diapers and keep Chris away from the electrical outlets for years. Chris had been the gap-toothed, adorable baby of the family who everyone loved, and then…

One day he woke up with hormones coursing through his veins and had been a prick ever since. His parents had doubled down on the niceness factor, hoping to sway Chris back into humanity through kindness, but Gage had seen over the intervening years that coddling had only made the problem worse.

If only he could convince his parents to let him be Chris' boss for a spell. It'd make a damn world of difference, in his humble opinion. Surely couldn't make him any worse than he was right now, anyway.

"Is everything okay?" Cady asked, sticking her head out of the dining room doorway, her mahogany curls swirling and bouncing around her angelic face as she looked worriedly past Gage and down into the basement. "Someone sounds really angry."

"It's just Chris," Gage said reassuringly. "He lost

the level he was playing on his video game. He'll be fine." He cupped his hand under Cady's elbow and steered her back into the dining room. His mom had added another leaf to the table, stretching the boundaries of the dining room to its limits and forcing Gage and Cady to sidle around the table, shuffling and knocking into the backs of chairs as they went. "Where's Jaxson, Rose, and the boys at?" he asked Sugar, who was already crammed up against Emma, as they went. Not that they had any room for them at the table if they had shown up but it only seemed polite to ask.

"Jaxson's ex has the boys this weekend, and Jaxson said he wanted to stay home and get some repair work done around the house. With a five-month-old underfoot, I don't know how much he expects to get done, but I guess we'll see." Sugar clearly looked amused at the idea of getting anything productive done with a baby in tow, and Gage didn't blame her. As adorable as Rose was, she tended to be a mess maker at this age, not a mess cleaner.

Much like Cream Puffs, actually. That day that she'd found a box of Kleenex…

Cady and Gage finally squeezed into their chairs – Cady able to maneuver in the tight space a lot easier than Gage was, yet another benefit of being so tiny – and after his father said a quick grace, they dug into the food, passing it around, laughing and teasing each other as the dinner progressed. Gage was impressed to see Cady holding her own, answering his grandmother's questions about the Smoothie Queen evenly; not visibly intimidated by his grandmother's stern expression. Grandpa wasn't saying much, but that was to be expected – he wasn't much for talking. Chris was sitting sullenly in his chair, picking at his food, clearly pissed at Gage, shooting him death looks whenever he thought their mom wasn't looking.

"Jaxson says you're doing great things at the fire department," Sugar said loudly, directing the comment in the general direction of Chris but clearly intending the entire family to hear her. "You and Angus have been showing up to all of the training meetings and learning a lot. At least, that's what Jaxson has been telling me. Are you thinking about becoming a firefighter now that you've graduated from high school?"

Chris'd just graduated at the end of May, and had spent the summer "contemplating his options." As far as Gage could tell, that'd meant Chris was spending his time debating between playing Call of Duty or Battlefield One. Was Chris going to be 42 and still living in their parents' basement?

God, he hoped not.

"Maybe," Chris said, straightening up a bit in his seat and looking interested for the first time in the meal's conversation. "He thinks I'm doing good?"

"He does," Sugar said firmly. "Says you're a natural."

Chris grinned proudly at the wife of the town's fire chief, stunning Gage into silence.

Chris, smiling? Since when did Chris smile? He threw pity parties for himself and acted like the whole world was out to get him. He had that typical teenager angst in spades.

But when he smiled, he was...he was almost *handsome*.

Gage felt like something in his brain just broke. Surely this wasn't happening. Chris didn't know how to be anything but a surly, snarling teenager.

He looked at Cady to see if she was catching this, if she was seeing the same thing he was, but she just sent him a cheerful smile of her own and then went back to listening to Chris, who'd started talking happily about the National Junior Firefighter training program, pitching in questions about pay and training as she listened, and he realized that she didn't know. She didn't know that Chris had had a personality transplant right there at the dining room table. She didn't know that this wasn't what Chris acted like.

Ever.

He looked down the table at Emma instead and caught her bemused smile as she stared at their younger brother. Gage knew her; knew she was wondering in that moment if this was all some sort of elaborate prank that someone had paid Chris to participate in, and what the final punchline would be.

Before the punchline could reveal itself, though, talk turned to the old mill in town – the whole reason Chris and his best friend Angus were involved in the junior firefighter program to begin with. A little over eighteen months previously, they'd been smoking outside of the mill before school one morning and a discarded cigarette butt had accidentally set a pile of greasy rags on fire. Angus had caught most of the flack from the debacle but Gage was sure Chris was just as much to blame. He was happy that both of them had ended up in the volunteer firefighter program. Chris deserved to be a part of the punishment as much as Angus did. It had been just like Chris to avoid the brunt of the blame.

"Angus and I have been helping out on Saturday mornings at the farmer's market," Chris said, jerking Gage back to the present. Chris? Just helping out? Since when?

"How much are you getting paid?" Gage asked bluntly, refusing to let Chris get credit for "helping out" when it was actually a job. Gage didn't "help out" at the Muffin Man – he *worked* there.

Big difference.

"Now, Gage—" began Mom.

"Jaxson says he's been working hard," Sugar put in. Gage wanted to glare at his employee and tell her to keep her nose out of this but he knew Emma would get pissy if he did, so he bit down on his tongue. Hard.

"We got paid a few times—" Chris retorted, and Gage snorted his derision – he *knew* Chris would only do something if paid, "—but most of the time, we've just been volunteering. After what happened… before…it just seemed…" The teenager trailed off, shrugging, staring down at the dining room table like its woodgrain contained all of the secrets of the universe.

Gage sat back, stunned for a second time that meal. Chris knew how to smile, *and* he had a conscience and could feel guilty about almost destroying a local landmark?

The conversation ebbed and flowed around Gage as he stared at his younger brother, lost in thought. They were still discussing something about the previously burned mill and the farmer's market that now happened there every Saturday, but Gage heard very little of it.

After the bakery had started turning a consistent profit, about two years ago or so, Gage had bought a house just a couple of streets behind the bakery, thinking he could then walk to work when the weather was nice. Living on his own, he'd missed a lot of the family drama and had been the happier for it — not seeing Chris disrespect his parents at every meal was best for all involved, honestly.

But had he also missed Chris growing up, even if it was just a little bit?

Chris caught Gage staring at him and sent him a, "What are you staring at?" defiant look in return. Gage cooly arched one eyebrow and then deliberately turned to listen to Emma talk about an especially awful client at the architecture firm.

Obviously, Chris may've grown up, but not *that* much.

"...a bell tower. On top of a bank! I asked the guy point-blank if he was going to ring the bells every time someone was late on their house payment, and my boss kicked me so hard in the ankle underneath the conference table, I had a bruise for a week. But *seriously*! *Bells* on top of a *bank*. Next, he's gonna want a moat filled with alligators to surround it, to protect the bank from the bank robbers or something." Emma shook her head in disgust as everyone laughed. "People be weird..." she mumbled loudly under her breath. "And rich people are the worst, because no one will tell them no. My boss keeps telling me that I can't tell clients that an idea is stupid, but if I don't, who will?"

Gage hid his grin behind his hand. One thing was for sure – you never had to guess how Emma felt about something or someone. She was liable to tell you, whether she probably ought to or not.

"How did you end up in Long Valley?" Grandma asked Cady bluntly, over the remaining chuckles. They all died off instantly, everyone's gaze swiveling to Cady. Her eyes got wide, and Gage knew that she'd been enjoying *not* being in the spotlight, and was probably wanting to crawl under the table any second now. "For a Boise girl," Grandma continued crisply in her most intimidating no-nonsense voice, "Sawyer doesn't offer much. What made you think you ought to move up here? And how do you like snow?"

"Grandma," Gage said defensively, "Cady doesn't

need to explain every little decision – Long Valley is beautiful. Of course she'd want to live here—"

"It's okay," Cady said, putting her hand on Gage's arm, sparks of pleasure shooting up his arm at the feel of her soft hand on him. He instantly shut up. "I was roommates with a girl from Sawyer while we were both at BSU," Cady continued, looking his grandmother straight in the eye as she spoke. "Hannah Lambert. Teacher over at the elementary school. Anyway, we came up here a couple of times and went hiking together. Just fell in love with the area. I hadn't been here for quite a while but I came up just after the new year and went hiking up in the Goldfork Mountains; found the empty storefront next to the Muffin Man on the way back to Boise. I didn't have anything tying me to Boise at that point, so…" She shrugged. "I bought the store and moved."

"You went hiking up in the mountains in January?" Emma asked, awe in her voice. "I guess you *do* like snow, then."

Cady laughed lightly, turning to Emma with another light shrug. "A lot of people really hate it but I love it. I struggle with the short days more than I do the cold and the snow. I think I have a touch of S.A.D. but I manage okay."

"Sad?" Chris asked. "You mean, you cry a lot?"

"Seasonal Affective Disorder – S.A.D.," Cady corrected him. "It means your body doesn't like winter months when the daylight hours are short.

You're affected by the lack of sunlight, in other words."

"We live in a deep valley," Dad said, speaking for the first time since he'd said grace over dinner. "We have even less daylight here than y'all have in Boise. When the sun sets behind the Goldforks to the west, we have hours of twilight before it actually gets dark."

"Winter is coming," Cady acknowledged, "so I'm just going to watch closely and see how it affects me. If it gets really bad, I'll order in a special light."

At the table of blank faces all staring at her, Cady clarified, "There are special lights made specifically for people with S.A.D. They put off light that's in the right spectrum. Helps provide enough real light – instead of artificial light – to fool your body into still functioning, even during the winter. They're pretty expensive but much better than hibernating every winter."

Even Grandma looked impressed by this information, which was really saying something.

As the conversation drifted again, Gage put his hand on Cady's thigh and squeezed, telling her without words how proud he was of her. She smiled shyly up at him, and he felt his blood heat up.

It'd been a whole summer now of hand holding that'd slowly morphed into kisses, but never anything more than that. Keeping his hands to himself had been agony, but today's meeting with his family was testing his self-control to the limits. He wouldn't have guessed that a family meal could be sexy as hell, but seeing Cady impress the people in his life who truly mattered to him; the people whose opinion he cared about…

Yeah, it'd made him horny.

Or, he was just in a constant state of horniness, to the point that watching paint dry would do the same thing.

He wished he could pull her discreetly down to his old bedroom and show her just how proud he was of her, but there was little chance of that. Dinner was finally ending and Cady was helping clear off the table, chatting with Emma and Sugar as she went, while Dad, Grandpa, Chris, and Gage went into the living room. It was such a bullshit male patriarchy thing – the women did the dishes while the men went and sat on their asses – but Gage was silently thankful that Cady wasn't protesting, at least openly, about it.

Traditions were hard to kill off, and Grandpa Dyer was certainly of *that* generation where men just didn't do dishes. Even when he and Grandma had owned the bakery, Gage had never once seen his grandfather wash a dish or a pan or even a whisk.

Gage knew the upcoming conversation would be dull, if it even happened at all – neither his grandfather, father, or brother tended to talk much – so he decided to make the excuse that he needed to take Cream Puffs for a walk so she could have a potty break. Dad waved him off, already settling into his easy chair to read a golfing magazine, so Gage slipped down the hall to the study where they'd kept the dogs locked up during dinner and hooked a leash onto Creamy's collar.

Hamlet, thrilled at the idea of getting to go for a walk, danced around, his giant tail whapping and thunking against every surface in the crowded room, his deep excited bark painfully loud in the enclosed space. Moments later, Sugar showed up at the door. "Hamlet, quit it," she scolded him and with what could only be described as a pout painted on his face, the Great Dane settled down with a low whine, crossing his paws over his nose dolefully as he watched Creamy get ready to leave.

"That is one picked on and abused dog," Gage said to Sugar, laughing. "I've never seen such sad eyes in all my life."

"He's the *master* of guilt," Sugar admitted, rolling her eyes. "Emma and I will take him here in a minute. He'll live. He just gets so damn excited every time he sees a leash in someone's hands. Are you going to take Cady with you?"

"I hadn't planned on it. I was just going to hurry out for a quick stroll around the block – keep Cream Puffs here from peeing on Mom's carpet. Do you think I can sneak Cady away from the kitchen?"

"It's super crowded in there. Your mom's kitchen isn't a bad size, but it isn't meant for that many people. Not to mention that I think your grandmother has come up with more questions to grill Cady on. You might want to save her."

"Shit," Gage muttered under his breath. "Okay, thanks. See you at work tomorrow?"

Sugar nodded as he wound his way out of the room, careful to keep Hamlet in the study as he closed the door behind him and Creamy. "Let's stop by the kitchen real quick," he told the puppy that was busy straining at the leash, trying to smell and lick every surface she could reach. "You can stop licking the end table leg now," he told her dryly. "Really, it's not necessary to taste everything you can reach, you know."

Cream Puffs was busy burrowing her way into a decorative basket of blankets and shawls, though, and obviously didn't think Gage's advice was worth worrying about as she emerged from the basket with his mother's prize cashmere shawl clamped tightly in her mouth, tail going a million miles an hour, a look of pure pride on her tiny face.

"Shit!" he yelped, dropping to his knees and trying to slowly pry the tiny puppy teeth off the shawl without hurting the fabric in the process. "Mom will *kill* you if she sees you chewing this thing up," he told the dog seriously, finally managing to extract the shawl without destroying it. *Thank God.* He lifted the small animal out of the basket and snuggled her against his chest, figuring there was only so much damage she could cause while wrapped up in his arms.

"It's a damn good thing you're so cute," he told her as he worked his way towards the kitchen.

"Otherwise, you wouldn't last a day. Hey, Mom," he said, poking his head into the kitchen, "mind if I steal my girlfriend away and we go for a walk?"

His mother's eyes lit up at the word "girlfriend" and he knew that in that moment, she would've said yes to any request at all. She'd badgered him for so long to bring home "a nice girl," he wasn't sure if she'd know what to do with herself now that he'd introduced Cady to the family.

*Hmmm…*Probably badger him about popping the question, actually. And then she'd be badgering him about when the wedding date would be. And then it'd become the question of when would she "finally" be able to get her hands on some grandchildren.

His mother was impossible, honestly.

"Of course, of course," Mom said brightly, shooing Cady towards the door, snatching the half-washed frying pan out of Cady's startled hands. "Us old married women don't need help anyway. Emma, come back here!"

Emma, who'd been oh-so-casually heading out of the kitchen alongside Cady, turned back to their mom, a guilty look on her face. "You said the married women didn't need help," she protested even as she began scooping up leftovers and tossing them into a Rubbermaid container. "I'm not married."

"And you also don't have a boyfriend here," Mom retorted. "Nice try."

Gage snagged Cady's still-wet hands and pulled her towards the front door, not daring to put Cream

Puffs down until they got outside. Once the puppy got her short legs underneath her, she took off like a rocket, chasing a leaf that was lazily drifting down from the sky. Cady had been right – it was starting to cool down and the leaves were changing. Soon, it'd be white as far as the eye could see.

"Sorry about that," Gage said, waving his hand back towards his parents' house as they set off down the sidewalk, tugging Creamy back onto the sidewalk every few steps as the overly excited pup tried to tear off in a new direction to chase something equally as fun and amazing as the leaf; rolly pollies, a grasshopper, and a moth all being chased down by the ferocious predator. Gage rolled his eyes at the dog's antics and then grinned down at Cady, snagging her hand in his and squeezing it. "My family can get sort of…overwhelming at times. They don't mean to be."

Except Grandma, and I'm not touching that bucket of worms with a ten-foot pole—

"Why doesn't your grandmother like me?" Cady asked as a few more leaves twirled down from the maples lining the street. "I *swear* I didn't do anything to her, but…"

She drew in a breath and continued on before Gage could say anything. Could think of what *to* say.

"And don't tell me that it's all in my imagination. She hasn't liked me from the word 'go.' She was shooting me frosty looks at Emma and Sugar's birthday party back in April! Your grandfather seems all right – at least, he hasn't said much – but your grandmother…makes me think that there's something to multiple lives after all, because I sure as hell didn't do anything to your grandmother in this life. I must've pissed her off in the last one."

Gage let out a belly laugh at that, surprising Creamy into stopping her attack of the leaf that had had the temerity of swirling and twirling through the air to land on Cream Puffs' back. Staring up at Gage for a moment, Cream Puffs debated whether this noise had anything to do with the possibility of getting a treat or pettings or a belly rub, and finally, deciding that it did not, went back to tearing the deserving leaf into shreds.

Gage stopped walking, pulling Cady to a stop next to him, giving the time necessary to Creamy to decimate her opponent that was somehow staying defiantly in one piece despite the tiny puppy's best ferocious attempts.

"So, I think I mentioned that my dad was in the Marine Corps for twenty years, right?" Deciding that if he was going to stand still, he might as well be holding Cady by more than just the hand, he pulled her into his arms, feeling her melt against him, bending over to bury his nose in her curls and breathe in deep. Her hair somehow smelled just like what he imagined sunshine would smell like, if such a thing could have a smell.

She nodded yes against his chest, and so he continued, forcing his lust-addled brain to string words together.

"My grandmother was pissed about it, to put it lightly. My father has two siblings – my uncle Dean and my aunt Patricia – but Dad was the oldest and he was supposed to be the one to take over the Dyer Bakery. He'd spent his whole childhood in that bakery, though, and had just wanted the hell out of Long Valley. He saw the Marines as his one-way ticket out of town. He was leaving, and he was *never* coming back. My mom was his high school sweetheart but a year behind him in school, so he waited around until she graduated and then they left Sawyer together on graduation night."

Creamy started pulling at her leash and Gage looked over and realized that she'd given up on her plans to destroy the leaf and instead had started back down the sidewalk without them.

"You're killing me, smalls," he told the puppy but still, he pulled back, letting his arms fall away from their natural position around Cady's tiny waist and instead snagged her left hand in his. If he couldn't hold her against his body, he would at least hold her hand. They began to wander up the street again, stopping every couple of feet or so, so Cream Puffs could attack another one of her enemies.

"She's going to be ready for a nice long nap when we get back to your parents' house," Cady said with a laugh as they watched Cream Puffs dive into a small pile of leaves, biting and snapping as she rolled in circles.

"Good thing we have such a fierce protector on

our hands," Gage agreed dryly. "She's going to be sawing logs here in a minute. Anyway, my grandma... she didn't want to admit that maybe her obsession with the bakery and the long days every kid had spent in it had just *perhaps* caused problems, and instead decided that my father joined the Marines because my mother pushed him to do it. Her reasoning went something like, 'He didn't join until Donelle graduated from high school, therefore it is Donelle's fault he joined.'"

Cady opened her mouth to object – to point out the obvious flaws in that argument – and Gage held up a hand to stop her.

"You don't have to tell *me* she had it wrong. I saw it with my own eyes. My father just doesn't like to bake. It completely skipped his generation – him, Uncle Dean, and Aunt Patricia all detest being in the kitchen. You can't pay them enough to spend their days slaving over a hot stove. But me? I've loved it since I was old enough to walk. I was the kid who made my own treats to bring to the bake sale at school. I was the kid who made my own cookies for my own after-school snack. There are some pictures of me when I was like three or four in frilly aprons of my mom's that she'd tied onto me…I tripped over the hem one time and split open my lip." He stopped and lifted Cady's finger to the tiny hairline scar that ran along the top of his lip. He kissed the tip of her finger and then forced himself to start walking down the street again before he made an utter fool of himself.

"My mom made me kid-sized aprons to use after that. I was into GI Joes as a kid – after all, my dad was in the Marines, right? So I had to love military stuff too, obviously – and so I had probably the only GI Joe apron in existence. I wore that thing until it fell apart."

They followed the curve of a cul-de-sac that led them, inexorably, back in the direction of his parents' house. Cream Puffs, perhaps realizing that her walk was heading towards finished territory, finally decided to get on with it and squatted in a bright green clump of grass. They stopped and waited patiently for her to finish, Gage more than happy to let the dog take all the time in the world that she needed.

"Although I now really, really want to see pictures of you in frilly aprons with flour all over your face," Cady said with a teasing grin, "what does any of this have to do with your grandmother not liking me? I'm pretty sure *I* wasn't there for any of this."

"Yeah, but you're a girl in case you didn't notice," Gage said wryly, "and the last time the apple of Grandma's eye fell in love with a girl, she lost him to the military and she didn't get to see much of him or of us grandkids for the next twenty years. It didn't matter that we were coming back here for most major holidays and every summer; we still didn't *live* here. And maybe my dad moved back here after he got out of the service, but that doesn't make up for the time lost. At least, not in my grandmother's eyes."

"So, she's afraid that you'll fall madly in love with

me and that'll cause you to join the military?" Cady asked, wide-eyed.

Gage let out a frustrated sigh and tugged his hand away from Cady's to run it through his hair. "I know it sounds a little nuts. And to be fair to my grandmother, I don't think she worries about me joining the military. I've bought the bakery. I've been running it for four years now. I'm 30 years old, which is a bit long in the tooth to be a new recruit. So, it's not that."

Creamy began kicking her back legs as hard as she could, intent on covering up the tiny brown pile on the grass, but Gage pulled a poo bag out of his pocket instead and scooped the shit up inside of it, twisting and tying it closed.

"Ready to go back?" he asked the tiny pup, but she was already at the end of her leash, straining to smell a nearby fire hydrant. They moved a little closer so Creamy could smell it and pee all over it without choking herself to death in the process.

"She's just…" Gage started again, and then sighed. How did he make his grandmother appear to be the loving, caring woman that he knew her to be, while also admitting that she had faults just like everyone else?

"It made her really possessive, you know? She isn't this way about Emma or Chris – just me. She'll eventually get over it; she and my mom get along great now, even though they didn't speak to each other for years. My grandma said some pretty nasty things about my mom to my father, and he didn't come visit them for the longest time. Wouldn't bring us grandkids home either. Finally, for the first and probably last time in her life, my grandmother apologized. Things started to get better after that. We began coming back to Long Valley for short visits when I was in elementary school; they became longer as I got older. My mother and grandmother became thick as thieves, and my mother started bringing us back to Idaho even when my dad didn't have any leave he could take. When they were fresh out of high school, they'd sworn that they'd never come back to this one-horse town, and now look at 'em – living here. On purpose." He chuckled a little at the irony, and then looked up to realize how close they were getting to his parents' house.

He slowed his pace to a crawl, not willing to give up the singular company of Cady just yet.

"With my grandmother, just…be polite, don't rise to her baiting, and wait her out. She's at least proven that she will eventually 'get over herself' and stop treating people like crap if given enough time. She simply takes a while. My mom, on the other hand, will love a person straight out of the gate. She's never met a stranger in her life. Until you prove to her that you're a jackass and not worth a bucket of warm spit, she'll be as friendly and kind as can be. But if you ever piss her off…boy howdy. Watch out. My grandmother will ice you out if she's angry; my mom will scream you out. Just duck and cover because things are probably going to go flying through the air when my mom's mad. Thankfully, she doesn't lose her temper now like she used to. In fact, I wish she'd lose her temper a little more with Chris, honestly. I don't miss the screaming fests, but she lets him walk all over her and Dad. He gets away with shit I could never have even dreamt about."

Cady tugged him to a stop at the head of the sidewalk that meandered up to the front door, lined with the orange and red and gold of mums and marigolds.

"Now that I've met this no good, terrible younger brother of yours, I have to say, I don't know why you hate him so much," Cady said bluntly. "He didn't seem half bad at dinner. Volunteering at the fire department? Helping out at the farmer's market? Not hardly the actions of a teenage delinquent."

Gage opened up his mouth to tell Cady exactly *why* it was that Chris "volunteered" at the fire department and farmer's market when Emma opened the front door. "There you two lovebirds are!" she called out. "I've been waiting for you to come back. Cady, if I'm going to go over things at the store with you, we better get on it. I need to get going for Denver soon."

"Where's Sugar?" Cady asked.

"Went home. Said Jaxson was probably in desperate need of help by now with Rose. He still doesn't like changing diapers."

"I don't think that's an activity that becomes more

pleasurable as time goes by," Gage muttered under his breath, and then, "Do you want me to come with you guys?" He was holding tight to the leash for Cream Puffs as she did her best to lunge towards Emma, clearly dead set on loving his sister – ie, lick her from head to toe. Realizing he was still holding onto the used baggie, he opened the trash can on the curb, ready for pickup the next morning, and tossed it in. *Speaking of poop...*

"I can stay out of it or I can come," he told Cady, keeping his voice studiously neutral. He didn't want to butt in where he wasn't wanted. "I'm good either way."

"I'd love to have you there," Cady said firmly. "After all, how are you supposed to know what your jobs are if you're not there to see what Emma thinks needs to be done?"

"Oh, *my* jobs, eh?" he said with a teasing laugh, and then leaned down and whispered, "And how, exactly, do you plan on paying me for all of my hard work?" He was a puff of breath away from her, wanting nothing more than to make her want him as much as he wanted her, and was rewarded with a sigh and a flick of a pink tongue across pink lips.

Pink, he decided just then, was his very favorite color.

"Well, I can't," she whispered breathlessly, "pay... uhhh...much, but..." She trailed off, apparently incapable of speech, her eyes drifting closed as she moved up on tiptoe, that delicious pink mouth *finally* coming into contact with his and his heart stopped and soared and the world flashed by and nothing existed, nothing at all except for Cady, her tiny, warm body snuggled up against him, every delicious curve on her pressing—

It was the wolf whistle that finally got through to him.

He pulled back, bleary-eyed, staring around him, trying to remember who he was and where he was and—

"*If* you two are done mauling each other in public," Emma said loudly, as if talking to a very deaf and very slow old man, "we really do need to get going. I have to leave for Denver in 45 minutes if I'm going to make it home at a decent hour."

"Emma, I do hate you," Gage said mildly, cupping Cady under the elbow and steering her towards the passenger side of his truck. "When you finally find a guy worth a hill of beans and bring him home, I plan on making your life miserable. Just so you know."

"As any good older brother would," Emma said with a dismissive wave of her hand. "Any less, and I would think you'd taken ill and would need to go see a doctor. See you over there?" she tossed over her shoulder, heading for her car. "Oh, whoops," she muttered, doubling back and sticking her head through the front door. "Bye, Mom! See you guys later!" She pulled the door shut and headed for her car again. "See you over there?" she asked rhetorically, and pulled her driver's side door shut.

Cady had settled into the passenger seat, her eyes still glassy with lust as she snuggled Cream Puffs onto her lap. Her swollen lips, her mussed hair…Gage had never seen such a delicious sight in all his life. Out of all of the tasty desserts that he'd made, he'd never wanted to eat anything as much as he wanted to nibble up one side of Cady and down the other in that moment.

Cursing his sister under his breath, he slammed the passenger side door closed and stalked around to the driver's side. A part of him wanted to just drive Cady to his house, his sister be damned – a very large, very hard part of him – but he wouldn't put it past his sister to drive to his house and knock on his door if he didn't follow her to the shop.

A living hell. I'm going to make her life a living hell when she finds a boyfriend. Please, dear God, let it be soon. I'd really, really like to exact revenge already.

Tomorrow would work fine for me, God. In case you were curious.

CHAPTER 20

CADY

Cady's head was spinning as she looked at the frantic notes and ideas she'd scribbled as Emma had talked, their pace frenetic as they'd tried to get through everything as quickly as possible. She was sure they'd missed some things. Probably a whole lot of things, actually, but Emma had been firm about her deadline and had left with a promise to make it back to Sawyer "soon" to go over things again if Cady felt like she needed the help.

Cady was very, very sure she would. How had it not occurred to her that she would need the shop to be wheelchair accessible? Somehow, this oh-so-obvious thought had completely passed her by. This totally changed the layout of the shelving that she'd put together before, and—

"It's going to be fine," Gage said soothingly, plucking the scribbled-on paper out of her hand and tossing it onto the counter next to them, pulling her up against him. "You came into this smart, with a nice, big cushion. You can make the changes you need to. It'll take a little longer, but I promise to help every step of the way."

She snuggled against his broad chest, feeling his muscular arms around her with the strength of two men contained in them. Instead of terrifying her like it would have a year ago, his muscles were comforting instead. He could carry the whole world on these shoulders.

She felt like he was carrying hers, at least.

She didn't like to be needy; she wanted to do it all on her own, but she couldn't. She didn't know enough; she wasn't strong enough; she wasn't well-versed enough in the law and building techniques and who to hire and—

"I'm damn proud of you, you know," Gage said softly, rubbing her back in small circles, going up and down her back, stroking the stress of it away. Cady snorted in disbelief, but Gage continued on as if he hadn't heard her. "Between Jackass the Football Player and then your parents…these are the kinds of things that by themselves would ruin a person's life, let alone *both* of them happening to you. Yet here you are, working so damn hard to make a go of the Smoothie Queen, instead of pulling in on yourself and hiding from the world. Speaking of all that…therapy. How do you feel like that's going?"

"Really well, actually," she said honestly. The prideful part of her wanted to hide the truth – that he'd been right, that she had needed the help – but she swallowed that pride. He deserved to know what a difference it'd made. "The Wellbutrin's been helping, too. I feel more stable, less…likely to fall apart at any moment, I guess. I used to feel like I was only just barely hanging onto the edges of my life, trying to stitch it together, trying to keep my life from flying to pieces. It's more manageable now. Life. You know? But it isn't just Dr. Wethersmith and the Wellbutrin. It's…you." She pulled back just a little to crane her neck and see up past the square jaw and into the handsome face of Gage Dyer. "You're so solid, so stable. You're here, always. I don't know what I'd do without you—"

"Then let's never find out," Gage broke in, but instead of kissing her like she'd thought – all right, hoped – he would, he stroked back an errant strand of hair, pressed a kiss to her forehead, and pulled away. She watched, stunned – a kiss to the forehead? Did he see her like he would view an elderly *aunt*?! – as he scooped up the discarded leash from the top of the counter and snapped it onto Cream Puffs' collar, waking her from what appeared to be *quite* the dream. She slowly blinked awake, staring up at Gage in confusion, but he still didn't share his plan with the dog or Cady.

"C'mon, Creamsicle," Gage said, tugging lightly on the leash. The puppy sprang to her feet, finally awake enough to realize that she was about to go outside again, making this a most auspicious day.

"Creamsicle?" Cady repeated with a laugh as she knew he'd intended, watching as he walked back towards her, scooping up her purse and list off the counter as he went, stuffing the list inside of the purse. "Cream Puffs isn't going to know what her real name is if you call her—"

"Creamsicle," Gage repeated as he scooped Cady up into his arms, grinning broadly at her loud squeal of surprise, clearly reveling in his ability to carry her around as if she weighed nothing at all. "Creamy, Cream Puffs, Puffy, Puffs, Creamsy, Puffers…I'm sure I could come up with more variations if you gave me a minute to work on it."

"Where are we going?!" Cady demanded in a half-shriek, half-laugh as they headed for the back door of the store. "You can't just carry me around if you want me to go somewhere," she informed him, trying to keep her face serious and stern. "I'm not a doll you can rearrange whenever you'd like." Damn her own dirty hide, she couldn't stay as dour-faced as she intended to be, perhaps because he felt and smelled so damn good. She buried her nose in the crook of his neck and breathed in deep.

Damn good.

"You're a lot more fun than a doll, it's true." He kicked the door to the smoothie shop closed behind them with the heel of his boot, and then carried her to the passenger side of his truck, sliding her onto the buttery soft leather seat. He scooped Cream Puffs up and deposited her into Cady's arms. "You'll hold onto her for me?" he asked, pressing another kiss to her forehead before closing the door and hurrying around to the driver's side.

"Why do you keep kissing me on the forehead?" Cady asked as he slid into the driver's seat. "I'm not your Great-Aunt Bertha, you know."

Gage let out a roar of laughter at that. "Because, if I kissed you on the mouth right now, we might just end up in the backseat of the truck," he said baldly. "My self-control is only so good, and you're testing every inch of it."

"Oh," Cady breathed, and then her brain stopped. Were they going back to his place? Or her place?

Despite her brave words, a part of her panicked at the idea of doing anything more than having Gage kiss her forehead. What if he tried to pull off her shirt and she hyperventilated and hit him upside the head with her shoe? What if she freaked out again, like she had that day in the shop, when everything had overwhelmed her and she'd been so sure that he was going to rape her?

When she was calm, rational, not stressed, the idea of Gage raping her was ludicrous beyond words but the part of her that worried about him raping her – about any man getting too close to her – never showed its face when she was calm, rational, not stressed. It lurked in the corners of her mind, ready to spring out and snap its jaws around her, drowning her in terror, when she wasn't looking.

When she let her guard down.

They pulled up in front of Gage's house, a sprawling two-story Craftsman with a huge front porch, but no decorations or comfy chairs were to be found on the plain porch. It begged for a homey touch, and the last (and only) time they'd been there together, Cady had asked him why the dearth of personality. He'd shrugged, saying that decorating wasn't his thing. Apparently, the bakery only looked as homey as it did because of Sugar.

The true selling point of the house was its kitchen, of course. Cady was sure Gage had told the real estate agent not to bother showing him anything that didn't have a stellar kitchen in it, and that agent must've known their stuff because the kitchen in this house was to die for. Double ovens, granite countertops, two prep stations, wine cooler, oversized fridge and freezer…it looked like it'd be right at home in a *Homes & Garden* spread on the joys of a high-quality kitchen remodel. The house had been built in the late 1920s and had originally had a cramped kitchen in it, but the previous owners had knocked out a wall, combining a storage closet with the kitchen, bringing it up to modern standards.

Last time she'd come over here, he'd cooked her dinner, making her sit on a stool and only watch as he moved around, clearly in his comfort zone, whistling cheerfully as he'd worked.

He'd finished that evening with a kiss on the tip of her nose.

Cream Puffs pawed at the window, barking with delight to see that they were at her house, and when Gage opened the passenger door, the puppy jumped down and streaked towards the front porch, sniffing and peeing on every clump and flower along the way. It was hard to see through the gloom of the evening, but Cady would've sworn the dog was grinning ear to ear as she practically flew up the steps to the front porch, dragging her leash on the ground behind her.

Gage and Cady looked back at each other, suddenly awkward without the buffer of Creamy between them. "I didn't bring you here to push anything on you," Gage said in a rush. "I just thought you looked like you could use an evening of relaxation. I know Emma threw a lot at you and I thought you might enjoy an evening of watching movies and getting your feet rubbed."

"Oooohhhhhh…" Cady sighed happily. "You said the magic words."

Gage grinned boyishly, his gorgeous white teeth glinting in the gathering darkness, and then he was scooping her up into his arms again, hip-checking the passenger door to close it as he carried her up to the front door, his boots thunking on the boards of the porch.

"I really can walk," Cady protested…and then buried her nose in the crook of Gage's neck again, breathing in deep. How was it that this man always smelled so delicious? It really wasn't fair, honestly.

How was she supposed to resist him when he smelled like heaven?

It almost made a girl not want to resist him.

"But why test that theory?" Gage asked with a naughty grin. "Best if I just carry you around. Just in case."

He opened the front door and carried her through — he didn't have to unlock it, she noticed — and Cream Puffs came bounding in on his heels, barking and dancing around Gage's feet with the excitement of it all.

"One day, I'm going to be 1/10th as interesting as Creamsy thinks I am," Gage said dryly as he carried Cady over to the deep leather couch and carefully let her slide out of his arms and into the depths of its cool embrace. "And have 1/20th of her energy. How is it that she can still tear around here like this after all of those leaves she defeated on our walk earlier?"

"It does make you wish you could bottle up energy," Cady said wistfully. She began to push herself off the couch as Gage headed to the kitchen, but he pushed her — gently — back down.

"I'm just going to grab a few snacks and drinks," he said. He grabbed the remote off the coffee table and hit a few buttons, bringing up the menu before handing it over. "I'm putting you in charge of picking a movie off Netflix. That way, you can feel like you've contributed to the evening."

She stuck out her tongue at his back — he'd sounded so damn patronizing just then — and then turned her attention to the selection. She idly stroked Cream Puffs' head behind the ears until she found the cheesiest romantic movie available.

Teach him to be patronizing…

He returned with thick, soft snickerdoodles, mugs of milk, and a bottle of lotion.

"It's not rose scented," he said with a disarming smile, "but at least it doesn't smell like men's aftershave either. Cucumber scented, which I guess means that if we get hungry, we'll just have to eat your toes."

Cady shook her head as she laughed. She would've thrown her cookie at his head but honestly, that was blasphemous. It was warm – had he microwaved it to warm it up? He certainly hadn't had time to whip up a batch of cookies in the last five minutes – and soft and oh-so-delicious.

"How did you make the cookie warm?" she asked after swallowing her last bite and a swig of milk to wash it down. "I know you didn't just pull these out of the oven."

"Microwave," Gage said simply. "People really underestimate how much a quick reheat of the item increases your enjoyment of it. You can't nuke it for very long, and you can't nuke it multiple times, or it'll turn into a brick that's more likely to chip your tooth than bring you pleasure. But if you know you're about to eat it, throw it in the microwave for 15 seconds. Makes all the difference in the world. Even passable cookies become delicious."

After they finished their cookies, Cady looking longingly at her empty napkin and wishing she wasn't quite such a glutton, she stacked the pillows behind her head and lay sideways on the couch, placing her feet on the pillow on Gage's lap where he began to rub them. The opening credits started rolling for the movie, but Cady hardly noticed. She was in seventh heaven. Cream Puffs was snuggled up against her, snoring her adorable puppy dog snore; her feet were in Gage's lap, being rubbed; she'd just eaten one of the most delicious cookies of her life...

She wasn't sure when it started. They'd been almost like platonic friends at the start of the movie, just lounging on the couch and watching the sappiest, most over-the-top movie filled to the brim with declarations of love, of life not being worth living without the other, when Cady began to sink further and further into the couch. Gage's hands were like magic – more than just rubbing, they were making her feel like she'd never felt before. Safe, loved, desired, wanted...

Needed.

But safe most of all. These were hands that would protect her, not hurt her.

He tugged on her legs, easily moving her down the couch, sliding her along the soft leather, her upper thighs, her waist all within his reach now. She felt like she was melting into him, as if her body no longer contained hard, straight bones but was now just a boneless being of feeling and lust as his fingers continued to stroke higher and higher, getting closer and closer to the top of her thighs where her body positively ached for him…

His fingers nimbly undid the button of her jean shorts, unzipping the zipper, fingers dipping inside where just the tiniest scrap of lace was covering her. Perhaps a part of her had known what was going to happen – maybe was hoping for what was going to happen – because she'd worn her skimpiest, sexiest panties she owned. They were just a bit of lace, really, hardly even enough there to qualify for the word "panties," but either way, she was very, very grateful. If she'd been wearing her old-grandma panties, ancient and stretched out and faded, she would've died of embarrassment.

"How are you?" Gage whispered, pulling Cady up through a few layers of lust, forcing her to concentrate on his words, and thus on the real world, instead of being able to slide into the world of desire where everything could just be decided and done and orchestrated by Gage. "Are you okay with me doing this?"

She paused, not sure what to say. Not wanting to say anything at all. She'd been happy just floating along, letting Gage be in charge. Him making all of the decisions.

Gage stretched, reaching up to her face where he wiped a few curls out of her eyes. "I want to make sure that you're all right before we go any further," he said, refusing to accept her silence as consent. "I don't want you to be afraid of me."

"I could never be afraid of you," Cady said without thinking, but all the more true because of their impulsiveness. Not this gentle giant that she was mostly draped across. Not this man who was treating her like spun glass. He'd chew off his right arm before hurting her. She knew that now. She caught his hand and brought it up to her lips, pressing a kiss to the palm of his calloused hand.

"I'm fine," she whispered, not brave enough to tell the whole truth – that she was more than fine. That she'd never been so wonderful, actually. She wanted him in that moment, more than she wanted to breathe or wake up the next morning or open up her own store.

She wanted him and nothing else.

She was too shy to say those words to him, so she told him the only way she knew how: She planted her feet on the arm of the couch and pushed her hips up in the air, freeing her ass to shove the shorts down and off her, leaving her in just the barest whisper of lace from the waist down.

Apparently this was a language that Gage spoke because he sucked in his breath and then let out a heart-felt groan. "You're killing me, smalls," he said, and the pain in his voice was almost palpable. "I was going to take this slow. Make you whimper with need before I even touched my lips to your skin."

She wanted to tell him that she was already there

– as his hands stroked up and down her legs, she felt trails of fire and she was sure her skin wouldn't be able to contain her much longer – but speaking was too complex, too difficult in that moment. Instead, she reached over and squeezed his arm, trying to tell him without words how much she needed him.

Inside of her, right then, please dear God...

Before she could force the tangle of lust and phrases in her mind to come out of her mouth in words that would be understandable, Gage took pity on her, scooped her up into his arms, and carried her down the hallway and then up the stairs to the second story. She didn't even bother protesting this time – if her life depended upon it, she wasn't sure if she could walk just then. Instead, she nuzzled his neck, breathing in his scent and then kissing the skin she'd been craving for what felt like years.

He carried her into a room and turned on a small lamp on the dresser as he passed, shedding gentle light in the evening darkness and then she was on a bed, lying there and just watching as Gage quickly shucked his shoes, his belt, his clothing, sure that this was all just a dream but because it was the best dream she'd ever had, she wasn't about to make any sudden movements and wake herself up from it. She could just lie there and watch his body of valleys and ridges and dips come uncovered, just for her eyes only, and then when he was done stripping, he would...lie down next to her?

She was frozen for a moment, in shock as he just

laid next to her, like they were going to just lounge around in bed and stare at the ceiling together.

"Gage?" she squeaked, and then cleared her throat. She rolled onto her side, suddenly grateful that she still had a t-shirt, bra, and panties on, not sure what was going on but wanting to be covered up while it was happening. A part of her wanted nothing more than to crawl underneath the coverlet, hide there until she knew what they were doing. "What's going on?"

She was pulling in on herself, embarrassed. Her bones were back again, and she suddenly felt awkward and ugly and unwanted. *He* obviously didn't want her. Was it her boobs? She'd always known she was small up top but then again, if she had DD breasts, she wouldn't be able to stand up straight because of the weight of them, constantly tipping her forward.

Or maybe it was how her hip bones stuck out—

She noticed the sheen of sweat on Gage's face then, and peered closer, fighting through the haze of self-doubt and worry to look – really look – at him. He looked like he was fighting himself, and losing. His hands were clenched by his sides and he had a pinched look on his face, like every bit of self control he could muster was keeping him in just that position.

"I'm yours," he croaked, and then cleared his throat. "I'm going to lie here. I won't move. Whatever you want to do, you can. I want you to be in charge. On top. No worries about me overpowering you."

It was dead silent in the room as she stared at him,

almost incapable of understanding what he was trying to say. Her? In charge? But she'd wanted him to be in charge. She'd wanted him to take over so she didn't have to think. So she *couldn't* think. She wanted to be swept away.

"Please," Gage whispered, and his voice broke on the one-syllable word. "I need…"

He trailed off to nothing, his hands still clenched by his sides, his face in what she could only describe as agony.

In agony because he wanted *her*.

She reached out a tentative hand and stroked her way down his abs, letting her fingers follow the ripples of the skin, soft over the hard muscles, his gasp of pleasure telling her that he wanted this.

A little bolder now, she followed the light happy trail from his belly button to his dick, standing straight up in the air, a drop of precum glistening on the tip. Somehow, this Greek god wanted *her*. He could have any woman in the world, dripping with muscles like he was, his square jaw, his brilliant blue eyes, and yet, he wanted her with the wild curls that got frizzy on a humid day and too-small boobs and a height that was more suitable to a junior high girl than a grown woman.

Even lying on his back, though, his muscles seemed too large, too ready to do anything he wanted to her, and she realized that he was oh-so-very-wrong in his approach. By giving her the space to be in charge, he was also giving her the space to think, and thus to worry.

Gage won't hurt me.

She knew that, and yet remembering it and acting on the information was a totally different ball of wax.

I can do what I want to, and he'll just lie here. He'll let me. I'm not in danger. He won't hurt me.

Testing his self-control, she ran her nails lightly up his thighs, running over the ridges and valleys, heading for his dick, still straining in the air, still glistening with pre-cum.

He didn't flinch. He did close his eyes tightly and mutter what sounded like a plea for help, but he didn't spring on her like a giant jack-in-the-box.

She wrapped her fingers around his red, almost purple dick, and could feel his heartbeat in it, pulsing through it, through him. His eyes squeezed tighter and this time she was *sure* he was muttering a prayer.

This made her giggle, which turned into a laugh, which turned into a snort, which made her laugh harder. She collapsed against him, letting every bit of panic in her drain away. No would-be rapist would pray for the self-control necessary to keep his hands to himself.

"Wanna share with the class?" Gage asked, his voice rough with need. He still had his face screwed up, his eyes tightly shut as he lay on his back, defenseless against anything she might get a hankering to do.

"I've not had a lot of guys pray while having sex,"

Cady finally said, once she got her giggles under control. "I just wasn't expecting it."

A quirk of the corner of his lips was his only acknowledgment, and then, "I love being all noble and shit, but Cady, I'm about a hair's breadth away from going completely insane. Either help me out, or I'll go into the bathroom and help myself out."

Her laughter died away completely then. He was being serious. There was nothing playful or funny about him in that moment. He was in desperate need…of *her*.

Sucking in a breath for courage, she ran her hand over his abs, following his happy trail, wrapping her fingers around the heat of him. She began stroking him up and down, the rhythm familiar from eons of ancestors doing just the same thing, and then she bent over and wrapped her lips around his dick.

He was scrabbling at the sheets, groaning with pain and want and need, but she was oblivious to it all as she ran her mouth up and down and around, dipping and swirling with her tongue, tasting and probing and trying anything that seemed like a good idea. She was busy running her tongue across the slit and around the head, wondering what would happen if she tried using her teeth to lightly graze the sides of his dick, when his words finally broke through the haze of desire that was swirling around her.

"Please Cady please Cady please Cady," he was chanting, another prayer but this time to her, pleading for her…

She swung her right leg over his body and then began slowly, ever-so-slowly, lowering herself down on top of him, pausing to let her body expand to take in his girth, until she was seated completely against him, her warmth, his warmth, melding together, and finally he was moving again – rocking his hips against her while wrapping his fingers around her thighs, lifting and dropping her body, their pants and screams rending the air as Cady threw back her head and screamed with pleasure, the world contracting to the point between her legs, nothing else existing, explosions and flying apart and coming together until finally, her body collapsed forward, the rigidity gone, sprawled across him, a giant pillow under her as she slept.

CHAPTER 21

GAGE

November, 2019

Gage had never been one to struggle with self-control. His mom had tried telling him one time that not everyone was as tightly wound as he was – she'd been trying to tell him to give Chris a break but had been couching the argument in vague terms, as if she really could be talking about anyone at all – but his legendary self-control was being tested to its absolute limits by a certain Cady Walcott.

He couldn't blame her – she wasn't trying to be temptation on a stick – but that didn't make it any easier, honestly. Watching her relax around him, around everyone, slowly gaining confidence, losing her instinctive, protective layer and revealing the soft, gooey Cady underneath…it was heaven.

Or hell.

He hadn't quite decided which, yet.

He was falling in love with her more every day, but was forcing himself to take it slow, not say anything, not scare her into running the other direction. He couldn't risk their relationship now. Not after it'd taken so long just to get to this point.

He found himself relying on Sugar more than ever, even hiring a second teenager to come in after school to get caught up on the tasks she usually took care of during the day, so she could do his job and he could be next door, helping Cady put the finishing touches on the Smoothie Queen. The electrical wiring was up to code; the aisles between the shelves on the right-hand side of the store were wide and accommodating; the tables on the left-hand side of the store sturdy but cute, giving the store the welcoming vibe Cady was striving so hard for.

She had a few overhead lights but had paid for outlets to be placed everywhere, making it possible to light the store via lamps without also creating a trip hazard in the process. The hodgepodge of lamps that Cady had bought from Second Time Around were especially useful in creating that eclectic yet homey feel.

After the delivery men brought in the shelving boxes a few weeks earlier, Gage had spent his two days off that week doing nothing but assembling shelves. He'd been surprised at first when he realized how short they were. Unlike a normal store where the shelves were 12-ft tall, these shelves were so short, even Cady could see over them without a problem.

Even Cady can see over them…

Which was when he'd realized, of course, why it was that the shelves were so short. No man was going to be able to sneak up on her without her seeing him coming.

She was also careful not to create any dead ends, where a man could corner her. Every aisle, every table, every corner of the store had an escape route built in.

As he saw it, she had a healthy fear of what could happen. Not an irrational fear that overpowered her and kept her from living her life, but a healthy fear that kept her aware of her surroundings at all times.

He was damn proud of her – every week, changing and growing and expanding just a little more.

He'd never lived in another person's pocket like this. Even when he was at the bakery, working away in the kitchen, it seemed like there was the constant excuse available for him to go to the smoothie shop, or for her to go to the bakery. Taste testing. Pricing discussions. Supplier debates. Buy new appliances and walk-in coolers with all of the latest features, or used with a much more affordable price tag? She understood what it was like to be a small business owner, unlike any other woman he'd ever tried to date. She didn't make him feel guilty for staying late and doing inventory; quite often, she'd join in and help.

The crossing back and forth between stores was getting to be obnoxious, though. Whether they went through the front doors or the back doors, it was still a walk around the wall in the middle – a solid wall without the smallest connection in it to the other side.

Much like our relationship was in the beginning. Solid, impenetrable, not a crack or a bit of wiggle room in sight. She stayed on that side; I stayed on this side. But now...

Gage pulled a large cake sheet pan forward, the peanut butter bars cooled enough to cut, and began slicing them into 3" squares for the display case out front. He took a corner piece and slipped it onto a napkin. He'd go over and visit Cady with a cup of coffee and the peanut butter bar. See how she was doing. Take a peek at the other side of the wall. Do some mental measurements. Decide if he was brave enough to pull this off.

With a wave to Sugar, he headed out the front door and over to the still-closed Smoothie Queen. Another two weeks, and Cady would be open for business; she was opening the week before Thanksgiving. It was crazy how quickly her self-imposed deadline had snuck up on them.

But all of this meant that it was now or never to make this happen.

CHAPTER 22

CADY

*L*IFE, Cady decided, was pretty damn awesome.

This wasn't a normal state of being for her. Well, at least not since *that* had happened. And especially not since her parents had died.

Previous to that, she'd been a positive person. Or she thought she had been. It was hard to remember that far back, really.

And then, it was the Dark Times, and she'd been miserable and scared and oh-so-afraid all the time, and she hadn't been able to believe that life would get any better. Life would always be that awful.

Always.

But Gage Dyer came into her life and had changed everything for her. No longer afraid of shadows. No longer afraid of planes, although she still didn't want to fly on one. She was happy to never step onto a plane for the rest of her life.

But at least she didn't cower and cry every time a crop duster flew overhead, which was a hell of an improvement.

She wanted to tell Gage how much she loved him; she felt the words on her lips almost constantly, but she was afraid. What if he didn't feel the same way? What if she was a fun companion for him – compatible in and out of bed – but he wanted nothing more than that?

Afraid to lose what they had, Cady swallowed her words of love and tried to show it through her actions instead. He'd changed her life – he *was* her life – and she told him this with every look, every back rub, every graze of her hand across his chest.

"We have *got* to do girls' weekends more often," Sugar said, laughing as she piled out of Emma's car, leaning back in to retrieve Rose. The 8-month-old was bundled up against the frigid air of the November day but she didn't seem to mind. She grinned up at her momma, showing off her bottom teeth – the only ones that'd come in so far – and waved her pudgy hands in the air. "The men in our lives can survive without us for three days."

"In *your* lives, maybe," Emma grumbled good-naturedly under her breath. "I don't have a man in my life to miss me. Other than my boss, and quite frankly, we need the weekends as breathers so we don't kill each other."

"Well, thanks for taking off during the week," Cady said. "I know it was a lot to talk your boss into letting you have Wednesday through Friday off, but with everything I still have left to get ready for the grand opening, nothing else would've worked."

They headed for the front door of the Smoothie Queen where they would try out Cady's newest creation – blueberries and pineapple, which she knew sounded disgusting but had promised everyone that it tasted marvelous – and then Emma had to head back to Denver.

Cady inwardly sighed at the thought of Emma leaving again. She'd never had friends like Sugar and Emma before, and although Sugar was fun when Emma wasn't there, it was like she completed the circuit or something, making life even more amazing when the three of them were together.

Life was just better with the Dyers around.

"Do you ever hear from Nicholas?" Sugar asked Emma as Cady fumbled with her keys for the front door. "Is he still in the Marines?"

"Nicholas?" Cady echoed. "Who's Nicholas?" She finally got the deadbolt to slide back and she pushed into the store, holding the door open for Emma and Sugar to pass through. "How have I not heard about a hot Marine before this?"

But both Emma and Sugar were just standing there with gleeful looks on their faces, looking meaningfully at Cady as if she was supposed to be excited about something. Even Rose was getting in on the scene, waving her slobbery fist in the air and screeching happily.

"Why are you guys staring at me like that?" Cady asked slowly, a tingle going up her spine. Something was going on here, and she couldn't tell what, and the way they were acting made it *seem* like it'd be good, but—

"Because they keep expecting you to notice that I'm standing right here," Gage said out of the darkness, leaning against the wall that separated their businesses.

Cady yelped and jumped at least a foot in the air, staring through the dim evening light, trying to read the look on Gage's face. "Gage!" she squeaked, her hand over her heart. "Oh heavens. You scared the *shit* outta me. Why are you standing here in the dark? You should turn on—" she reached over and flicked on one of the table lamps on top of a shelving unit and turned back to Gage, "the lighhhtttssss..."

She sounded a bit like a toy running out of battery – a rundown talking doll – but she couldn't make herself care in that moment. Her brain was too stunned as she tried to take in what she was seeing.

It was Gage standing there all right, but he wasn't in front of the wall between the bakery and the smoothie shop. He was in front of the glass door between the bakery and the smoothie shop.

"Where...what..." She was sputtering like an engine running out of gas. "Where did the door come from?!" she finally got out. She was crossing to it, pushing at it and letting it swing open into the bakery, looking for all the world like it'd always been there.

Except it hadn't. It wasn't like she would've missed seeing a glass-and-aluminum door between their businesses all this time.

"Surprise," Gage said softly, and even through the haze of shock, she could sense the nervousness in his voice. "It locks from both sides. I can install curtains if you'd like, blocking the view. We can lock it and pretend this never happened. I wanted to surprise you – a present for your grand opening on Monday. But if you hate it, I can make it go—"

"Hate it?" Cady whispered, still pushing at the door and watching it swing. "Hate it?! I *love* it." She turned to Gage and threw her arms around his neck, wrapping her legs around his hips and kissing him enthusiastically. His hands slipped under her ass and he supported her there as if she weighed nothing more than a small sack of sugar.

A tiny part of Cady's brain registered words and sounds and then it was just her and Gage in the store, kissing as if they'd never kissed before.

No, Cady decided, better than that. Kissing as if they knew each other intimately. Kissing as if they'd been apart for ages but now were ready to become one. Right then, right there, against the wall right next to the swinging door, Gage was going to take her and...

Barking. Loud barking. What was that noise? Gage was kissing down the side of her neck as she practically melted into the wall, her head tilted to the side to give him better access, her ankles hooked at the small of Gage's back, but still, there was barking.

Finally, she forced her eyes open and she saw Cream Puffs dancing around their feet, barking excitedly, thrilled that Cady was gone from her three-day weekend with Sugar and Emma and quite ready for some attention. Like, now.

"I need…" Cady moaned, pushing at Gage's shoulders. She let her ankles unlock and she slid down the front of him, every delicious inch pressing against her body on the descent.

"*I* need—" Gage said, his voice husky with that need, but Cady pushed lightly at his shoulders again.

"Cream Puffs hasn't seen me in three days," she said, dropping to her knees and letting the teenage dog bathe her face in kisses. "She misses me."

"*I* haven't seen you in three days either," Gage grumbled good-naturedly, and then pushed the door open between the two businesses again, clearly ready for more praise on the topic now that it was obvious they weren't going to make passionate love against the wall of the smoothie shop. "I really wanted to ask you before I did this, but I couldn't figure out how and still have it be a surprise. Asking 'Can I do this?' tends to take away the surprise factor."

Cady snorted with laughter against Cream Puffs' neck. "Just a bit," she murmured.

"So I decided to make it mostly reversible. In case you hated it. Like I said, a lock on either side plus curtains would pretty much turn this into a no-go. It wasn't hard to convince Sugar and Emma to take you out for some girls' time together—"

"Oooohhhhh…" Cady breathed, the pieces all falling into place. Their insistence that they *had* to take these three days off, even though it was just days before the grand opening. Their insistence that Cady make them the blueberry and pineapple smoothie once they got back, even though Cady had thought they'd both just want to go home and relax.

"They didn't want to try my smoothie after all!" she said, half indignant, looking around and realizing that they were both gone. She vaguely remembered the noises and the words while she'd had her legs wrapped around Gage, and guessed that it was them saying goodbye.

Or telling them to get a room.

Probably both, honestly.

"They just wanted to be here when you saw the door," Gage agreed. "Emma was absolutely insistent. Said she wouldn't leave for Denver until she saw your face."

Finally having given Cream Puffs enough love – at least for the moment – Cady stood and walked back to the door, the dog trailing in her wake. "So you just cut through the cinder block wall?" she asked, looking at the carefully crafted door frame. If Gage ever decided to give up making cakes, he could do handyman work instead. She'd never met such a meticulous worker before, other than her own father, of course.

"Just? *Just?!*" he repeated, mock outraged by the word. "I busted through concrete for *you*. Not every girl can say that her boyfriend broke through a concrete wall for her."

She laughed as she grinned up at him. "It is a very romantic story," she whispered as she stood up on her tiptoes, sliding her arms around his neck. "I shall be sure to give it its full due when I retell it, I promise."

As she kissed him again, and he pressed her against the wall of the shop again, and began making his way down her neck again, she decided that actually, life was even better than "pretty damn awesome." Perhaps "really damn awesome" was more appropriate. Or "stupendously damn awesome."

Whatever way she cut it, though, "awesome" was definitely true.

CHAPTER 23

CADY

*E*XHAUSTION. Had she ever been this tired before in her life? Those dark days where she hadn't gotten out of bed for weeks at a time except to go pee…she'd been exhausted then.

But that had been a different type of exhaustion. Today…this came from hard work. From pushing herself to the limits and succeeding, not lying in bed and wishing the world would just leave her the hell alone already.

No, this was a very different kind of exhaustion indeed. *This* exhaustion felt good. Accomplished.

Gage had already left for the day – headed back to his place to start on dinner while she cleaned up her store. It was the end of her first full week of being an open and operating business owner and it had gone pretty damn well if she did say so herself. There'd been learning curves galore – overfilling of the blender; under-ordering of the frozen strawberries – but no one had died, and she figured that was an achievement in and of itself.

It was true that she was making smoothies and selling health food which didn't tend to kill people off, but still...

She'd take the win.

She locked the back door of the Smoothie Queen, able to do it even in the dark without having to flick on the flashlight app on her phone. She wasn't sure what this said about her – she was so comfortable leaving work after dark, was she turning into a workaholic? – but at least it meant that she wasn't liable to trip and hurt herself—

"You bitch," a malevolent voice growled in her ear as a gloved hand slid around her face and another around her waist. "Staying late, with *him*?"

But whatever else he was going to say was drowned out in Cady's screams. She fought and thrashed against him, using every bit of muscle she had to go for his soft parts – his vulnerable spots – the places that would make a grown man cry.

He was holding her too tightly though, and she couldn't get at his groin or his throat. Who was this man? Why was he attacking her? She was slamming her elbow against him as hard as she could, feeling like a tiny gnat struggling against the arms of a giant.

He shoved something foul and dirty into her mouth and then clamped his hand over her mouth again, keeping her from spitting the rag out onto the ground.

"Shut up!" he growled. "You cheating whore. You'd have his child and then still work for another man? You deserve this. If Jaxson won't teach you your place in the world, I will."

That got Cady's attention and she stopped for a moment, suspended mostly off the ground as her attacker held her from behind.

Have a child? Work for a man? None of this…

Oh.

Ohhhhhhhh…

It didn't help her escape to know who was holding her from behind, but still, it strangely made her feel better. It gave a reason for the otherwise inexplicable situation that she'd found herself in. It was Sugar's ex – the town drunk. That asshole who'd crashed Sugar and Emma's party. He thought she was Sugar and was trying to…kidnap? Kill her?

Her mind went spinning in a million different directions. It was dark, they both had brown hair, they were both petite, and the back door to the Smoothie Queen was just a couple of feet away from the back door to the Muffin Man.

Plus, Richard was drunk. Stinking drunk, based on the fumes rolling off him. As intoxicated as he was right now, he probably wouldn't have been able to tell she wasn't Sugar even in broad daylight. Sugar's chest was larger than Cady's, and then there were Cady's curls compared to Sugar's stick-straight hair, but apparently those weren't the kinds of details that a drunk-off-his-ass Richard was capable of picking up on.

Bastard. Bastard. I'm going to kick you in the nuts, you bastard. You rat bastard.

Feet still dangling off the ground, he began carrying her like a wiggling sack of potatoes, his hand clamped hard over her mouth, keeping the disgusting rag in place. "You think you have every right to prance around in public. Everyone loves Sugar. Sweet as pie, they say. They don't understand why I'd divorce you. But you made me. I can't tell people that. They would laugh at me."

She kicked backwards again and actually made contact this time, slamming her foot into his knee, the howl of pain in her ear almost deafening her. "You *bitch*!" he howled, but still, he didn't drop her. She was suspended in mid-air, his arm pinning hers by her side. She wanted to get at him. She wanted to dig her fingers into his eye sockets like the self-defense coach had taught her but he was behind her and she couldn't reach up and get at him. Her breath was short and choppy and black spots swirled in along the sides of her vision and she was going to pass out – she couldn't breathe, he was holding her so tight and the nasty rag was in her mouth, forcing her to only breathe through her nose, and the stench of alcohol fumes rolling off him was going to choke her all by itself—

She couldn't blackout. She had to concentrate. Where were they going?

She squinted through the darkness and spotted a fluorescent orange Jeep at the end of the employee-only parking lot, a vehicle she'd never seen before. It had to be his.

Good. She was fighting the blackness, fighting him. She knew where he was trying to take her. When he tried to push her inside of the Jeep, she'd throw her arms and legs wide. Keep him from shoving her in.

Fight him. Fight him. Every step will cost him. I won't let him win. I won't—

Beams of headlights turned into the parking lot, cutting through the darkness, and even above the panic pulsing through her veins, making it difficult to think clearly, she recognized the sound of the engine. It was Gage's truck. She didn't know how she knew; she couldn't see him. But she knew it anyway. He'd come for her.

How did he know? Thank God he did, but—

Richard let out a string of nasty curse words in Cady's ear as he hobbled faster towards his Jeep, trying to reach it before Gage could reach them, and then they were in the path of the headlights. Screeching tires and a dog barking wildly; a door opening and boots pounding on the asphalt; a wall of muscle was hitting them, slamming them to the ground and Cady felt agony shoot up her arm, the pain so intense she lost track of the world as she just tried to breathe, curled up on the ground, the dirty rag still in her mouth and keeping her from breathing and she pushed at it with her tongue, wanting it out of the way, wanting a lungful of fresh air more than anything else but she couldn't get the damn thing out; it was too limp and large and somehow clinging to her teeth like barnacles on a ship.

It finally registered somewhere in the back of her scattered mind that her arms were free now, and maybe she couldn't use her right arm to pull out the rag, but she could use her left.

She rolled off her left arm that'd been pinned beneath her and tugged at the rag, throwing it as far as she could away from her, and her mouth, dry as the Sahara, had the most awful taste in it. She tried to spit but she couldn't gather up enough moisture. Heaving, breathing, trying to push the darkness away, trying to focus on something other than the pain radiating through her upper arm.

The sounds started to register then – flesh striking flesh. The growls of a dog. "I'll kill you," Gage was roaring as the blows kept going. "Teach you to pick on women half your size. *Kill* you!"

Cady rolled to her knees and then to her feet, cradling her arm, trying to see through the darkness. The beams from the truck headlights almost made it more difficult to see what was going on, as the two men showed up in sharp relief in the light and then disappeared into the darkness under the beams, rolling on the ground.

Cady scrambled for her purse, digging through it

for her phone. *Hurry, hurry, hurry! You need to get help! Find the phone! Where's the phone?!* Adrenaline was making her shaky but finally, *finally*, her hand closed around the slim device and she pulled it out with a shout of triumph. Shaking, her vision intermittently clouding and then clearing from the panic shooting through her, she dialed 9-1-1.

"Sawyer City dispatch, how may I help you?" an old, querulous sounding man said on the second ring.

"Need help. Please, send someone. We've been attacked." She could hear the fists and the yells and the barks and she thought she might throw up. "Please."

"Where are you?" The grumpiness was gone from the man's voice and he was all business. Calm. "What is around you?"

"Behind the smoothie shop. And the bakery. In the parking lot behind. Dickwad attacked me. Gage saved me."

"Dickwad?" And now the man sounded slightly amused. "Don't hang up," he said, professional again. "Stay on the line with me. I'm dispatching officers right now. Gage who?"

"Gage Dyer. Owns the Muffin Man."

"That must make you Cady Walcott," the dispatcher said under his breath; a statement, not a question.

This cut through the panic and pain washing over her. *What the hell...* "How do you know that?" Cady demanded, shocked to her core.

"Small towns," the dispatcher said dismissively. "Officer Miller is on her way. Can you see what's going on? Talk to me – tell me the scene in front of you."

Even as Cady turned, trying to focus through the bright lights and the inky midnight darkness, she could hear the faint wail of sirens. *They're coming. Thank God, the police are coming. A* woman. *Can she handle two grown men, though? They're both so big.*

"Cady, what's happening in front of you?" the dispatcher snapped, bringing her attention back to the present. "Talk to me."

"They're fighting," she said. "I think Gage is on top now. Our dog is biting Dickwad's ankle. Good girl!" she called to Cream Puffs. "Bite him hard."

The dispatcher let out a rusty laugh that sounded as if it hadn't been used in years. "What's your dog's name?" he asked through his chuckles.

"Creamsicle. No, Cream Puffs," she corrected herself. "Sometimes Gage calls her Creamsy or Puffers, though."

She shouldn't be telling him this – he didn't care, and a part of her knew it – but her brain was so disconnected from the moment, she felt like an alien was possessing her body. Red and blue lights were flashing intermittently and the sirens were getting louder and then the police car screeched to a halt on the far side of Gage's truck, another one pulling in behind.

"They're here," she said gratefully.

"Officer Miller and Officer Morland will take care of you. Be careful, honey," and then the line went dead.

Honey? I just got called honey *by an old man I don't know.*

Small towns. They're a breed of their own.

A stoutly built woman was running past her, yelling, her service pistol pulled and trained on the men on the ground. "Hands up! Get your hands up! Move! Gage, I know he deserves it, but you gotta stop swinging now."

A wet tongue swiped the palm of Cady's right hand, jostling her broken arm, sending a sharp wave of pain through her body, an involuntary shout spilling from her lips. Cream Puffs whined uncertainly, and then a male officer was there, putting his arm around Cady. "You're okay, ma'am, you're going to be fine," he said in a deep soothing voice. He spoke into his shoulder. "We will need an ambulance here. One hurt female. Two potentially hurt males. Send two buses – I don't think we ought to cart them to the hospital together." He let off on the button on the radio as it crackled to life, people calling back and forth as he turned back to her. "Where does it hurt?"

Cady shook her head, mute. There was a big man standing right there. His arm was around her. She knew he was there to help her – at least, the sane, calm side of her did. But still, underneath it all, it throbbed. *What if, what if, what if…*

She was shaking so hard she couldn't stand any

longer and she found she was on the ground, sitting on the dirty asphalt, Cream Puffs licking her face and whining, the cop trying to talk to her, the lights flashing, and then the darkness closed in and she knew no more.

CHAPTER 24

GAGE

How was it that it kept being Abby who had to break up the fights between him and Dickwad? Gage didn't tend to get into many fistfights, but the last two that he'd been in had both been with this worthless piece of shit, and both had been broken up by Officer Abby Miller.

It was a damn good thing he liked her so much; when she'd tried to pull him off Dick, he'd almost punched her instead. He'd checked his swing just inches from her face as he'd realized who it was that was pulling on him, the momentum of the swing making him stumble forward, almost pitching to the ground himself.

"It's Abby," she'd shouted, bringing up an arm to deflect his wild swing.

Gage was grateful that he'd managed to check himself at the last moment – not only because he genuinely liked Abby and would never punch her if he was in full control of the situation, but also because he didn't figure Wyatt would be too understanding about his wife sporting a black eye because of him. Wyatt was more lanky than Gage and Gage could probably take him in a fair fight but still...

A pissed-off Wyatt Miller wasn't a pretty sight.

Gage pressed the cold compress the hospital had given him harder into his eye socket as he looked down at Cady's sleeping form. She'd been in and out of it since the police had arrived and then the ambulance had taken the two of them to the county hospital, Dickwad trailing in his own ambulance behind – a damn good thing or Gage might've been tempted to get a few more punches in while the bastard was strapped to a gurney. Fair or not, Gage didn't care. Dickwad obviously didn't mind beating up on women half his size, so why should Gage care about taking a few swings at the guy when he couldn't defend himself?

They'd drugged Cady up good and well when they got there because she'd kept fighting everyone, even him, as they'd tried to run x-rays on her arm, put an IV into the back of her hand, even clean her superficial wounds with alcohol wipes. She hadn't been there with them in the room, though – she'd been fighting her own demons, screaming and flailing around, shouting gibberish, and he knew that she didn't have a damn clue of what was going on. The medical professionals, clearly confused by her reaction, had struggled to figure out how to handle her until Gage had told them bluntly that she'd been sexually attacked previously. She was reliving that.

One of the aides jabbed her in the thigh with a sedative then, and she'd been heavily drugged ever since. Gage had hated breaking her confidence; had hated telling these people who were strangers to her about the darkest, deepest secret of her life, but they had to know. The situation didn't make sense otherwise, and they wouldn't have been able to help her.

He only hoped Cady would understand when she woke up.

He stroked the frizzy curls away from her delicate face, her elfin features perfectly matching her tiny body. She looked like one strong wind would blow her away, but Gage knew better. The fight she'd put up earlier…

She was a damn sight tougher than she looked.

She stirred a bit under his hand and he sucked in a breath of anticipation. She was going to wake up, and then…how would she view the world? Would she be back to hating everyone and everything, distrusting every man because of the actions of Richard Schmidt?

"Water," she croaked, flicking her tongue across her lips, but unlike the countless times that she'd done that before and desire had flooded through him at the sight, this time only worry and love filled him. There wasn't a damn thing about Cady in that moment that cried out for sexual attention, but love?

That's what she needed in that moment.

Well, and water.

He hurriedly picked up the plastic cup fitted with a lid and straw that the nurse had left on the tray earlier, and held it up to Cady's lips. She sucked the water greedily, the water dribbling out of the side of her mouth in her clumsiness, but she wouldn't let him pull it away.

Finally, after sucking the cup dry, she lay back against the pillow, looking drained. "Where are we?" she croaked, her eyes closed, looking as if she was going to drift back to sleep at any moment.

"The hospital. Valley County Hospital, to be exact. You broke your arm; they had to cast it."

She shook her head violently. "I didn't break it," she rasped, and Gage paused, trying to figure out how to respond to that comment. Was she still not in touch with reality? He'd seen the x-rays. Her humerus was most definitely broken. A clean break, the doctor assured him, and she would make a complete recovery. "That rat bastard broke it."

Gage choked for air, sputtering, and then roared with laughter. "I thought we'd decided to call him Dickwad," he said, wiping the tears of laughter from the corners of his eyes. He couldn't believe she'd had it in her to make him laugh like that. Not at a time like this.

"*You* may call him Dickwad if you like," she retorted weakly. "I prefer Rat Bastard."

He picked up her hand, stroking the top of her

thumb with his. "Well, that rat bastard is just down the hallway from us," Gage said. Only a slight tightening of her hand on his revealed that she'd heard him. "Last I heard, they're thinking about transferring him to Boise. He might need reconstructive surgery on his face. Again."

"May he hit every pothole along the way," Cady said solemnly, as if pronouncing an Irish blessing upon her attacker's head, and then finally forced her eyes open. He gazed down into her golden brown eyes, squeezing her hand, stroking her hair, trying to direct his love towards her, like an invisible ray of feelings. "You're bandaged up," she said, pulling his hand up into the air so she could look at it closer.

"Dickwad's face kept getting in the way of my knuckles," he said with a shrug. "Funny, that. No matter where my fist was aimed, it always seemed to meet with his face. Or his stomach. I'll admit that it met his stomach a couple of times. Oh, and my elbow seemed to make frequent contact with his windpipe." He shrugged casually as she snorted a little with laughter. Listening to her laugh – he could do that for the rest of his life. "Now that you're awake, we need to call the police, though. They'll want to take your statement. They already took mine, but they said they'll need yours in order to really make the charges stick."

Her relaxed demeanor, her laughter, her open trusting expression, disappeared. "'Make the charges stick'?" she repeated, and he could feel her body tense up on the hospital bed. "What do you mean? Surely they couldn't let him out *again*."

They both heard a knock on the doorframe and looked up to see a pretty teenager standing there, holding a tray piled high with implements, bandages, and ointments. "Hi, Cady," the girl said cheerfully. "I'm Zara Garrett, and I'll be your CNA while you're here. I heard voices and wanted to come check on you. I need to clean your abrasions and check you over for other wounds. Can you tell me where you hurt?"

With one final squeeze of her hand, Gage stepped out of the room and into the hallway, giving the two privacy while he called dispatch. Hopefully Abby would still be on and could be the questioning officer. Things would go much, much better if it was a woman who was asking the questions. The grumpy dispatcher wouldn't say, though, only promising to send an officer over now that Cady was awake.

"Shit," Gage mumbled, stuffing his phone into his back pocket, wincing when his split knuckles hit the edge of his jeans pocket. He looked down with a grimace. He was disgusting. Rolling around on the asphalt with that asshat, he'd probably rolled across a couple of rusty nails and some broken glass. He really ought to ask for a tetanus shot while he was here.

He saw the flash of red and blue lights out of the corner of his eye and he looked up quickly, watching as the front doors to the hospital slid open to reveal Officer Aaron Morland.

"Dammit," Gage grumbled as he headed down the hallway to greet him. He didn't mind Aaron – they didn't know each other real well, but from the few interactions with the cop that Gage'd had, he seemed like a nice enough guy.

But that was the problem – he was a *guy*.

Morland looked up from his discussion with the receptionist and spotted Gage. "Hey," he called out, leaving the receptionist behind and heading down the hallway to him. "Dispatch called in and said Cady is awake. Is she ready to give a statement?"

Gage pulled him to the side of the wide hallway. "Don't take this personally, but is Officer Miller available?" he asked in a low voice. "Cady's had some bad experiences with men in the past. She'd do a lot better with a female officer."

"No, sorry. She's got the day off – won't be back to work until the late shift tomorrow."

"Of course," Gage muttered. "All right. Last I checked, she was getting cleaned up by a CNA. Wait here – I'll see if she's decent."

As he walked into Cady's room, he found a slightly bemused Cady and a chattering Zara. "So *I* told him that if he didn't stop being such an ass, I'd kick him in the nuts. I have brothers – I know where to hit. Don't ever mess with girls who have brothers. Do you have any?"

"You must've taken lessons from the same place as my sister Emma," Gage said, stepping in to save Cady from having to answer and admit to her sibling-less state. "She doesn't put up with much gruff from us poor abused brothers."

"As if," Zara sniffed. "She'd tell us a different story if she were here."

"I'm sure she would," Gage said mildly. "Cady, the officer is here. You ready?"

"Which one?" Cady asked, not answering his question, shifting higher in the hospital bed, cradling her right arm to her.

Gage looked over at Zara, eyebrows raised, waiting for the teen to leave before answering Cady's question.

"Right!" Zara said after a moment, finally catching onto the hint. "I'm sure there are bed pans that need to be emptied anyway." She sounded less than thrilled at the idea but left quietly.

"It's Officer Morland," Gage said, turning back to Cady. "A guy. He's the same one who questioned me." She was already shaking her head no, and he clasped her hand in his. "It's going to be okay," he said softly. "I can stay right here if you want me to."

"They'd let you stay in the room with me?" She looked skeptical at the idea. Gage suppressed a laugh. She wouldn't take kindly to him laughing at her.

"You're not under suspicion. They aren't going to be cross-examining you. The police just need to know what happened out of your own mouth. I can only tell them what happened after I got there."

"Why did you come back?" Cady asked, a hint of desperation in her voice. It was clear as daylight that she wanted to postpone the questioning as much as possible. "You were supposed to be gone for the night. I've been meaning to ask you why you came back."

"I left my cell phone on my desk in the bakery. I went to text you to tell you that dinner was ready, and couldn't find it anywhere. I don't have a landline, of course, so I couldn't call you and ask you to pick it up on the way to my place, so I drove back instead. Figured I'd talk you into leaving if you hadn't already. I half thought I'd see you heading to my place as I was heading to the bakery, but your Jeep wasn't on the road. Then I pulled into the parking lot and there were *two* Jeeps parked there, one a fluorescent orange, and…" He shuddered, trying to push down the panic that threatened to overwhelm him.

Seeing Cady struggling in Richard's arms had stopped his heart, he was sure of it. It was Cream Puffs that got him going again. When he'd been leaving the house, she'd gleefully jumped in the back of his truck, excited for a chance to go for a ride, ignoring his stern order to stay behind. He'd given into her – it wasn't worth arguing with the dog and anyway, she was getting pretty good about staying safely in the bed of the truck while they drove around town.

When he'd pulled into the tight, dark parking lot, hemmed in by buildings and detritus that every business seemed to accumulate, she jumped out and took off like a shot before he could even bring the truck to a standstill. She'd growled and barked ferociously as she'd tried to tear off Richard's leg.

He figured she deserved a treat a day for the rest of her life for her bravery last night.

"I'll go get Officer Morland. I'll come back with him, he'll ask you questions, and it'll all be over in a jiffy." He squeezed her hand and then went to the doorway of the room, not willing to take no as an answer. The sooner they could get this done and over with, the sooner they could make sure they kept this asshole locked up for life. "Morland?" he said, and the officer hurried over. "I'll stay in the room as you talk to her," he said bluntly, and the officer nodded.

"As long as you're not doing the talking, I'm good with that."

The understanding clear between them, they headed back through Cady's hospital door. Some questions, and then he could get Cady out of the hospital and ensconced in bed. He could feed her chocolate pie and cream puffs until she got better. The Smoothie Queen had only been open for a week, and it sucked to close it down so quickly, but the town would understand. She could reopen it again when she had use of both of her arms, and Dickwad was securely locked behind bars.

Until then, he'd make sure that she was okay. That was all that mattered.

CHAPTER 25

CADY

*C*ady's heart was galloping fast in her chest, feeling for all the world like it was going to tear right out of her. Officer Morland? Did she *have* to talk to a male cop? Couldn't she just hide in her house and pretend for the rest of her life that there were no men in existence?

Except for Gage, of course, but he didn't count.

Hmmmm...I should probably not tell him that I don't count him as a male. He may not take that in the right spirit...

It was this thought that had her smiling slightly as Officer Morland entered the room, Gage right on his heels, but as soon as she spotted the bulk of the officer, the smile disappeared. He wasn't quite as muscular as Gage – honestly, no one was, so that wasn't saying much, but still, she could see his bulging biceps straining against the sleeves of his uniform as though threatening her, promising that if she didn't do what he wanted, he'd hold her down and...

Her breath was coming in short, choppy gasps now and the edges of her vision darkened, sound warping and distorting, like everyone was suddenly at the other end of a very long tunnel.

Gage's hand, calloused and large, slipped into hers, and she heard him talking even as her eyes clung to the curve of Morland's bicep. *So much power right there. He could hurt—*

"No one's gonna hurt you," Gage whispered, stroking his fingers through her hair.

Could he hear me? Was I talking out loud?

Shit, shit, shit.

This realization, finally, was the reason she could pull her eyes away from the unwanted male in the room and up to Gage. "You'll stay?" she whispered. He'd already told her yes but she needed to hear it again. She needed to know that he wouldn't abandon her.

"I'm not going anywhere," Gage whispered, and then pressed a kiss to the tip of her nose. "I'm just going to sit here quietly while you chat with Morland. He'll be *extra* nice to you because he knows that if he isn't, he won't get any more of those bear claws that he just loves."

Cady nodded. Withholding bakery treats from someone was a pretty big threat. Morland was a cop, ergo the main staple of his diet was donuts, ergo he'd hate to lose access to the only bakery in town that sold them.

Satisfied with the severity of this threat, she turned

back to the police officer and found that he'd pulled up a chair and was sitting beside the bed, a notepad and pen in hand, no longer looming menacingly over her. Cady instantly liked him about 10 times better. Gray-green eyes, a curl to his dark brown hair, and a square jaw… Cady supposed that women probably thought he was handsome, although he was certainly no Gage Dyer.

Still, she clung to Gage's hand, as if scared he was going to pull it away at any moment. She knew he wouldn't, but…

It felt good to hold it tight anyway.

"Hi, Cady," the officer said with a small smile that reached his eyes. "I heard that you've had a run-in with Richard Schmidt previously. Why don't we start with that encounter, and then move to last night's activities?"

"I call him Rat Bastard," Cady said, figuring that she should start with the important information.

She heard Gage choking on his laughter as the gray-green eyes of the officer went round.

"An applicable nickname if I've ever heard one," the officer finally said in a strangled voice that sounded suspiciously like he was trying to choke back his own laughter.

Cady decided he might be all right after all.

"So," Cady continued, "Rat Bastard showed up to Emma and Sugar's big birthday party they hold every year. Have you gone to it?"

"Not personally, but I've heard it's fun."

"Well, Rat Bastard decided to take Sugar hostage because he was pissed that she had Jaxson's baby, which is honestly ridiculous. This sounds like a plot line from *Days of Our Lives*, but I swear it's true. Like she's really going to say," and Cady intentionally pitched her voice in a high falsetto that sounded *nothing* like Sugar, "'Oh gosh, Rat Bastard, I thought you were a real asshole before, but now that you've attacked me and held a gun to my head, I'll love you forever!' Said no woman ever."

This time, the choking laughter spilled out as Morland let out a roar of laughter.

Cady grinned up at him, pleased with herself. She'd been so damn terrified before this hulk of a man came into the room, sure that she'd be attacked again but Gage's presence by her side had made her feel relaxed. Protected. If something bad happened, he'd stand between her and the bad guy every step of the way.

He'd proven that last night.

And now, Officer Morland had proven that he had a sense of humor. Cady decided to tell Sugar and Emma that he should hold a permanent spot on the guest list each year. Not that she was personally in charge of who they invited and who they didn't, but she knew they'd be more than happy to add another guest to the list.

She told the cop about how Gage had saved Sugar, and then Abby had taken the rat bastard away in handcuffs. She hadn't seen him since; had mostly forgotten about him, actually.

The truth was – although she didn't share this insight with the cop – was that if she'd remembered him living there, lurking in the shadows, always ready to jump out at her and hurt her, she never would've relaxed as much as she had over the past seven months. It would've been a guillotine, always hanging over her, ready to fall at any moment.

"So you two didn't interact at any point during that encounter?" the officer probed. "You didn't yell at him to leave your friend alone, or take a swing at him?"

Cady shook her head. "I hardly knew Sugar and Emma at that point. I'd just met Sugar 30 minutes before Rat Bastard showed up, and Emma 15 minutes before that. I didn't know their history; I hardly knew anyone in Long Valley at that point. I just stood in the crowd and watched. I didn't know what to do, and he had a gun…Honestly, he was so drunk off his ass, even if we'd had an entire conversation, he wouldn't have remembered it the next day. But he didn't attack me last night because I'm me." At the officer's blank look, she plowed on. "He thought I was Sugar."

She felt more than heard Gage's sharp intake of breath next to her, and she realized that somehow, no one had figured out this piece of crucial information.

"Did he call you Sugar?" the officer asked, and Cady shook her head. "Then how do you know he thought he was attacking her?"

"He called me a bitch and a whore," Cady said slowly, struggling to remember everything that had happened. It'd been dark and so surprising, and then the adrenaline rushing through her veins…it was a giant blur of fear and panic and anger. "Well, maybe he called me Sugar. Dammit. I'm sorry. It's all a big mess up here." She waved a hand next to her temple.

"Well, whether or not he actually used the name 'Sugar,' you seem really sure that he thought he was attacking her. Can you tell me why?"

"Oh. Right. Well, because he kept talking about Jaxson. How I had a baby with him, but I was still working for Gage," she squeezed his hand but didn't look at him, "and how someone needed to teach me manners. Or that wasn't how a married woman was supposed to act. Something along those lines." She waved her hand dismissively. "But I realized that in the dark, and the back doors for the bakery and my smoothie shop right next to each other…it'd be easy to get them mixed up. Plus, we're about the same build, both have dark brown hair – mine is curly and hers is straight, but he might've thought that Sugar got a perm." She shrugged. "I don't know if y'all ran a blood alcohol test on him or not, but he was stinkin' drunk. Literally. The smell rolling off him…I could hardly breathe. You guys are going to lock him up this time, right?" she demanded. It was ludicrous enough that he'd gotten off without punishment after bringing a gun to a birthday party. Surely he couldn't get away with a second attempted kidnapping.

Gage and Officer Morland exchanged glances, as if they'd been discussing this exact point before Cady had come along. "What?" she asked sharply.

That look. It wasn't good, that was for damn sure.

"You know who his father is, right?" the cop said after a moment's pause.

"Yeah. The town's judge. The only judge for the whole county, actually. But that shouldn't matter. Justice is blind, and he should have to—"

"Justice is sometimes a little less blind than she should be," Morland broke in. "We've tried to nail this guy's ass to the wall before – this ain't our first rodeo with him. But the county prosecutor says that making the son pay for what he's doing will screw up every other case coming through the system as the judge takes his anger out about Richard's case on everything else. We can't get the prosecutor to prosecute any of Richard's drunk driving arrests – of which he's had *plenty* – and the birthday party incident was dropped for 'lack of evidence.'"

Cady sputtered in shock but the cop just held up his hand wearily. "There were probably a hundred people there who could've testified to what Richard did. If my other cases had *half* that amount of evidence, I could die a happy man. But us cops can't force a prosecutor to take on a case, no matter how much we wish we could. Which," he said with a quiet pride, "is why we're going to move jurisdictions. The county prosecutor is pissed at us for taking this out of his hands, but as soon as this got called in, we started working on getting everything moved to the state level. Usually the state won't take on cases like this – they have enough on their hands without taking over county cases, too – but we made it clear what's happening, and convinced the state that they needed to step in. It's obviously a conflict of interest but since none of the prior cases actually went to court, the judge could claim that he hasn't had any say in any of it. It'd been working pretty slick for him, but now..."

The cop trailed off meaningfully, and Cady grinned at him, feeling happy for the first time since the attack. *Finally*, Rat Bastard was going to get what was coming to him. Turns out, justice was a little more blind than some people wanted her to be after all. Oh, what a glorious day!

"I've already talked to Sugar and Gage," Officer Morland said with a jerk of his head towards Gage, "but your cooperation will be most important of all. Otherwise, we won't be able to connect the two attacks together, and the defense lawyers might argue that these have been nothing more than a couple of fistfights between two guys. Certainly not something to lock a man away for; otherwise, half our county would be in jail." He laughed at his own little joke and then stopped, looking Cady straight in the eye. He could see the panic building up inside of her, she could tell, and she tore her gaze away. She didn't want him to see the vulnerability. He couldn't. She didn't want him to know. No one should know.

"Cooperation?" she asked, her voice cracking

partway through with fear. "What kind?" She wetted her lips and then to give herself something to do, picked up the cup with the straw and tried to take a sip. It made a faint gurgling sound – she'd already drained the cup dry. Gage took the cup and filled it from the sink in the corner.

Without something to hold and hide behind, Cady twisted the pendant around her neck instead, sliding it back and forth along the chain. Maybe the cop just meant she'd have to give her statement and that'd be it. That was fine. She could do that. As long as—

"You have to be willing to testify in court," Officer Morland said bluntly as Gage handed the cup back to her. "Maybe Richard will take a plea deal and it won't come to that, but you have to be willing to do so, or the whole thing falls apart. The state prosecutor was very clear on that."

Her hands were shaking so hard, she was suddenly glad that the hospital had felt like she needed a sippy cup to drink from, like a small child would use. The lid kept the water from sloshing over its sides.

"Gage and Sugar both..." she said desperately, hoping that the answer would be no. She couldn't look her boyfriend in the face. He was sitting right there next to her, but the implied question was directed at the cop.

Say no, say no, say no—

"We both agreed to testify in court," Gage answered softly, squeezing her hand. "It's the only way—"

"But then he'll come after *me*," she broke in, the panic breaking and washing over its banks. "This last time, he attacked me on accident. If he'd known who I was, he wouldn't have touched me. I become a marked woman if I testify against him. Next time, he's attacking me because I *am* me." Her breath was coming in short, shallow pants now, her voice far away, belonging to someone else.

"Well, I'm going to leave you to think it over," the police officer said tactfully, rising to his feet. "For now, we have enough to go on – we're at least pointed in the right direction. I know the last 24 hours has been a lot – try to think over the attack and remember every word he said. Courts aren't kind to people who say vague statements. We will want to get this nailed down. Come down to the station tomorrow and we can do an official statement then." He nodded to Cady and Gage in turn, and then left, closing the door behind him.

Before Cady could figure out what to say in the strained silence, though, the door swung back open. An older woman with iron gray hair swept up into a bun came striding into the room. "You are awake," she said. "Good. I'm Nurse Knutsen. I helped set the break and cast your arm while you were out. Do you have any questions?"

Cady shook her head slightly in an attempt to clear the swirling thoughts all fighting for attention, but before she could marshall her thoughts into some semblance of order, the nurse continued on, clearly taking Cady's shake of the head as an answer. "Good. We'll go over your discharge instructions orally, but I will also give you a paper with them summarized on it. Are you going to be the one taking care of her once she gets home?" she asked Gage.

"No!" Cady yelped at the same time that Gage firmly said, "Yes."

The nurse looked back and forth between them, clearly unsure whose answer to go with, but Gage was faster on the draw and spoke before Cady could. "I'll be watching over her for the next few days," he said smoothly. "What's the best way to take care of her arm while it's in that cast? Can she get it wet in the shower? And will she be having physical therapy for that arm once the cast is off?"

Cady wanted ever so dearly to tell him to go jump off a cliff – this was *her* arm, not his, and she should be the one asking the questions – but just then, waves of pain began washing over her, obliterating any coherent thought. She felt a sheen of cold sweat sweep over her body as she struggled not to throw up.

It was as if her mind had forgotten about the break in her arm but now that it'd been reminded it was there, everything was now focused on the pain radiating up and down her arm.

I was just fine two minutes ago. Obviously, it can't be hurting that bad, right? This is all in my mind.

But still, when two white pills were placed in her hand and the cup of water held out by the ever efficient nurse, Cady took them gratefully. Anything to cut the pain. She'd never broken a bone in her life, and she was starting to think that it wasn't an experience she was especially keen to repeat.

Faintly, she heard the nurse talk to Gage, giving him instructions on how to care for her while also helping Cady out of her hospital gown and back into her ragged clothes. Gage tactfully looked the other direction as the nurse efficiently stripped Cady and then redressed her like a giant mannequin.

A mannequin with hobo taste in clothing, that was. Cady vowed to throw her clothes in the trash as soon as she got home. She never wanted to see these jeans or this t-shirt again.

The checkout procedure passed in a blur of pain and then the fogginess of drugs invaded and Cady found herself just nodding at people no matter what they asked or said, hoping that they'd take the hint and just let her go home. Zara wished her luck on the way out the front door, and Cady awkwardly waved at her with her left hand when she realized that her right hurt too much to lift up in the air.

This, she decided with an inward groan, was going to be a massive pain in the ass. How long was she going to have this thing on her? She realized that they'd probably told her while she was doing her best wobbly head doll imitation, her head bobbing in time with the flow of their words, but she'd had no comprehension of what was being said.

She'd just have to ask Gage. Later. When her brain wasn't so…mushy.

Mush. Muuuussshhh. Mushy.

She rolled the word around in her head, suddenly weirded out by it. Was that a real word? Or had she just made it up?

"It's a real word," Gage said in her ear as he scooped her up in his arms and carried her to his front door.

She wanted to ask him how he knew what she was thinking when her brain finally caught up to the situation and she realized that they were at *his* house. She couldn't even remember getting into his truck, let alone the drive over here.

"This is *your* house," she said weakly, pushing against his chest with her free left hand, her right trapped between her and his muscular chest.

"It is, and a good thing, too. Otherwise, the last couple of years would've been pretty awkward," Gage said lightly. "Turns out, people don't want you to live in places that aren't yours."

They were going up the stairs to the second floor, Cream Puffs dancing around Gage's feet, barking with excitement, her toenails clicking on the hardwood floors. Cady couldn't see her from her vantage point in Gage's arms, but she could practically feel the intense pleasure rolling off the dog in waves at having her there.

"But I was shupposed to go home," she said, her mouth not forming words right. "Supposed to," she said again, forcing her mouth to cooperate.

"We'll discuss this when you wake up," Gage said

firmly, pulling her shoes and belt off and sliding her under the covers. "For now, you need to keep these pillows from floating away. They were looking a little light-footed just a minute or two ago."

Cady wanted to argue but the world was already sliding into darkness around her and she knew no more.

CHAPTER 26

GAGE

*G*AGE SHIFTED IN HIS CHAIR, putting one foot up on the edge of the bed as he turned the page of Diane Capri's thriller novel. He loved this take on the Lee Child series—

Cady groaned and moved around a little in bed, and Gage snapped the book shut, jerking forward, both stockinged feet landing hard on the oak floors.

"Water," Cady murmured, and Gage hurried to grab her water bottle from the nightstand, holding it up against her lips as she sucked down the liquid.

"How are you feeling?" he asked her, stroking some stray strands of hair off her face. Her hair was curling and springing every which way; he knew that she would think she looked horrible if she saw herself in the mirror, but he'd never seen a prettier sight in all his life.

He'd almost lost her. If it wasn't for a forgotten cell phone, what would've happened?

He felt sick at the thought.

They *had* to put that man away. Cady had to be willing to testify against him. Gage didn't care how much it terrified her – letting Dickwad roam free was *not* an option.

"Better now," she said, finally pulling her mouth off the built-in straw of the water bottle. Her hand moved up to her neck and she patted her necklace, a habitual checking to make sure that it was still there.

"I've been meaning to ask you," he said casually, wanting to keep away from the fraught topic of testifying for a moment. "Where did you get that necklace from? I've noticed you only take it off in the shower." She didn't take it off anywhere else – not to sleep, or go out hiking, or even while having sex. It stayed around her neck no matter what.

"Mom and Dad." For the first time, her eyes fluttered open and she smiled sadly at him. "Eighteenth birthday present. I love emeralds – green and full of life, you know? Diamonds are so colorless and boring, and rubies are like blood…" She shivered a little.

Creamsicle came bounding into the room just then, having heard the voices and realizing Cady was awake. The dog propelled herself up onto the bed, the height of it no match against sheer willpower, despite her short, stubby legs. Nothing would hold her back from giving Cady the face bath she so obviously deserved.

"Hi, goofball," she said, laughing between strokes

of the pink tongue. "I've missed you, and I can see you missed me, too. Hey, just a second." She looked at Gage with panic in her eyes. "Where's Skittles? She's probably freaking out—"

"Rochelle is taking care of her," Gage broke in, before she could wind herself up into a true frenzy. "She lost her cat just a month or so before you moved to Sawyer, and I think she's been missing the companionship. I didn't want to bring her over here; I didn't want her and Puffers fighting and tearing around underfoot with you in a cast."

"Thank you," Cady said gratefully.

Cream Puffs, obviously feeling neglected, began nudging her side, hoping for more pettings. Cady lifted her right arm to pet her and then dropped it back down to the mattress with a groan. "This," she said through gritted teeth, "is really going to suck." She switched to her left arm and scratched Creamsy behind the ears, and then looked at Gage, her eyes haunted. "How am I supposed to make smoothies and run a cash register when I only have one arm? And it's my *right* arm. If it'd at least been my left…"

Gage picked up her right hand and squeezed it softly.

"You really can't," he said bluntly. It was best if she just faced the truth now. "Your whole arm is in a fixed cast from shoulder to wrist. There's no way you can work. I already asked Sugar to put a sign up on the front door of the Smoothie Queen, and to tell anyone who asked what was going on. Dickwad isn't exactly a popular man around town – no one can stand him, to be honest. Driving drunk everywhere you go, especially after your own sister and niece died in a drunk driving accident…" He shook his head.

He could almost see the gears whirring as Cady tried to decide which topic to tackle first. Finally, "His sister and niece died in a drunk driving accident? I didn't know that!"

"I keep forgetting that you don't know all of the dirty secrets of this town," Gage said with a small chuckle, holding the water bottle back up to her lips, encouraging her to drink more. "It's kind of refreshing, honestly."

"I want you to tell me that story – or I'll get it from Sugar – but right now, we need to back this train up to the station. What do you mean, I'm not going to reopen the Smoothie Queen? I can't just abandon my business a week after opening it! Hold on, what's today?"

"Wednesday. Tomorrow is Thanksgiving. Everyone will be busy with preparations for Turkey Day – I promise you, business would be slow today anyway. You were already planning on being closed tomorrow, of course, and then it's the start of the biggest shopping weekend of the year, which means everybody and their dog will be in Boise, scouting for the good deals, and *not* here in Sawyer, buying health food. That means you have until *at least* Monday before anyone will even think to wonder where you're at. We can see how this weekend goes; play it by ear."

He helped her sit up in bed, stuffing the pillows behind her back, fishing out two pain pills and handing them over along with the water bottle. Her groans of pain just from trying to sit up in bed…

He had a feeling that by Monday morning, it wouldn't be so hard to convince Cady to stay in bed after all.

"Tomorrow is Thanksgiving?" she moaned, looking frazzled. "I can't go eat dinner with your family like this. I can't eat with my left hand – at least, I've never tried. I'll probably miss my mouth half the time."

"Don't worry. I've already told Mom what's going on; I'll run over and pick up some plates loaded down with turkey and all the trimmings and bring them back here. I promise to point and laugh every time you spill gravy down the front of your shirt, and I'm sure Cream Puffs here will help you by licking it all off."

She glowered at him. "I've decided to upgrade to balloons and flowers on Emma's next birthday. I don't think I need to wait another ten years after all."

Gage burst out laughing. God, it was good to laugh again. After the scare two nights ago, laughter was a precious thing.

"I love you," he said, still chuckling and wiping at the corners of his eyes. "I—"

They both froze. His casual admission hadn't been on purpose but now that the words were finally out, he refused to take them back. Almost losing her…

Life was too short. He had to tell her how he felt and if it freaked her out, too damn bad. It was the truth.

"I love you too," she whispered, her eyes glistening. She dashed the tears away with the back of her left hand. "I love you so damn much."

"I love you," he whispered, and this time it was sincere, not a flippant remark, his heart feeling a thousand times happier than just minutes before. "Watching Dickwad…" He shook the memory away, and then leaned forward to softly kiss her on the lips. She was still fragile, but he couldn't hold the kiss inside any longer.

It didn't take long for Cream Puffs to start nudging her nose underneath his arm, whining and reminding them that she was there too.

"Do you love us too?" Cady asked teasingly as she and Gage broke apart and she began scratching the dog behind the ears. Her tail thumped on the bed as her eyes closed in bliss, happy to be loved on. "I think that's a yes…"

Just then, her stomach rumbled, and Gage grinned at her. "You don't eat much, but you sure do eat often," he told her. "C'mon, let's go downstairs and I'll make you some chicken noodle soup. My grandmother's recipe. Your broken arm will be healed by tomorrow."

He scooped her up in his arms as Cream Puffs jumped off the bed and pranced around their feet, happily barking as Cady laughed. "I broke my arm, not my leg," she protested as he headed for the bedroom door.

She broke off then, yawning hard, looking exhausted. "I hate those pain pills," she grumbled. "They keep putting me to sleep. No more of them. Only over-the-counter stuff from now on."

As long as she wasn't in pain, Gage didn't care what she took. He just wanted her to be okay. Nothing else mattered.

He settled her down onto the leather couch and turned on a movie, then hurried into the kitchen to make soup. By the time he was done, though, she was fast asleep, curled up on the couch with Creamsy tucked in beside her. They were adorable together, even with the thick cast of her arm in the middle of it all.

At least she's okay – that's what matters…

He went upstairs to grab Capri's book. It looked like he had another couple of hours of Cady-watching duty, just making sure she was all right. After what she'd been through…

He eased himself onto the couch, careful not to wake her, and then opened up his book, flipping back to where he'd left off.

He would make sure that she was never hurt again.

CHAPTER 27

CADY

"*H*ELLO?" Her former roommate sounded distracted, like her mind was somewhere else; the indistinct chattering in the background making it hard to hear Hannah's naturally quiet voice.

"Hey, Hannah," Cady said, stifling the quaver in her voice. She would not cry; she would not cry; she would not cry. "It's Cady. How are things going for you?"

"Cady!" Hannah half yelled in her ear over a round of high-pitched squeals of joy and laughter in the background. "Damn, I'm so happy to hear from you." The quiet voice was gone, replaced by one filled with excitement. "I keep thinking that I need to call you and set up a lunch date or something but this school year has just been nuts and *how* is it that we can be living in the same tiny town and yet never see each other?! It seems like we should've at least run into each other down at the Stop 'N Go or Mr. Petrol's or something. Hold on, let me get to a better place to talk."

Cady heard a shuffle, a muffled whisper, a thunk, and then quiet. "Ah, that's better," Hannah sighed in satisfaction. "Brooklyn has a bunch of friends over today and...well, little girls. Drama, drama, drama. I just put Elijah in charge of making sure no one kills anyone else, or even worse, says something mean to someone else." She chuckled dryly. "I wished him luck with that one," she said sarcastically. "If I don't hear hysterics in the next five minutes, I'll count myself lucky. *Any*way! Enough about me. How are things going for you?"

As soon as the words were out of Hannah's mouth, Cady could sense the regret Hannah was feeling for having said them. Which meant that somehow, Hannah had heard about the attack.

'Somehow'? C'mon, Cady. This is Sawyer. You know how this works.

But before she could assemble an answer that didn't include tears, Hannah continued. "Aaron was telling us about the attack and having to pull some strings to get the case moved to the state level. It's about darn time if you ask me. That piece of crap has been getting away with attacking women for far too long—"

"Aaron?" Cady interrupted, instinctively trying to rub her forehead with her right hand, biting back the pain that came from trying to move her right arm, and rubbing her forehead awkwardly with her left hand instead. Somehow, it wasn't nearly as helpful to do this move when forced to do it with the wrong hand. "Who's Aaron?"

"Aaron Morland?" Hannah said tentatively, almost as a question, not an answer. "Elijah's older brother?"

"Hold on, your fiancé's brother is Officer Morland?" Cady asked, stunned. This was taking the whole everyone-knows-your-name, small-town-bullshit a little too far.

"Oh. Yeah. I thought you knew that."

"I saw Elijah's last name on the wedding invitation, but it didn't occur to me…" Cady broke off with a laugh. "Is there *anyone* in this town who isn't related to someone else?"

"You!" Hannah said with a teasing laugh. "You're an outsider. I heard that guys have been flipping Gage shit because he snapped up the only single, not-related-to-anyone woman in town, leaving the rest of them with no one to date besides their second cousin, once removed."

"The flattery of it all," Cady grumbled underneath her breath, but she chuckled anyway. It was a small miracle that anyone found someone to marry in Sawyer, honestly. "Hey, speaking of weddings, how much longer until you get married?"

"Two weeks and two days. And I'm totally not counting, in case you're wondering," Hannah added dryly.

"Of course not!" Cady said, laughing. "I'm sorry I haven't been over to help you with the planning – the opening of the smoothie shop—"

"Don't apologize," Hannah hurried to say. "I haven't been over to help you with the fixing up of the Smoothie Queen either. And anyway, I have a close friend in town – Carla, she owns the flower shop, Happy Petals – and I think she's died and gone to heaven. Helping me plan my wedding has been the highlight of her life. I think she should've become a wedding planner, not a florist, but she's good at them both, soo…" She chuckled lightly and then things got quiet between them. Hannah knew that this wasn't a just-calling-to-catch-up sort of call, and was patiently waiting for Cady to spit out the problem.

"Well, I called because," deep breath, "I wanted to talk to you about…you know, what happened. I need to…" And then it came out in a rush. "I can't talk to Gage about it because he's a guy, and I can't talk to Sugar about it because he attacked me because of her. Of course she wants me to say yes. Emma is in Denver but she's bold and brave and nothing scares her so she'd tell me to stop—" Cady felt the tears closing off her throat, the worry and panic and fear and guilt all battling for supremacy. She wanted to be brave like everyone said she was, but they weren't painting a bull's eye on their backs. It was easy for *them* to say words of platitude.

Be strong. Be brave. Take this guy down. Testify against him in open court.

And have him hating her, hunting her for the rest of her life?

"I'm going to come pick you up," Hannah said with an air of authority that Cady still had a hard time associating with her former roommate. She used to be so timid and shy, not wanting to give offense. But now… "It's Black Friday so I actually have the day off, hence me being here in the house with seven hundred prepubescent girls. I'll leave Elijah in charge of them and we can go to Franklin for lunch. There's that great new Mexican restaurant over there. We'll eat our way through buckets of chips and salsa, and you can tell me everything. Are you at Gage's house?"

"Yes. Only because he's taking care of me because of my arm." She didn't know why she felt like she had to justify being at her boyfriend's house. She had every right to be there. But still, it felt weird. She'd never lived with a boyfriend before.

Just one more new event in her life.

"Perfect," Hannah said, tactfully choosing to ignore the defensiveness in Cady's voice. "I'll tell Elijah he's in charge of the girls, which is only fair – I have to put up with giggling, crying, laughing, hysterical preteens all day long – and then I'll be over. See you soon."

Cady tossed her phone to the side and then pulled off her ratty robe – its ease of donning and disrobing had made it a favorite of hers over the past few days – and struggled first to fit into a t-shirt, giving up after being unable to get it past her cast, and then turning her attentions to an overly large button-up shirt. She'd never worn it before; she'd bought it several sizes too big on accident and had been too lazy to return it to the store, but was finding now that its tent size was plenty useful.

It was after one of her drug-induced naps that she'd woken up to find that Gage had sent Sugar to her apartment and together with Cady's landlord, they'd packed up a bunch of clothes and toiletries to bring back to Gage's house. It had all been snuggly ensconced at Gage's house in the guest bedroom while she'd been sleeping off the drugs and the trauma.

She'd tried to muster a small amount of anger over his high-handedness, moving her like that without her permission, but had failed completely. It was lovely to have someone take over the reins for once. It was lovely to rely on someone else.

How did I survive before I moved to a small town, where everyone helps you just because they care about you?

If she'd lived in Sawyer when her parents had died in that dreadful plane crash, she never would've retreated into her own world for months at a time. It was the size of Boise – the impersonality of such a big city – that had allowed her to disappear into its depths.

It was true that it was a little creepy that the city dispatcher had known who she was even though she'd never met him, but the upsides of small town living? They made it worth it.

Except Rat Bastard will always know how to find me in a town like this. If I stand up on that witness stand and I send him away for ten years, then what? He gets out and can find me within hours. I can't hide in a town like Sawyer.

She heard the doorbell ring then, causing Cream Puffs to start barking wildly, and slipped on her flip-flops. It was too cold to be wearing sandals but they were also the only footwear she had that didn't require tying laces and for that reason alone, they won out.

"Hi, Hannah," she heard Gage's voice drift up the stairs as she headed for them. "How's it going? Here to see Cady?"

"We're going to go out to lunch," Cady called out from the top of the stairs as she hurried down them. She saw Hannah was petting Cream Puffs who was flat on her back, pink tongue lolling out, tail swishing across the floor, joy radiating out of the pup. Her former roommate's gorgeous red hair was in a braid, falling over her shoulder, and the thick glasses she'd worn for years were gone.

She was beautiful. Older than she had been back when they were at BSU together, of course, but her change in personality had apparently extended to clothing and hair, too.

This Elijah guy sure has been good for her.

Gage looked up at Cady, grinning at her as she came down the stairs – leering at her, really. Despite the fact that Cady was wearing a shirt better suited for use as a tent and her hair was in a crooked ponytail –

doing her hair was almost impossible with only one hand – he somehow found her beautiful.

If he wasn't wearing glasses at that very moment, she would've told him to go get some. His vision was *clearly* impaired.

"You're driving?" he asked Hannah. "One-Arm Cady over here isn't safe behind the wheel."

"One-Arm Cady?!" Cady yelped over Hannah's laughter. "You're supposed to be coming up with sweet endearments. Honey, darlin', sweetie—"

"—Cupcake, Love Muffin, Sugar Pie," Gage broke in.

"Why is it that all of your nicknames have something to do with food?" she demanded when she got to the foot of the stairs. "You make it sound like you're going to eat me for dessert."

"Oh, I'll eat you," Gage whispered in her ear, carefully gathering her up against his broad chest, making sure not to jostle her right arm. "There are parts of you that I'd love to eat right up." He began nibbling on her ear, and Cady, a brilliant red flushing her face and neck, pulled away.

Hannah snorted with poorly contained laughter, and Cady was just sure she'd heard every word Gage had just said. She could feel the heat of the flush reach her toes.

"Leaving now," she told him pertly, swinging her purse over her shoulder. "Since you don't have me to mother over, you could go down to the bakery. See what's happening there."

Gage nodded enthusiastically. "I was just thinking the same thing. See you tonight." He gave her a thorough kiss and then smacked her on the ass as she walked through the front door, leaving a sad Cream Puffs and a laughing Gage behind.

"Sooooo…" Hannah said as they piled into her car, Cady hurrying through the short snow drifts, teeth chattering from the cold. Thankfully it wasn't the heart of winter yet; Cady would have to figure out how to put boots on one handed soon, though. "Things seem to be going well between you and Gage."

Cady shook her head, even as she laughed. "It took us a while to get past the just-friends stage, and even when we got to the dating stage, it took us a while to get to the sleeping together stage. I took my time learning to trust him. Once we started sleeping together, though…" She shook her head again and laughed. "Let's just say that I think Gage's self-control, waiting for me to be ready, is all the more impressive now that I know how horny the man is. He's a damn smart guy, but I think he uses 98.2% of his brain power up by thinking about sex."

She tried to insinuate that she wasn't exactly the same way, but was pretty sure she hadn't fooled Hannah, at least not if the smirk on her friend's face was anything to judge by. It was just so hard to think about anything *but* sex when Gage was around. Those mountains and valleys of muscles, his happy trail, his square jaw…

He was sex on a stick. Even with her arm in a cast, they'd made it work. What was a little broken bone when it came to sex with a Greek god?

"I have a couple of friends here in Sawyer – Michelle and Carla – and I swear they spent years of their lives drooling over Gage," Hannah confided. "We used to have our weekly Early Spinster's Club meeting at the bakery just so they could drool over him. It's a good thing you're my friend. When they first heard an out-of-towner had snagged his attention…" She shook her head in mock disapproval. "Hearts were broken all over Sawyer at the news, I can tell you that. Women have been throwing themselves at him for years and I don't think he's ever noticed any of 'em. Too focused on the bakery and making a go of it, not to mention that everyone thought he and Sugar were an item for a long time."

"Sugar and Gage?" Cady asked, shocked. She'd seen Sugar with Jaxson; had seen how in love they were. The idea of her being in love with Gage had somehow never even crossed her mind. They ribbed each other endlessly; he treated her exactly like he treated Emma.

Exactly like he would treat a sister.

"Both single, both cute, both working at the bakery…it was a rumor that was bound to happen." Hannah shrugged. "I never thought there was anything between them, but you know how small towns are."

The discussion drifted then, first to how her class

was doing this school year, and then to how Elijah was doing going back to school himself to become an electrician. "He kept telling me he's too stupid to learn, but he's been doing great," Hannah gushed, the stars in her eyes so bright, astronauts in space were probably wondering what the twinkling lights were below them. "He has to work hard, but that's okay. It shouldn't be easy to become an electrician. You want as few imbeciles running around as possible. Have the locals forgiven you for taking out the power in town by hiring Watson, by the way?"

Cady laughed. It was easy to laugh now at the whole thing. It seemed so long ago. "Memories are long, but I'm hearing about it less and less as time goes by. Thank God."

They pulled into the parking lot of a small Mexican joint. The smells wafting out into the cold air were mouth-watering. Hannah caught the look on Cady's face and laughed. "Yes, it is as good as it smells," she said. "Let's go. I hear the chips and salsa calling my name from here."

They were seated and after a quick scan of the menu, they ordered, the pretty, quiet Hispanic woman scurrying off to the kitchen with their order in hand. Hannah turned to Cady and an expectant hush fell over them. Cady knew that it was time. Thankfully, they were in a booth in the farthest corner from the front door and the kitchen, allowing her to keep her voice low. Even still, Hannah had to lean forward to hear her.

"What I never told you," Cady said, sucking in a steadying breath and then letting it out slowly, trying to calm her racing heart, "is that I was attacked while working at the physical therapist's office." Hannah sucked in a quick breath but otherwise did nothing, just watching Cady intently, listening to her story. "The BSU football player had been a patient of mine. Came at me from behind during his last appointment with me. I didn't…I never went back to work there again. I tried, but I just couldn't."

"Why didn't you tell me?" Hannah asked quietly, reaching across the table and squeezing Cady's hand. "I wouldn't have judged you."

"I didn't tell many people," Cady said with a small shrug. "My parents, the cops, the lawyer…"

Hannah had graduated and headed back to Sawyer while Cady was still attending BSU, so they hadn't been roommates when the attack had happened. Cady had never quite figured out how to call Hannah and say, "Hey, having a great day? Me too! Except, I almost got raped, so you know, that happened."

Somehow, she'd managed to skip that conversation.

"Anyway, BSU offered me a settlement in return for never speaking publicly about it. I can't tell you his name or anything about him – just that he's now playing in the NFL back east. Bastard. At least he isn't still in Idaho."

The waitress returned just then with steaming

plates of food, warning them that the dishes were hot as she put them down on the table. They waited until she left, and then Cady continued, pushing her food around with her fork, not eating much. No matter how good it smelled, she found she wasn't hungry.

"Our family's lawyer told us that we could probably get a larger settlement if we took him to court, especially because there had been other women and BSU had helped cover it all up. He was their star; he was going places. They wanted to be able to claim producing a top pick for the NFL draft. Allegations of rape might keep that from happening. Turns out, people don't like rape and violence." She snorted as she stirred her lemonade with her straw, knowing she should be eating but…

She forced herself to take a small sip of the tart liquid.

"But if we took the case to court, my name would get dragged through the mud. Maybe I had been leading him on. Maybe I really deserved this. You know how people can be." She flapped her hand in the air, wishing she could just as easily brush away all of the assholes of the world who'd dare defend a rapist. "Plus, the guy was huge. If I did a quiet settlement, he'd probably let me move on with my life. If I took it to court and 'ruined' his life like it deserved to be ruined, then maybe he'd come after me. Maybe he'd do his best to make my life miserable. Track me down. It was easier to just let him walk away."

Damn tears were sliding down her face now as she

looked at her friend across the table, wavy and indistinct through the liquid.

"I was a coward. I hated myself for that. I should've made him pay. And now, it's my chance to rectify that – to not be a coward this time – and all I want to do is be a coward again. I haven't grown all that much as a human being after all. Officer Morland…I mean, Aaron – that is *so weird* that he's Elijah's older brother! – says that the state prosecutor in Boise told him that it all hinges on me. If I don't testify against him in court, a good lawyer can make the argument that Gage and Rat Bastard just got into a couple of fistfights. Certainly nothing to lock the guy up over."

"'Rat Bastard'?" Hannah broke in.

"Richard Schmidt. But that's such a normal name. I think Rat Bastard is a much better name – much more applicable. You might want to be friends with a guy named Richard Schmidt, but no one would want to be friends with Rat Bastard."

Hannah threw back her head and laughed so loud, some of the other patrons in the restaurant turned to look at them, curious what was so funny. It was such a free and jubilant move, so unlike the quiet, cautious Hannah of yesteryear.

She's changed so much, and it's all been for the better. But not me – I'm still stuck in the past, wanting to hide from the jackasses of the world. Hannah would never let a rapist walk because she was too scared to take the stand.

"It was the summer between my junior and senior

year at college," Hannah said quietly after a moment's pause, both of them lost in thought. Cady looked at Hannah curiously, wondering where this was going. "You spent it with your parents, helping them remodel the downstair's bathroom. Remember that? I spent mine here in Sawyer. It was the Fourth of July and I was going to watch the fireworks with Dad. This was back when he was still...you know. With it. Anyway, I was walking up towards City Park as night was falling – the fireworks were going to be starting soon. I knew I needed to hurry. I went past the row of poplars at the edge of the park, and then, he was grabbing me. Pulling me into the cover of the trees. He'd clapped his hand over my mouth to keep me from screaming, and then..."

She trailed off, staring into the distance, not meeting Cady's eyes. "He told me that I wanted it," she whispered, "because I didn't fight him. I don't know why I didn't. I just lay there and let him...Then he told me that I couldn't tell the police. He'd tell them that I'd spent months trying to seduce him, and as a 15-year-old boy, he'd fallen under the spell of my charms and so of course he couldn't be blamed for it. For having sex with me."

"Fifteen?" Cady asked in a quiet voice, horrified. To think of Hannah being raped by a fifteen year old when she was in her early twenties...

It added a whole new level to the nastiness of the situation.

"Said I'd ruin my teaching career before it even

started." She sucked in a breath and then looked straight at Cady. "He was the son of the town judge, after all, so the police would believe him over me."

"Town judge…" Cady just stared at Hannah, the world zooming in and out of focus as she tried to put this information into some sort of order that made sense. "Rat Bastard *raped* you?"

Hannah looked up, one corner of her mouth quirking for just a moment at the nickname, and then it was gone. "When I came back to school that fall, you kept asking me what was wrong. I couldn't bear to tell you the truth. You aren't the only one who's been keeping secrets." She laughed sadly. "That's when I started wearing my hair back in a bun and thick glasses and oversized clothes. I didn't want a man to look at me again. Not any man, for any reason. It took Elijah a good long while to work his way through those defenses.

"But Cady – I didn't stand up to Richard. Didn't tell a soul. Didn't stop him. I couldn't give up my career. It was all I wanted to do in my life. I *couldn't* give up teaching. So I said nothing. Then he and Sugar were trapped into marriage when those photos were taken, and Sugar had to live with that man for years, until she was finally able to escape him. He won't let her go, though, and his father will protect him from everything, so he'll continue to dog her steps until someone gets hurt. Or killed. A restraining order – what good does that do? It doesn't matter to a man like Richard Schmidt."

She drew in a deep breath, trying to stem the flow of tears cascading down her cheeks, and failing spectacularly. "I'm not telling you that you have to testify against him in court. Only you can make that decision. I just wanted you to know that more than possibly any other person on the planet, I understand. I know how hard this decision is. I won't tell you what to do; I'll support you no matter what your choice is. I'm on *your* side, no matter what side that is."

They reached across the table at the same moment, their hands drawn together almost like magnets, clinging together, each lost in their own pain caused by the bastards on the planet who thought that a woman was nothing more than a piece of meat to be used and discarded at will.

"Has he ever bothered you again?" Cady asked in the quiet that'd fallen between them. "You moved back here. He lives here. Surely you've seen him again."

"He doesn't seem to be obsessed with me like he is with Sugar, and we don't tend to run in the same circles," Hannah said with a shrug of her thin shoulders. "He's never managed to father a child, thank God, so I don't have his kid in my class, and I don't hang out in bars and in crack houses, shooting whatever I can find between my toes."

"He does drugs, too?" Cady asked, somehow stunned by this news. She'd only ever heard what a drunk he was. How had she missed drug use?

"I've heard a few rumors. His drug of choice is

alcohol, but he isn't beyond taking anything he can get his hands on. Aaron's told me about a few baggies they've found."

"Right. I keep forgetting that Officer Morland is going to be your new brother-in-law." Cady shook her head in surprise. "Small towns, small towns…"

They sat still for a while, both just lost in their own thoughts, in how one man had affected both of their lives, and who knew how many other lives.

Finally, Hannah paid for their meal above the protestations of Cady, and then they hurried back out into the frigid air. "We should go to I Don't Know," Cady said impulsively, not ready to go back to Sawyer and decisions and guilt just yet. "I've heard they make delicious Mexican hot chocolate."

"Brilliant," Hannah agreed. "I've only been there a few times, but I've heard the same thing." She started the engine and carefully backed out onto the street, her thick red hair shining in the dull, wintry sunlight.

"Thanks for listening," Hannah said suddenly, apropos of nothing at all. "I've only told a handful of people. It's not easy. I don't know how it is that our society makes it out so that it's a *woman's* fault that she's been attacked. And I don't know how to change it."

"I can change it," Cady said impulsively. "Well," she gulped, backtracking, "at least my own tiny corner of the world."

The words came spilling out of her as she felt a

rush of pride in what she was saying. It was the right choice – she was sure of it.

"I'm going to change Sawyer by standing up to a man who has been terrorizing women for over a decade now. It's stupid – I didn't want to be on his radar. I thought that if I didn't testify, he wouldn't notice me or try to hurt me. But I am on his radar now, no matter what. Maybe I got there by accident, but that doesn't really matter. Whether it's a case of mistaken identity or not, I'm still there. I can't let my fear of him ruin my life. I already spent so much of my life hiding in bed – after the football player, and then after my parents died. I won't let it happen again."

Hannah pulled into the parking lot of the quaint I Don't Know café and turned off the engine, pulling off her seat belt and leaning across to give Cady a huge hug. "I hope your parents are watching right now," she said, her warm breath skimming across the top of Cady's head. "They'd be so damn proud of you. I know that my dad would be, if he could…you know. Understand what's going on around him."

Hannah's father suffered from dementia and was living in the retirement home, slipping away from the world a little farther every day. Cady and Hannah headed into the café, hurrying towards the warmth promised inside, as Cady asked, "How is he doing?"

Hannah shook her head and then sent Cady an overbright smile. "Not well. He keeps yelling at the nurses, telling them to stop hiding his wife from him.

There's no point in telling him that Mom died years ago. He won't remember five minutes after you've told him, and during those five minutes, he's so heartbroken..." Hannah pulled the door open, ushering Cady inside, the doorbell jingling overhead. "It isn't kind. So they just keep telling him that Mom's gone to the bathroom."

Cady gratefully soaked in the warmth of the café as she listened to Hannah talk, thinking about what Hannah *wasn't* saying. Did her dad still recognize her? Or had his memory of her faded too? And what did Brooklyn think of it all?

From what Cady understood, Elijah's parents weren't supportive of their upcoming marriage, so she doubted Brooklyn had much interaction with them.

Meanwhile, Hannah's mother was gone; her dad was gone in all but body; and then there was Brooklyn's biological mother who was currently behind bars, serving five to ten years for almost killing Brooklyn one night by driving back from Boise drunk as a skunk, Brooklyn in the backseat.

Who did Brooklyn have to cling to? Cady's heart ached for the little girl. She at least had Elijah and Hannah behind her 110%.

After Hannah ordered and they got their to-go cups, they headed back out to the car. Cady had been willing to stay at the café and drink their cocoa there, but she could sense that Hannah hadn't wanted to dawdle. She was ready to go back home; back to her house full of screaming preteen girls because she'd already started missing Brooklyn and Elijah.

Hannah had a family now. She was no longer the single girl, able to simply hang out with Cady because she had no other pressures on her time.

Cady knew that this was what Gage wanted. He hadn't asked her – he wouldn't push her. He was giving her the space to learn who she was, just like she'd told him she needed. But in the long run, this was what he wanted.

They just had to make it through the trial, and then…she could figure out everything else.

One step at a time.

CHAPTER 28

CADY

APRIL, 2020

She was going to throw up. She should've asked the state prosecutor beforehand what the judge did when a witness threw up. Did they hold 'em in contempt of court? Would she be thrown out of the courtroom? Would Rat Bastard roam the streets free because she couldn't keep it down?

These suddenly seemed like Very Important Questions, and *how* had it not occurred to her to ask the prosecutor before now? It was so obvious that she should have.

She'd just kept believing that it wouldn't actually go to trial. Surely, with all of the evidence and eyewitnesses, Rat Bastard couldn't think he'd get a not-guilty verdict.

But he'd clung stubbornly to his chance in court, refusing the deal the state prosecutor had offered.

Perhaps he thought that with his father being a judge, they'd call the case to order, realize who he was and their tragic mistake in prosecuting him, and let him go.

It was the only reasoning Cady could come up with. Blind, stupid cockiness born of a lifetime of never having had to suffer the consequences of his actions.

"The state would like to call its next witness, Cady Walcott, to the stand."

Every eye in the courtroom swiveled to her. Staring at her. Drilling into her, and she realized that she'd been wrong.

So very, very wrong.

She wasn't going to throw up.

She was going to pass out.

Stupid her.

Gage squeezed her hand, his bulk beside her, comforting her, protecting her from Rat Bastard. No one would touch her with him around. Gage had proven that the night of the attack.

Except they wouldn't let him go up onto the stand with her. She'd asked. The prosecutor had given her a look that plainly said that he'd *thought* he'd heard it all but now he really had heard it all, and no, a 34-year-old woman could *not* take her boyfriend with her up to the stand.

Gage squeezed her hand again, a little more urgently this time, and Cady realized that the murmurs were breaking out in the courtroom, everyone wondering if she was actually going to move sometime this century.

A fission of fear ran up her spine but she forced herself to her feet, then scooted down the bench and out into the end aisle. Walking up to the front of the courtroom, it was like she was in a long tunnel, except even with the slow speed of her feet, the front still came all too quickly. The bailiff swore her in, and then she climbed the steps to the witness stand, legs shaking, knees knocking, no color in her face, and slid gratefully into the wooden chair. At least now she wasn't expected to bear her own weight any longer.

"Ms. Walcott, I understand that you originally met Richard Schmidt last April, at Emma Dyer and Sugar Anderson's dual birthday party. Is that correct?"

She nodded numbly.

"We need you to give your answers verbally," the prosecutor prodded.

Shit. He'd told her that beforehand. She'd told him that would be no problem.

But that had been years ago. Maybe centuries. Surely no one could expect her to remember that far back.

"Yes," she said, her voice cracking.

She found Gage's face in the audience and clung to it, like a person adrift at sea clinging to a life raft. His supermodel good looks; his bodybuilder physique; but much more important than that, his thoughtfulness. His soul. The goodness inside of him.

It was hard to remember all those months ago when she'd wanted Gage fired just for offering cream puffs to her. That was a different Cady. A Cady who was scared of her own shadow.

She straightened her back. That wasn't her anymore.

I'm doing this for all of the women that you've abused, Richard Schmidt. All of the pain that you've caused.

She turned her eyes back to the prosecutor.

"At this party, did you talk to Mr. Schmidt at all?" the prosecutor asked.

"No."

"Were you introduced?"

"No."

"How do you know that it was Mr. Schmidt that also attended that party, then?"

"The people around me. The other guests. They were saying his name. Also, I talked with Emma afterwards, and she told me who it was."

"Why were you there?"

"I was a guest of Gage Dyer, Emma's brother. He introduced me to Emma and Sugar at the party."

"And why was Richard Schmidt there?"

Finally. We're getting to the heart of the matter.

"Because he got drunk and decided that crashing the party with a loaded gun would be a lot of fun," she said sarcastically.

A ripple of laughter spread through the courtroom at the answer.

Cady clung to Gage's face, though. Nothing else

mattered. It was like she was telling him a story. Talking to just him.

"Did he threaten you at all with the gun?" the prosecutor went on, ignoring the laughter.

"No. He didn't see me or interact with me in any way at that party. All he cared about was Sugar. He was angry with her for having Jaxson's baby. He thought it should've been his."

"Objection, Your Honor!" the defense attorney cried, shooting to his feet. "That's speculation. Ms. Walcott could not possibly know what my client was thinking."

"He was yelling what he was thinking at the top of his lungs," Cady retorted, somehow forgetting to be scared for just a moment.

"If your client didn't want anyone to know what he was thinking, perhaps he shouldn't have shouted the thoughts out for the whole world to hear," the judge said mildly. "You may continue," he said to the prosecutor.

"How long had you lived in Sawyer by this point?" he asked her.

"Only three weeks or so."

"So you were attending a party for two ladies who you'd never met in a town you'd just moved to, and although you witnessed and heard Mr. Schmidt making threats, you had no interaction with him yourself."

"That is correct."

"With all of that in mind, why is it, do you think,

that Mr. Schmidt attacked you during the evening of the 25th of November?"

"Objection, Your Honor!" the defense attorney yelled again, jumping to his feet. "He is asking the witness to speculate on the motives of my client."

"Let me rephrase," the prosecutor said smoothly, before the judge could say anything. "Ms. Walcott, let's leave motives aside for a moment and just focus on what happened. What time did you leave work that evening?"

"Somewhere between 6 and 7 p.m., I would guess. It was getting dark. I remember thinking that I'd been staying late at work for too many nights, because I didn't need the flashlight app on my phone to lock the back door."

"And then what happened?"

"Richard—" she'd been warned not to call him Rat Bastard in court, "—attacked me from behind. One arm around my waist, and one around my face. It took me a minute to understand what he was saying and what was going on. He called me a bitch and a whore." There were gasps in the courtroom, but Cady plunged on, growing braver by the moment. Well, only so brave, really – her eyes were staying glued on Gage's face. She could see Rat Bastard out of the corner of her eye, but she wouldn't look at him. She might break down and—

"He asked me if I was staying late, with *him*." She emphasized the word just like he had that night. "I didn't know who he was talking about – what him? I don't have any employees, male or female. I didn't know at that point that he thought I was Sugar Anderson."

"Objection, Your Hon—"

"Shut up!" the judge roared. The courtroom fell deadly silent. "The witness is free to recount her story the way it happened to her. Ms. Walcott, please continue." The defense lawyer sank into his seat in defeat.

"Uhhh…" she stammered, every coherent thought completely gone. Her story. What had she been saying?

"You'd mentioned that Mr. Schmidt had said that you were staying late with a male," the state prosecutor said smoothly. "Then what happened?"

"Oh. Right." She picked up the thread of her story from there, Gage smiling reassuringly at her through it all. "Then he asked me how I could have Jaxson's baby and still work for Gage. Told me that if I wasn't going to learn my place in the world at the hands of my husband, then he'd have to teach me. This is when I figured out that he thought I was Sugar Anderson. Jaxson and Sugar got married before I even met them, but Richard has never forgiven her for divorcing him."

"Can you describe Sugar Anderson to me, please," the prosecutor said.

"Oh. Well, she's very nice – lives up to her name, honestly. Makes everyone feel wel—"

"What she *looks* like," the prosecutor interrupted to say.

Cady felt the tips of her ears go pink. *Stupid, stupid, stupid. Of course he wants a physical description.*

"Right. My height, my build, dark brown hair about the same length as mine, but hers is straight and mine is…well, not." She gestured to her mass of curls on her head and everyone laughed. "In the dark, from behind, to a man who smelled like he'd taken a bath in alcohol before he could gather up the courage to accost me…I can only imagine how easy it would've been to mix us up. Plus, the exit from the bakery where she works is right next door to the exit from the smoothie shop that I own."

"Was Sugar still at work?"

"No, the Muffin Man had closed. Sugar was at home with her husband at the time of the attack. Or," she shot a look at the overly eager attorney for Rat Bastard, who seemed to enjoy objecting to virtually everything she said, "at least that's what she told me later. She certainly didn't come outside during the fight."

Why isn't Sugar here today? I know she doesn't testify until tomorrow, but still. I could've just had her stand up and everyone could've looked at her. It isn't hard to see how the mistake was made.

Sugar had stayed behind, though, keeping the Muffin Man open for business while Gage had come to Boise with Cady.

"Let's discuss that fight for a moment," the

prosecutor said, and then led Cady through it, step by step. The nasty rag in her mouth. Gage showing up. Cream Puffs jumping out of the bed of the truck and attacking Richard. Gage tackling them, and her arm breaking. Calling 911 and talking to the dispatcher. Officer Miller and Officer Morland showing up.

Finally, the state was done with her, and Cady wanted to dissolve into a puddle of joy. She could not *wait* to get off the stand, but she couldn't. Not yet. It was the defense attorney's turn to try to tear her to pieces.

Except, his heart didn't seem to be in it. Whatever the strategy had been before the case went to trial, it seemed to have died a painful death, leaving the attorney to grasp at straws. He began a rambling monologue about this being some sort of conspiracy between Gage and herself to frame his client, shuffling back and forth in front of the witness stand but not looking at Cady once, until the judge interrupted him.

"This is your chance to cross-examine Ms. Walcott, not give your closing statement. Either ask Ms. Walcott questions, or *sit down*." The judge was pissed, the air in the courtroom crackling.

Cady could see Rat Bastard out of the corner of her eye, growing more agitated with every passing moment. She refused to look at him. She couldn't. She wouldn't give him that power over her that she instinctively knew he'd have if their eyes met.

"Are you and Gage Dyer dating?" asked the

attorney, his face beet red from anger and embarrassment from being verbally reprimanded by the judge.

"Yes."

"How long have you been dating?"

"It'll be a year next month."

"And Sugar Anderson is an employee of Gage Dyer's?"

"Yes."

"Is Sugar Anderson a good friend of yours?"

"Yes."

"That is all," the attorney said, sinking into his seat behind the defendant's table.

What

The

Hell

What was that supposed to prove? Did he change his mind halfway through? Did he give up? Has he realized that he doesn't have a snowflake's chance in hell of getting his client out of this one?

But almost as soon as the attorney's ass hit the seat, Rat Bastard shot to his feet.

"Do you know who I am?" he shouted at the judge, and this time, Cady couldn't help herself. She looked at him – his pummeled face, broken and distorted in ways that even the best plastic surgeons money could buy were unable to fix. After the attack, Sugar had showed Cady a picture of him back when they'd dated while in high school. Cady could objectively tell that he'd been a fairly cute guy at the time, although she'd honestly had a hard time seeing it. She just couldn't look past what she knew he'd become.

But now…finally, his face matched his soul. Blotchy, twisted, veins broken; a mask of hatred and anger. His attorney was tugging on his hand, but Rat Bastard yanked it free. "If you won't defend me, I'll do it myself!" he yelled, turning to face the judge, shoulders heaving. "I am Richard Schmidt, Jr., son of the judge for Long Valley County, Richard Schmidt, Sr. You cannot treat me like this! My father will—"

"Your father will do nothing at all," the judge said, his voice ice cold. "Your father has been using the power of his seat to protect you for far too long. He has kept you from feeling the consequences of your actions, turning you into a spoiled, nasty human being."

"I have done no such thing!" a man yelled from the audience directly behind the defendant's table, also jumping to his feet. Cady just stared in disbelief. Did this sort of thing happen all the time in courtrooms and she just didn't know it? She'd always thought of trials as being placid affairs – staid and straightforward and full of motions to do things that she couldn't begin to understand.

Not this shouting affair.

"Judge Schmidt, you will be quiet or I will have you removed from the courtroom!" the judge thundered, banging his gavel. "You are treading on thin ice – based on the situations I am finding in this case, I have already recommended a thorough review of your record to the state judicial board. I would not count on being a judge too much longer. And you, sir," he said, turning back to Rat Bastard whose chest was heaving with anger, his face almost purple from rage, "you will sit down and you will not interrupt these proceedings again. This is not your father's courtroom and I will not have you disrespect it." He banged his gavel again, as if to emphasize what he'd just said, and then turned to his bailiff, as if trying to regain his footing.

"Where were we…" he asked rhetorically.

"I do believe you were about to dismiss Ms. Walcott from the stand," the bailiff said, a twinkle in his eye.

"Right you are!" the judge said with a chuckle. "Ms. Walcott, you can step down now."

With a shuddering sigh of relief, Cady walked down the handful of steps to the main floor of the courtroom, her knees weak. She was just wondering if she was going to lose all capability to walk and simply collapse on the floor in a mess of jelly and nerves – wouldn't *that* be embarrassing – when the judge called for a recess, to "let everyone regroup." Gage was almost instantly beside her, his arm around her waist, and she felt herself melt into his side.

Again. He was there for her again – through thick and thin. Through the good times and the bad.

How had she gotten so lucky?

Feeling a bit like a swooning-prone actress from

the 1940s, she looked up at him through heavy-lidded eyes. "I did it," she mumbled, her steps faltering. If she didn't know any better, she would guess she was drunk.

Drunk on relief – was that a thing?

"You did," Gage said, pulling her to his side and squeezing her tight. "I asked the state prosecutor and he says that you're done. I still have to testify, but not until next week. You ready to go home?" They were already heading outside, into the weak spring sunshine.

Home. Such a gorgeous word. She rolled it around and around in her mind, pushing it, poking at it. It'd just been a year ago when she'd not known what "home" really meant. She'd been alone – no family, hardly any friends to speak of, and a broken-down building in desperate need of repairs.

And now…she did have a home. With Gage. After Rat Bastard attacked her five months previously, Gage had moved her in with him and she'd never left. She still had a lease on her basement apartment, was still paying the rent, but she'd decided to ignore all of that until after the trial was done. She could make decisions then.

But she realized that her heart had been making decisions when she wasn't looking, because when Gage had said "home," she hadn't thought of her apartment. She'd thought of the two-story Craftsman where they'd laughed and loved each other over the past five months.

"Yes, please," she said finally. "I would love to go home."

"Good. Because I have a surprise for you."

"Oh! What's the surprise?" she asked, climbing up into the passenger side of the truck with the help of Gage. At least her arm wasn't in a cast any longer. The day she'd been able to get that off…that'd been a glorious day.

He hurried around to his side and slid into place. "You suck at surprises, you know that?" he said mildly, starting the engine and backing out of the crowded parking lot. The small, tight parking lot was not large-truck friendly. They should've driven her Jeep, but getting ready to leave for Boise that morning, Cady had known that there was just no way she could drive, either there (from nerves) or back (from relief that it was finally over).

"The whole point of a surprise," Gage said, finally maneuvering his truck out onto an even more crowded one-way street, "is that you don't know what the surprise is beforehand."

She stuck her tongue out at him, and then unbuckled her seat belt and slid over to the middle seat. Crowded and uncomfortable as it was sitting over the hump that ran down the middle of the truck, it was still better because then she could sit right next to Gage. She pulled on her lap belt and then snuggled her head down onto his wide, muscular shoulder.

"I've almost forgiven you, you know," she said

mildly, the nerves and adrenaline fading away, leaving her feeling like a wrung-out dishrag.

"Yeah?" he said with a chuckle. "For what?"

"For being so damn muscular. I used to want to only date guys my size—"

"—So you were hitting up the 12 year olds in junior high?"

"—Buuutttt," she said, a little louder, drowning out his teasing laugh, "I've decided that you being strong has some advantages after all. Like beating up assholes in dark parking lots."

"I'm glad you could see your way to appreciating my muscles," Gage said dryly.

"Plus, I've spent my whole life not eating pickles because I couldn't get the lids off the jars! I've been missing them…"

"I'd offer to stop at the grocery store on the way home to buy some just so I can demonstrate my amazing pickle-jar-opening skills, but there's a surprise waiting for you and I want to see your face first. *Then* I'll buy 12 jars of pickles from the Stop 'N Go and wow you with jar after jar of the stuff."

"Very kind of you," Cady said dryly, burying her head down further, feeling her eyes fluttering shut. "I can't wait."

And then she was gone, drifting in the land of slumber, feeling at peace with the world with Gage by her side.

EPILOGUE

GAGE

He rolled to a gentle stop in the driveway of his house, looking down at the sleeping face of Cady, her long eyelashes dark against the paleness of her skin, her curls going every which way.

And then, the snoring. She had the most adorable snore on the face of the planet, as far as Gage was concerned, although she was convinced he was teasing her when he told her that she snored. He couldn't blame her too much for that – teasing Cady was his second favorite thing in the world, behind making love to Cady – but still, he was tempted to record her one night and play it back to her, just so she could hear herself.

Okay, Gage, it's time. He pulled his cell phone out of its dashboard holder and sent the pre-planned text to the predetermined list, patted his pockets, and then with a feeling of regret at waking Cady mingled with happiness that she was his to wake, he gently ran his fingertips down her face. "Hey, Sugar Plums," he whispered softly. "Time to wake up."

She surfaced slowly, stretching and blinking before finally registering what he said and bolting up right. "We're at your house," she said, peering eagerly through the dashboard to look at his home, as if the surprise was going to be painted across the side of it.

He hurried around and slid her into his arms, carrying her to the front porch over her laughing protests.

"The surprise is, I have working legs," she said gaily, running her fingers through his hair as he carried her. "It's not much of a surprise to me, but it seems like it is to you."

"Now you tell me," Gage grumbled, as if she'd been holding out on him all this time. He fumbled with the door knob – he'd intentionally left it unlocked when they'd left for Boise, knowing what they'd be coming back and doing, but even with it unlocked, his hands were slick with sweat.

What if she doesn't like it? What if she says no? What if? What if? What if…

He finally got the door open and Cream Puffs came bounding over, dancing, barking happily, tongue lolling out of her mouth as if she hadn't seen them in years and years.

"You goofy girl," Cady said, sliding out of his arms and down onto the floor. "I just saw you this morning." But still, she was intentionally holding her face within range of Cream Puffs' tongue, as if inviting the dog to give her a face bath.

An invitation the dog was all too happy to say yes to.

Gage stood behind her, discreetly looking around. It looked amazing in the house – way better than it had any right to. Of course, putting Sugar and Emma in charge of decorating always meant the results would be better than he could ever hope to do himself. He saw one eyeball peeking around the corner at them, a long brown braid dangling below it and he shook his head silently.

The hair and eyeball disappeared. Gage let out a tiny sigh of relief.

"Are you okay?" Cady asked absentmindedly. "That was a big sigh…what the *hell*?!" she yelped, staring at the wall behind Gage's head. There, Sugar and Emma had hung the last family portrait Cady and her parents had done before leaving for their trip. An exact replica of Cady's smile graced an older woman, but Cady's golden brown eyes were from her father.

Golden brown eyes that were now staring up at Gage in shock. She scrambled to her feet and then reflexively looked around the house, as if searching for other changes.

And other changes there were. There were her school pictures, twelve photos arranged in an oval around the large senior picture in the middle. There was the end table she'd made together with her father.

There were the throw pillows on the couch she'd bought when she'd moved out on her own and wanted to feel oh-so-grown-up now that she had her own place that she could decorate. It should've felt crowded, adding Cady's stuff in with his, but of course, the talents of Emma and Sugar were at play, not to mention that Gage had always been horrible at actually decorating. Finally, his house had that woman's touch that made it feel like a home.

Their home.

"Cady, will you move in with me?" he asked, digging frantically for the key in his pocket. "I never want your home to be somewhere else. I want you to spend tonight, and every night, here with me."

He held out the key towards her, which was just when Skittles decided to make her presence known. She let out a loud meow, alternating between rubbing against Cady's legs and hissing at Cream Puffs, who seemed to be delighted to have a friend to play with.

Not surprisingly, Skittles didn't seem to return the feeling.

"How…when…" Cady shook her head, as if trying to clear it of cobwebs. "We were together in Boise!" she burst out. "How did you get all of my stuff over here?"

"Magical fairies," Gage said, at the same time that Sugar and Emma piped up, "Us!" as they burst around the corner, apparently incapable of hanging back any longer. "Although, I like the name 'magical fairies,'" Sugar said to Emma seriously. "I think we should go with that instead."

Gage was shooting death rays at the two of them as Cady squealed with delight. "So *this* is why you guys couldn't be at the courthouse!" she said, throwing her arms around one and then the other in turn. "I thought it was bullshit that you guys couldn't bring someone else in to run the bakery for a few hours."

"We just shut it down completely," Sugar said, waving her hand dismissively. "Put a sign on the door, stating that we were busy trying to put Richard Schmidt behind bars. The assholes in this town who don't like it can stuff it. I don't want to sell them donuts anyway."

Gage cleared his throat, and then when the girls didn't seem to hear him, he cleared it again, louder this time. Emma and Sugar both looked guilty – as they damn well should – and backed off. He'd told them not until—

"Will you move in with me?" Gage repeated, holding out the key again.

"Yes!" Cady shouted, throwing herself at him. Cream Puffs yipped and danced; Skittles hissed and pounced, landing on the dog's side. Cream Puffs took off like a shot, yipping in pain, Skittles holding on for dear life, and they heard a thunk and then a crash as they skittered together into the dining room.

"We'll go take care of that," Emma said with a

grimace, grabbing Sugar's hand and dragging her towards the dining room.

"I love you, I love you, I love you," Cady murmured, pressing kisses all over his face between every word. "I'm even starting to love surprises."

"Oh good," he said, allowing himself one kiss on her lips before dropping to one knee in front of her. "Because I have something else to ask you." He dug in his other pocket, pulling out the intricate engagement ring, the swirls and interlocking hearts reminding him of Cady's hair. In the center sat a giant emerald.

"Cady, will you marry me?" he asked, holding up the ring between thumb and forefinger.

Please God, please God, please God—

"Yes!" she said in a strangled voice as he slid the ring onto her finger. He was thrilled to see that it fit perfectly. He'd asked Emma and Sugar to take her shopping at a cheap costume jewelry shop in the Boise Mall. They were supposed to find some new fun jewelry to wear, and get her to try on rings while she was there. Report back on the proper size to him.

After all of their help in making it happen, he could *almost* forgive them for interrupting his proposal.

"It's so beautiful," she whispered, staring at her finger and then up at him. Her huge brown eyes were filled with tears, but they were happy tears. With any luck at all, those would be the only kind of tears she'd ever shed on his account again.

As they kissed, Gage was dimly aware of the stream of people coming into the house, oohing and aahing over all of the hard work that Sugar and Emma had done, there to celebrate Cady's time on the witness stand *and* her moving in with him *and* their engagement. It'd been a risk to ask people to show up to a party that was to take place just minutes after he proposed to Cady – what if she'd said no?! – but it had felt right. He knew she'd want to see all of her friends and customers from the smoothie shop – people who could celebrate her big day with her, even if her parents couldn't.

Finally, the catcalling and wolf whistles got too loud for even Gage to ignore and he regretfully broke off the kiss, suddenly regretting inviting half of Sawyer into their living room. If they'd been by themselves, he could've taken Cady upstairs and shown her just how happy he was that she said yes, but as it was, he was pretty sure people would notice if they disappeared.

"Congratulations, son," Mom said, appearing at his side and pulling him into a big hug. "You found a keeper. And you," she said, turning to Cady to give her a huge hug too, "welcome to the family. Now I have two daughters I can dote on."

Their first meeting seven months ago, when his mother had pulled Cady into a hug, she'd had a look of 'What the hell is going on here?' on her face, and had hardly known what to do. Now, she enthusiastically hugged her future mother-in-law back. "Thank you," she whispered. "I would love to have a mom again."

Then his dad, not much for emotion, pulled Cady into a bear hug of his own. "Welcome," he said gruffly, his tough Marine Corps façade cracking just a little. "Glad to have you."

Gage grinned a little to himself. In his father's world, that was practically a speech.

Grandpa hugged her and kissed her on the cheek, and then it was Grandma, her steel-gray hair pulled back in its tight bun like always. She looked intimidating as hell, but Gage knew that was her resting bitch face at work. She wasn't nearly as scary as she appeared to be, especially when she liked someone.

It just took her a while to like someone, was all.

"Welcome to the family," his grandmother said formally, but eschewed Cady's proffered hand for a hug instead. "You've got a really special man here," she said softly into Cady's curls. "Take care of him for me."

Gage, who wasn't much for being emotional, felt a bit choked up at the sentiment. His grandmother was finally giving her blessing on their relationship.

He didn't know how much he'd wanted that until it had happened. His grandmother had taught him how to cook; had had the belief in him that he could succeed when they sold the bakery to him; had helped him pay for culinary arts school. He'd wanted that side of her – the loving, sweet, caring side – to be the side she showed Cady, too.

Before anyone could pull them apart again to wish

them well or ask for a tour of the house, Gage snagged Cady's hand and pulled her against his chest. "Are you sure about this?" he whispered, staring down into her golden brown eyes. "I know I sprung a lot onto you."

"I love you, Gage, like I've never loved another soul, and never will. You are it for me. I would go with you to the moon and back if you wanted."

"I think we can keep it right here in little ol' Sawyer, but I'll keep that in mind," he whispered against her lips, and then kissed her to the cheers and laughter of his friends and family.

Their friends and family. Because they'd all come to love Cady just as much as he did. Which just went to show that the townspeople of Sawyer had very good taste indeed.

~

Quick Author's Note

Baked with Love has been one of those hard labors where in the afterglow, you forget all of the pain and fuss and sweat and tears, and simply stare in awe at the beautiful thing that you just produced.

Much like having a baby, but with a lot less stinky diapers.

After *Arrested by Love* (when Wyatt did a beat-down on Richard Schmidt for daring to drive drunk), and then *Flames of Love* (where we found out the history behind Sugar and Richard's forced marriage), and then *Lessons in Love* (where we found out the pain and destruction that Richard caused in Hannah's life, too), I had a lot of readers who were calling for justice to happen in Richard's pathetic, worthless life. Who doesn't want the bad guy to finally lose in the end, right?

So with all of that in mind, I hope this book lived up to y'all's expectations. 😊

Being a small town, though, the consequences of this will continue to reverberate through the years. In other words, this won't be the last time you've seen Richard Schmidt, Sr and Richard Schmidt, Jr in the Long Valley world. #FairWarning

Assholes aside, one of my absolute *favorite* parts about writing in one world is that I never have to say goodbye to anyone. There are the people I would *like* to say goodbye (and good riddance!) to, of course, but for the most part, it's a town filled with good people just trying their best to succeed in this not-always-so-friendly world. They are as real to me as my friends and family are, and it's one of the great blessings of my life that I get paid to share them with y'all. Life really doesn't get any better than this.

I wanted to touch on the subject of Cady (soon-to-be Dyer) Walcott for just a moment. As human beings, we're drawn to stories of bravery and leadership, and it's easy as an author to write stories about women who kick ass and take names – who are fearless and tough – but what about the women who've gone through a lot of trauma in their lives? Who are afraid of their own shadows? Who have overwhelming phobias and fears that keep them from living a "normal" life? I wanted to write about these women also, to let people see themselves in the fears…and thus in the triumphs, too.

I know that Cady (and Hannah) are not your typical tiny-waisted, big-boobed, violet-eyed, sassy, fearless heroines. I hope that you'll draw inspiration from them for this very reason.

Hugs and love,
Erin Wright

ALSO BY ERIN WRIGHT

~ LONG VALLEY ~

Accounting for Love

Blizzard of Love

Arrested by Love

Returning for Love

Christmas of Love

Overdue for Love

Bundle of Love

Lessons in Love

Baked with Love

Bloom of Love (2021)

Holly and Love (TBA)

Banking on Love (TBA)

Sheltered by Love (TBA)

Conflicted by Love (TBA)

~ FIREFIGHTERS OF LONG VALLEY ~

Flames of Love

Inferno of Love

Fire and Love

Burned by Love

~ MUSICIANS OF LONG VALLEY ~

Strummin' Up Love

Melody of Love (TBA)

Rock 'N Love (TBA)

Rhapsody of Love (TBA)

~ SERVICEMEN OF LONG VALLEY ~

Thankful for Love (2021)

Commanded to Love (TBA)

Salute to Love (TBA)

Harbored by Love (TBA)

ABOUT ERIN WRIGHT

USA TODAY BESTSELLING AUTHOR ERIN WRIGHT has worked every job under the sun, including library director, barista, teacher, website designer, and ranch hand helping brand cattle, before settling into the career she's always dreamed about: Author.

She still loves coffee, doesn't love the smell of cow flesh burning, and has embarked on the adventure of a lifetime, traveling the country full-time in an RV. (No one has died yet in the confined 250-square-foot space – which she considers a real win – but let's be real, next week isn't looking so good…)

Find her updates on ErinWright.net, where you can sign up for her newsletter along with the requisite pictures of Jasmine the Writing Cat, her kitty cat muse and snuggle buddy extraordinaire.

Wanna get in touch?
www.erinwright.net
erin@erinwright.net

Or reach out to Erin on your favorite social media platform:

- facebook.com/AuthorErinWright
- twitter.com/erinwrightlv
- pinterest.com/erinwrightbooks
- goodreads.com/erinwright
- bookbub.com/profile/erin-wright
- instagram.com/authorerinwright

Made in the USA
Coppell, TX
09 February 2024

28817447R00205